it is what it is

it is what it is

A Novel

Adam Tyson

iUniverse, Inc.
New York Lincoln Shanghai

it is what it is

iUniverse books may be ordered through booksellers or by contacting:

iUniverse
2021 Pine Lake Road, Suite 100
Lincoln, NE 68512
www.iuniverse.com
1-800-Authors (1-800-288-4677)

This is a work of fiction. All of the characters, names, incidents, organizations, and dialogue in this novel are either the products of the author's imagination or are used fictitiously.

ISBN: 978-0-595-43189-2

Printed in the United States of America

CHAPTER 1

Walk out doors of art gallery – down stairs – swing round - to walking on Lafayette – heading towards orange 'JAV' truck for a 3:00 cup -

"Zach."

Turn round… no one… "hm…"

Walk on –

"Zach." –

~I *heard* that~ – swivel head, survey. . . no one. . . "I *heard* that…"

Look for a construction worker - yelling to a co-worker – or someone calling from a car….

Scan for any chance of it being a prank… - but who do I know here? – setting up for an art show – there's Brent (curator) – but he's inside, cutting labels …

Continue – replaying voice in head – so clear - *real*…. think of accounts – seen on TV - where people claimed to hear voices – religious fanatics, or… people in asylums - schitzos. . – ~but this was *outside* – outside my head - from a distance…~

"You're going to go on an adventure greater than any have experienced throughout all history, Zach."

Stop. Close eyes. Deep breathes… ~have I sniffed too many fumes today – paint or chemicals - hanging up the pictures?… – we didn't deal with any fumes today… – wire, nails, pins, hammers, chord, canvases, frames, levels…~

Open eyes, turn round, slow, again. . . arms open, palms out, "hello?" I say as a lady in a Russian babushka darts fearful hazel eyes at mine a second in passing …

Forego coffee truck – head for café – nooked here on MacDougal by NYU... grab cell from pocket, call Brent. . . – "So you're all set for today, right?"

"All good... See you at the opening tomorrow..."

Sit by massive front window... look out as clouds roll in, heavy rain falls – man runs by in trench – clutching newspaper overhead. . . Song playing overhead is metal – guitar speeding into crescendo... –

~What's this 'greatest adventure' – and of all time? – what would that *be*... -

Do I travel around the world? – that's been done by many... – Conquer some huge foe? – been done by many... Get that top babe? – been done by many...~ –

pretty waitress walks up – flips lil' book open, clicks open, readies, pen ...

Listen to myself say "bacon double cheese burger." - ~where did *that* come from?~ –

Look over to right – table across the way – guy sitting at it – dressed in a tiger mascot costume – smiling tiger head on floor - on his plate: a large... horseshoe crab – overturned – on its back – struggling – its spike tail lashing about – smacking, launching salt and pepper shakers – rattling silverware – he raises steak knife, the lash down, drives it into center between squiggling, stiffening, limp cluster of claw-legs... – sitting next him... it's... Uncle Sam – white beard, brows, striped hat – whole getup – lines of definition rip visible across forehead – and in jowls as his jaw mechanically hydrolic-locks into massive burger – stuff spilling out other end into pile on plate ...

Turn back to waitress - "Fries with thaaaa-" – her mouth stretches huge - surreal – out from it soars a big bright red boxing glove – *PAP*!!! – explosion of stars: head, snapt back... Eyes... open... falling from... bunk – "CLAM!!!" – cabin door smashes open – water, gushes in... hitting ground "Oohf!" head, reels, getting it... together – as, cold water ignites nerves, washing over body – taste salt water in mouth – all the things on shelves raining down now – light bulb flickering on-off... on, off, on – everything rocking, loud – sit up - water shoots cold in face –. . . – ~Craig's boat (Dad's posh yacht), that's right...~ ~daytrip – fishing...~ – things clicking into place – ~in Jersey somewhere – they've a beach house around here – his Mom grew up vacationing summers here – now they've a place right by the beach – and this big boat they dock at the harbor – we took it out miles and miles this morning~ – recall the gray clouds rolling in as I reclined for that nap - storm *hard* upon us now – fiercest I've seen – another gush smashes cabin door open again – pots fly from wall – clang off stove – heavy one bounces off back - cabinets burst open – contents gush forth down - tumble over back as I languor, stumbling over them, toward door – here, a twenty dollar bill, floating serene on the black-green-clear water in the flickering light – instinctual jolt to grab it up – but let it be - ~what's that now?~ and boat heaves a drastic nosedive – sending me into a bellyslide on floor - out cabin – wind, rushing loud – throttling sails which tear to long shreds, whip about... see Craig – leaned - back to wall – possessed look in eyes – staring straight ahead, transfixed – grasping up-side-down-U-shaped fishing rod... - "I gotta *monster* on the line!" –

Waves – like moving midnight-blue peaks – sizes of houses – creep, lurk, surge, rush by on all sides – one curls – crashes in – damage, felt, done to boat. . . - another "CRAM!" – white foam covers floor of deck... feel for the boat – feel it hurting, trembling, doomed ...

"We're taking in water!" I yell as he's knocked over – slides on stomach – scrambles to feet – squats – heaves a growling yank. -

"You ain't getting away! – you're *mine! – aaaall miiine!* yeah I'm gonna cook you up and *eat you dooown yeeeeeaaaah!*" – another strained crank of rod - reeling in hard... –

up wriggles over the edge a massive, lumbering, stupid – yet wise – wild, beast of a fish – midnight-blue and gleaming silver, flailing visible in lightning flashes – 'KLUMPHF!' – floor shakes at its landing – Craig already raising bat in hand – tiny wooden Louisville – his veins apop out on arm – another wave curling over, - crashing onto him as he clamps fish in headlock – both knocked tumbling into the wall – fish looking about his size, weight -

"*We're taking in water!*" – can't... get to him... to shake him out of it – boat swaying so fierce... – he and the fish are wrestling – he's growling like a crazy person as the fish writhes for its life – and flails - vibrating whole boat with each slam-down of its powerful tail – its mouth opening and closing insane in lightning flashes – "*Craaaaiiiig!*" – boat jolts a wheelie - see the bottoms of Craig's sneakers - then his hand, locked grip on (half-in) gill hole – now, struggling to kneeling position, it's up with bat again - 'WHAP!' – I let go of ladder – head towards him – trying to keep balance - bat lashes up and down to thunder claps – 'WHAP! WHAK! WHAP!' – boat juts hard diagonal left – sliding on belly towards him – bat's hitting harder – 'WHAM!' – "ALL MINE!" 'WHAP! WHAP! WHAP!' fish blood spraying, stringing, spilling – catch split-second light of life still aflicker in fish's neon green eye in here, the brightest flash yet – looks to me in an resigned sort of way (the fight, leaving it) - seems to communicate "what an absurd situation this is, no?... – can't you... *do something* about this? or'... but 'WHAP!WHAP!' drawing close now, tumbling – reach a hand out, sliding by, to grab hold on... Craig's ankle... ~*got it*~

– "Craig! The boat is *sinking!*" – fish tail whooshes over – hits side of head – knocks face into side of cabin – scramble to feet - mast – soaring straight for - **KAK!** multi-color stars – sharp, distinct – strobey now – stark-bright – to… fading. . .

Make quite the entrance into café – heads turning, smiles cracking on - Roma – Roma style - Shannon on arm – 10ish… having just… dined on pizzas over in Piazza delle Coppelle… to… moonlit stroll through winding stairs - Friday night vibes rejoicing atmospheres the world over… right lighting here, right crowd, table, – waiter – bottle, chosen – glasses, poured – toast – duet band – one on violin, other on triangular guitar – feeling hearty tune – transference of it - into air, into our hearts… air, *acrackle* - wine infusing into play – Shannon's eyes aglisten – shine forth joy – into mine – mine into hers - like, visible beams, shooting out from her head… whole room, everyone in it… *ecstatic* …

Eyes open… sun stings them to clamping shut… open again… gaze into clear blue sky… – feel belly convulse - compress – feel fluid rush through esophagus - watch stream exit – watch it ascend upwards – like a pole – mushrooming at end – bouncing around on itself up top – see tiny pieces of pink clam, potato skins, bits of carrot – corn (still in tact), this, last night's homemade chowder, ate over that game of Rummy 500, drinking Coronas – everything seeming gelly slo-mo as frothing mix jiggles about up top – ~how can it be up that high?~ – and… down it all falls, on face, splashing off… no attempt to dodge… lay unmoved… as… time prolongs its abstraction… feel drained at all that leaving body… eyes… closed …

registrations clickle in brain… perceive I'm… lying flat on back… in sand by water's edge – its cold foam, here, kissing at heels… hear seagulls… waves, crashing close by… ~there's… something up with my eyes…~ try opening them again – the intensity – *radiance* of the blue – with its one puff cloud afloat therein - clamps them shut ~my *God*~ …

~thirsty~… just… stay… lying… cool breeze washes over body… another – stronger – lots of sand in it – over face, bare chest… ~cold~

pictures of the boat chaos flash to mind… ~what about Craig?~ -

scene of him bashing that fish's spattering broken panicking head… ~Craig… did he… make it? … no way of knowing for a while I suppose… there's *no way* he could have died… no way… but it's… likely so… ~

~I've survived a shipwreck… I'm washed-up on shore here…~

~I have to get up… I have to get up… and get water… why? why stay alive, really, when one really gets to thinking about it…~ ~because it might be grand(?), is that it?~

ears hone in on the waves… ~water, water, everywhere… – not a… drop to… drink…~

'zzzzzzz' – faint – 'zzzzzzz' – growing louder – 'zzzzzZZZ' – a motor… – 'ZZZZZ' – ~motor(s)(?)~… crane head up… – to chin nearly touching chest… open eyes… 'ZZZZZ' - it's two… waverunners… approaching… approaching… – streams of water, soaring up, out behind them in archs… 'ZZZZZZZ'' - see them in such *sharp* clarity – make out the details - the yellow buckles on their new bright-orange life vests… their tan bodies – a man and woman – a couple – both blond – bright white teeth – smiling huge – 'ZZZZZ!' – their pairs of sunglasses – Oakleys – with florescent orange lanyards affixing them to heads… – both going same fast speed – a safe fast - - - passing now 'ZZZZZZZZZ!!!' - - - - see through guy's sunglasses as he passes – see his eyeballs zip a quick shot at me – ascertain - see 'em zip straight ahead again – see thumb snap-press accelerator in far as it goes – hear engine spike louder ~he doesn't want to be bothered… they are enjoying themselves – they are experiencing a pleasurable moment for themselves - no crimps must pinch on his current groove~

turn head with them as they go 'ZZzzzzzzz' watch them fade away… gone… clamp eyes shut – feel them stinging …

"RRrrrrrRR!" rolling over on right side "*rrrrr*", seaweed, tumbling off chest… open eyes again …

the sand… see every grain of it… close eyes, shake head… open… see… all the grains – distinct – shadows of each even – cast on lower grains – also seen with sharp clarity… a little crab skittering sideways comes into view, stops right in front of face – its black dotty eyes - at realizing I'm alive – zaps off a stunned vibe – its purple claw opening and closing, sending a message …

every detail on this crab is fully seen – its shell - every stubby hair on its little legs, every little bubble popping at its mouth – see *into* it's mouth – through its shell even – all its functioning little bits inside – snap eyes shut again – rub at them with hand ~something is definitely up with my eyes.~ … roll onto stomach… open eyes again… every sand grain, still in fine detail – see the crevices – the millions of color differentiations… swivel neck round, look on ocean – ~good *God*~ every wave, clearly defined, distinct – every ripple – *ripples within ripples*… snap eyes shut – let it register… ~something's changed here…. a… deepening, widening, clarification, a new sharpness of vision – an *uber clar-*

ity… – *really* seeing…~ reopen… crab skitters off… blink, play with eyes, blur them, squint… ~ultra-clarity~ remains in tact …

and it's taxed the brain… roll over on back again and fall sleep. . . . .

'boop-boop… boop-boop…' coming to… 'boop-boop… boop-boop…' feel waves at feet… lift head from sand, swivel neck, open eyes …

An old guy, waving beachcomber to and fro just above sand… white tank top, orthopedic sunglasses – see details in face – nose hairs, red skin pores, moles… faded blue beach hat, yellow Sony radio headphones – chunky - with antenna, faded lime green shorts, thin wrinkled flesh sagging over knees… standing now, close, staring, studying me, open-mouthed… – fully gauge his… dimensionality in space too – his *essence* – periphery as well – beach houses in background – see a woman - through sliding screen door – asleep on a lazyboy chair - mouth open… see the show on TV - five day forecast – calling for rain tomorrow… close eyes …

"You ok there son?…"

~hmm, what to do here~

open mouth: "lllllllrrrrreeeeeeeeuuuuuuuuu' - leave off… sudden shock-waves fire through spine – convulsing body into some sort of epileptic fit – prompting snap call to crank a push up – whoosh! – flow into a sprint – sand, shells, seaweed strands, flying off in wake. . . "hey now!" hear the guy say – keep eyes half shut, turning left into soft sand, heading for dunes. . . – watch my tan feet pop in and out of view in horizontal slit. . . – turn back - open eyes wider to see (jiggly though perfectly clearly) that the old man has his sun-glasses slid down to tip of nose – looking over them – to old model cell phone – where he dials 9…1…1 …

Eyes shift to shaking semi-circle sun, rising on horizon – and – its rays soar-ing in – leers the feet drastic – here now atop a dune – inside head - innumera-ble beams shooting in - explosions - every direction – surrealistic, spinning, radiating – body thrown into spasms again – loose footing, falling through air - into dune – tumble, roll – ~steep, deep dune here~ to a stop… feel… at rest, at peace, catching breath… ~c'mon, get up man~

Eyes shut, slip into a quick sleep… – snapping awake – looking at top of dune – see a greenhead horsefly on blade of grass – see its many eyes… shift to – rising into view - the faded blue hat – sunglasses – red nose - tank top – he's… climbing over –

Scurrying to feet – squinting at him …

"Now-now… (he says, hand outstretched, making a motion like he's pet-ting a dog) "now-now… it's ok… gonna be aaalright… just… just… taaake it

eeeaasyy" – eyes perceive every thread of his shirt – see small faded palm tree
sown on breast pocket – see faded spaghetti sauce stain – look at sunglasses –
eyes wide behind them - he's close now - detector (in right hand) is turned off
- not making a sound – look at his face again – "*eeeasy* does it, that's right…" –
perceive a strain in him – tension - real close now – inches – he's tall - mouth
suddenly snarls into a yellow-toothed grit as vieny hand shoots forth in a red
streak – latches on my wrist - a stinging vice-like pressure – his sunglasses slide
down on bridge of shining sweaty red nose – revealing glossy blue/brown eyeballs swimming in yellow gels – I see every fine rose and blue vein – his eye
brows: complete diagonal slants – and he's actually growling as I try wriggling
my hand free… "rrrr-yyouuur not going anywhere young man *rrrrrr* – you just
hooold tight till the police come – every thing's gonna be juuust fine –
rrrrrr…" –

I manage stringing words together – "It's ok sir" - though it sounds like
someone outside of myself is speaking - "everything's fine – if you'd just go
ahead and… let go… that'd be…" – other hand joining in, working on loosing
the grip, which somehow increases in pressure -

"rrrrrr-you're just gonna wait here for help that's all-*rrrrr*- everything will
be sorted out just fine…" he's shaking and breathing heavy, loudly ~is he trying to be a hero?~ it strikes in that I must break free – that I must get away and
clear head a while – consider next steps …

cock free arm back… hit the old man in the face with open hand – causing
his hat to pop off - sunglasses to shift all crooked – "why you little *ffffffffff* – 'hit
him again – open hand – harder - on side of head – his white hair blasting
instantly unkempt – sunglasses fly through air – he's growling hard, wriggling
arm free from beach comber – it rattles loud – parts flying off before it clumps
to a heap on ground – he raises a high right arm – down it comes – head –
another - ear, blow after blow - shoulder, head, chin – but… not much power
in them - I thrust an arm up through the flurry, clamp it on his throat – ~so
delicate~ – push his whole body towards the sand comber –his feet tangle into
it - perfect tripping block – hear the plastic crackle crazily as he goes over – his
hand releasing from my wrist to help break his fall – hear the 'AARRRR!' and
more cracking plastic as I scurry over other side of dune… - three or four more
– and into a woodsy area – curvy pine needle trees – thick, dense – every needle distinct – pungent odors flooding memory banks as I accelerate – feel the
soft pine needles under feet – a rabbit dashes across path – but it's neon pink -
and transparent… listen to steady footfalls a while… ~maybe I've run a mile
now – maybe two~ all the delicate shadows of the needles ~could say I'm…

seeing the 'bigger picture' now - of everything – everything in light of it… this… new perspective… outlook… world view~ … winded, hungry, thirsty… turn left, walk… to bumbling out onto a street… quiet… – lined with beach mansions – their lights all out – must be very early – 5ish - judging by dark orange lighting and vibe in air… 4 or 5 in the morning …

Hear laughter …

Group of high school kids ~Senior Week~ four - five of them - all drunk – rowdy – laughing - one has another in a headlock… I put my hand on a car hood to stabilize self, catching breath as they approach… big, stocky, football types – college hats on backwards… – one double-takes – hones in on me, curls on a smile – "Well, well heh-heh what have we got here – *welcome to the freakshow* – check this guy out." – All hone in – burst into laughter… - "we got a regular *tarzan* on our hands heh-heh" – "have another dude." about to wheeze a request for water, think better of it – ~gotta be a store around here somewhere…~ guy in the headlock breaks free – serious look on face – shoving match begins – the others whooping it on – circling them "*yyyeeeeaaah!*" – one performing a kind of rain dance – punches throwing now - landing, both sides - to here, growling wrestling – the one picking the other up – suplexing him down on car hood, denting it in, setting off alarm – snapping them out of it – into nervous laughing – all breaking into jog, which, at seeing colored lights flashing on trees, turns into ("*run for it!*") scattered all-out sprints - Caprice leaning hard into turn – front shocks depress low – tires chirp screech - two cops bound, determined, from vehicle – time slows a second as the guy just brawling runs at me, eyes wide, mouth open – watch him morph into the position of a hockey player about to check someone - "*outta the way!*" – as impact shoots nerves through body – floating sensation – more nerves shock as scrape, roll on asphalt… – roll right up into a sprint – "*Stop!*" I hear - ~he's got sights set on me~ -"*stop right there!*" hear his black combat cop boots – those super-lightweight kind - with big treads – pounding louder and louder on ground behind me – hear grunts from his mouth - turning neck round – he's right here – reaching out hand to grab – cut hard right – hear "AAAR – GH!" – look back and he's tumbling in a sandy cloud… ~I've got the youth factor on him… – and I'm lighter…~ - jut right, hop fence, run into pine trees – needles like clouds under padding feet – breathing heavy – hear his feet again – turn, see him gaining ~fast for his weight~ - jut right again – into dunes – over a few – onto beach – run left, look back – see a police car tear onto beach, engine roars, spotlight flashes on, beams into woods as it rushes towards… ~*man!*~ - but then its doors fling open - two cops scramble into the dunes after one of the football guys… – another squad car veers onto beach – in distance – search light beams into woods, heads slow this way… – I see a batch of high dune grass and dive in – as grass bends and crackles in descent to ground – see lil' purple clawed crabs skittering off – disappearing in lil' holes – feel reeds cutting at arms - "Oof!" – on ground - army crawl on elbows in deeper – lay flat, dead still, lungs pumping… hear motor purr by – hear CB crackle messages – engulfed in light a second – shadows cast thousands of lines – the details! – flashback to Craig – whaling that fish 'WhaM!' – expression radiating forth from that insano, gobby fish eye as club smashed its skull to bits… – note vines now - shimmery three-leafers- ~damn~ loads of it – I'm *in it* - *lying* on it (all the running having taxed system – vines even morph into slithering snakes a second – shake head - vines again) – engine – its duel exhaust blubbing tuffy - purrs out of earshot… – and I'm up and running again – noting cop from before – much closer now – renewed in purpose at seeing me "*Hey!*" I accelerate and - "BRRRRRRR!!!" - beach-combing tractor – out of blue - bouncing towards – driver wearing gun muffler earphones squints at me… cut around it… – feel the soft sand sapping energy – sucking it from body with each stride – ~and so out in open here~ - swiveling head – see cop making his way over dune – lethargic, on verge of turning back – ~but probably not till I'm out of his sight again~ - he… flags down the tractor… I stop, hands on head, catching breath… watch cop climb onto tractor, standing on a step of ladder leading to cab, holding a handle – he points like an army general at me, hollering to driver, who cranks engine – black puff of smoke shooting from vertical exhaust as tractor leers into a U turn and it's bouncing quick towards - cop unsheathes billyclub from side, points it, frown-smiling… I turn towards pine trees, run… into them, turn left, up speed – hear engine zoom past, fade away… run for a long time – emerge close to where I'd entered – cop car still there – lights off… – an officer talking with a guy wearing a robe next to the dented car… ~must… get… water… soon… or… pass out~… head in search of a 24 hour store …

examining forearm… has an 8 inch patch (the shape of Florida) of red… bumps, forming… – and chest – red blotches – back too, it feels – and back of neck… – fine slashes on outsides of arms from reeds, blood drops, trailed away a bit, dried… – calves too – further developed - stop to scratch hard at them – itch leaves at each fingernail scrape-over – returns stronger though at leaving off… over and over, stop to… have at it… ~like life – one thing after next – what more than a series of… pain, relief, pain relief…~ …

Approaching front doors of Wawa, a batch of beat partiers exit, climb into long 1960's Buick convertible, rumble engine to life, pull away …

'beeeeeee-booooo' sounds sensor, passing through threshold… music overhead: "Dreeeeeamm weeaaaverrr – I believe you can get me through the ni-iiight." bleary patrons bumble about, doubletake at me – here, experiencing… hallucinations – cartoon polar bear on ICEE machine grows fangs, leaps at me – candy hops off racks, runs around…. Ketchup bottles doing battle with mustard jars… really scratching at back of neck now… take hold on a tall Poland Spring bottle in cooler, unscrew cap, tip up, watch bubbles rise… feel it… filling voids within…. ~conveyering life into shell…~ … - ~a *liquid*, giving life!~ (glug, glug… where there is water… there is life – notion springs in - think of the desserts – compare them to rainforests - colorful lizards zipping about - monkeys playing in trees)… hm, entire thing drunk in one tilt… Hungry now… very… dawns… no money… Facing cashier – cute blonde – probably from Poland – here working the summer on a Visa deal – loads of them crop up summer to summer – work the Boardwalk stores – up in Nantucket it's the Irish, summer influx of 'em… turn head, note a group of three guys standing at deli… The one bites deep into just-bought hoagie - educated-looking, red-headed, bearded, guy …

I approach, "I'm trying to pay for this…" voice is raspy "anyone have any money?" He, chewing big, smirks, reaches in pocket, pulls out a money clip – one-handedly extracts a five, hands it, gives a nod, mashes another bite …

~enough for a hotdog~ pull one from heated box – out from under the hot yellow lights… pile on relish, onions, kraut… half it with a bite… another finishes it off… big chews, grabbing an iced tea from cooler… remove pair of 99 cent red sun glasses from white plastic display cylinder, slide them on, laying five on counter, walk out… – a little brighter now… tipping a glug from iced tea, look at newspaper truck - parked - its rear open towards front door – guy inside throwing cubes of papers out from it onto ground – Philadelphia Inquirers and New York Times… a stack of Inquirers tumbles to by feet… Eyes hone in on date, Thursday, June 5… – hone in on picture, bottom right: wrecked boat laying on side in dark green water:

"Two Lost at Sea,

One Found Dead

As Search Continues…" Our two high school pictures …

swivel head… cashier's eyes give her away, on phone, mouth moving… look down at paper again… ~guess I'm supposed to… turn myself in to the police… tell them everything is ok… call everyone up, tell them I'm fine…~

~hm… more into moving forward with this new vision… experiencing it – getting a better feel for it – aside from all the fingers meddling in a while… giving it time…~

looking down at article again ~well, it… is what it is… I suppose… past is past - no changing it… no right for it to interfere with present, really – it's in the realm of unchangeable fact now – it… is what it is… going to police… all those hoops – to jump through… drama… - gonna give it a while… 'clear head' 'sort head out' – apart from distractions – impediments – littleness – tedium - obstacles to… potential new goals… – what about your family, friends – Shannon? - ~well, that all is… what it is… pretty much…~ - just the now – and what's to come – matters – ~holds any sway~ now, it seems… - rendering these paper cubes here at feet… insignificant – ~save a few snips of upcoming events perhaps – and how interesting a reading experience can that offer?~

The hotdog has me feeling energy, standing, itching at poison ivy, wearing new sunglasses… ~what's next?~…. ~Is it just… back to what was… back to the routine – back to "heading to college in the fall?" like all the others… – accruing the ball and chain loans – to get paper diploma - which supposedly opens doors to getting this, that job… No, clearly not an option now – is exactly what it is – 'was what it was' now…~ ~it's this… *new* life now – this 'all-out' style – 'go for it' mode… it's like… fears, inhibitions - any vestige of pretense – have all… left the building… – fear of man, gone… – took that whole old-guy-fight-on-beach experience in stride – cop chase too – it all, just, so, what it was at the time, that was that, and, here, getting walking, this… is this~ vision forming – ~what to… *go do*?~ - and… all that… seems to… make sense now is… to go and be an artist… - ~what with this new way of seeing…~ … ~ok, where?~ – in the thick of where the energy, action, *life* is - rather than in some New Haven classroom – *first hand* experience over nose in a textbook… – ~ax straight to root over flicking at branches…~… ~where then?… where's the… epicenter? … well, just about the all top artists have gone to New York… is this still where it's at…~ – mind reels, assessing…. – ~yeah… well, go there then… – right smack in beating heart of Village…~

start walking again as heavy Chevy cop car bounces shocks dramatic into lot – they open, slam doors – hurrying into Wawa, hands on holstered guns… –

kick into a jog - next block over, run five straight blocks …

Transitioning into walk, Shannon appears in mind…. ~I'll contact her soon enough – Dad and Mom, Jerry and Ruth too… high time to ('high'?) establish a position in the world – have monkeyed around long enough on the broad road of falling in line…~ …

~how do I get up to New York?~ turn around, walking backwards, stick up thumb – old Jeep pulls right over – huge tires – open cab (roll bars w/big KC lights), stereo blasting – shirtless surfer, red hat on backwards, mirror sunglasses "where ya headin' dude?"

"New York."

"hop in – can take ya far as A.C. man – you can catch a bus from there."

Climb up into ripped vinyl seat… – thrown in gear – roar off …

"That's some wicked poison ivy bro!" yelling over engine.

"Yeah, wash the seat when I'm gone!"

Onto AC Expressway… engine and blasting wind limiting conversation… Mom appears in mind… Dad… Jerry – older bro – living at home a while before heading off to Air Force. – Ruth – very bright, somewhat to-herself in-her-own-world younger sister… ~what are they going through?~ - play out each of their reactions in head – that first registration of the news in brain… how they're coping… – their fielding questions to neighbors, friends – extended family… – think of Uncle Earl – living out in the woods of Jersey – my stay with him part of last summer – think of my dirtbike there – riding it everyday, adventuring, contemplating, mapping out, strategizing senior year as the wheels went where they would …

Loop an exit… ~I'll call them soon as I get in New York~ we roar through Margate - past massive elephant sculpture… and into mid-day Atlantic City – bright sunlight, kind of… *exposing* the place – a bizarro, tired haze hanging in air… the Casinos looming - emanating their vibes - as we weave through a set of faux Caesar columns… –

"Such a dodgy place!" he hollers "heh-heh - I'm just passing through! – picking up some buddies!"

blankstare at Casinos again… ~like… machines…~ see buses rolling up to them, unloading… ~machines feeding on the downtrodden, the oppressed, the masses… while the rich… sit, running the machines – toasting behind the scenes… taking baths in hundred dollar bills… having another steak… all on the coins slid into slots of dazzling machines by proletarians by the sea…~

Front right wheel bounces up on curb – "Alright, bus station's right over there – enjoy NYC man…"

"Thanks bro", hopping down, turning, facing, "do you have a twenty for me to catch a bus by any chance?"

just looking at me through sunglasses, sustaining a goofy smile… "Are you homeless man?"

"For now…"

Processing, holding smile, engine idling 'blub-blub-blub…'

"Spare me a begging session on the boards y'know…"

Shoving hand in orange bathing suit pocket, "tell you what…" unvelcroing wallet… "I'll give you all I got." slides a ten from it, hands… "Here go… hope everything works out ok for ya…"

"Yeah, thanks man, definitely appreciate…"

Cranks in gear 'RUM! RUM!' wobbles off curb – 'BRAAAAAaaaaaaa'

Everything seems quiet after the ride, here, walking towards beach, hot, itching at shoulder …

~will have to beg the other $10 on the boardwalk…~ – see a Rite Aid ~more than 10~ swing in, get a tube of anti-itch cream, swing out …

About to slather it on, heading for beach - ~go in water first~ - seem to recall salt water being good for rashes …

crossing crowded boardwalk – smell the food – poofs of smoke from grills… – as if under a spell, jut a sharp left, step to counter, order a "cheeseburger, cheese fries and a black and white shake."… – carry it over to here, an orange plastic table, sit, close eyes, take in a deep sniff… open eyes, look to left: a guy, scratching furiously with a penny at a lotto card – looks up - into my eyes… black dots swimming in a yellow and red ooze seem to zap a… bad energy into mine… notice I'm scratching poison ivy on arm and leave off - grab up red plastic bottle, squirt ketchup on – which makes a loud farting sound… and get wolfing down burger – greasy – a big one - quarter pounder – as seagulls start dive-bombing in for cheese fries – I'm shooing them – swinging arm - growling open-mouthed chewing "*GRAAA!*" bits flying from mouth – hit one with fist – feel its buoyant little chest on knuckles – knock it flapping into 300 pound woman eating nachos next table over – the squeal – chips hurled high in air – raining down on customers snapping heads over – she's pointing, cursing… scurry off, gulping milkshake through straw – chuck cup in trashcan, as stomach takes a turn - ~burger was a bad idea~… – belly does a kind of… gurgle as I cross boardwalk, clutching it - start down wooden stairs – "ex*cuse* me *hellooo*" – turning round, dark-haired teen-age girl in sunglasses, sleeves-rolled-up polo shirt, "a beach day-pass is *8 dollars*…" …

"Oh, right…" back up stars… walk a block – no bathroom in sight - slip through railing on other side, stroll under boardwalk – shady, cool, essence, stirring memories, thoughts on transience of life – out other side – few lil' dunes – step over half-swallowed-up-by-sand wooden fence, and blend in to the colorful umbrellas and people - laid out, reading, or, here, throwing a Frisbee, - here, building a sand castle… tighten cap on anti-itch cream, stick it in back pocket – long belch – quicken pace – another 'RaaAURP' – as itching sensations spike – scratching hard - draw blood on forearm – transition into jog – faster – water cold on feet – the dive '*Swoosh!*' – feel green salt water penetrate bumpy red pores – taking over - soothing – ~healing in its wings~… under for a while… cool green liquid light haze… play dead… hear heart, beating… ~thanks for keeping it beating… Source? - what through all those years – experiences…~ roll over… surface… inhale deep – feel wind gust over body – triggering sensations – ~definitely alive here~ let bladder go… going a while… feel the relief… "aaahhh" – ears in water hear a faint 'twee-tweeeeeeeeet'… shift to doggy paddling… – 'tweeeeet-tweet-tweeeeeeeeet-tweeeeet!' swivel head… Lifeguards, standing on their white-wooded stoop, one peering through binoculars, the other waving arms franticly, whistle in mouth, cheeks bulging 'tweet-*tweeeeeet!*' I just… stare… apparently I'm between guards here – while I'm supposed to be in front – with all the others – some of whose heads turn, stare… – the one guard puts megaphone to mouth - as other – Army-looking guy with crew cut - climbs down – grabs orange rocket-shaped floating device – throws it round neck, dives in – swimming - olympic-speed - towards… "*You* there!" calls the megaphone – "over this way – *move over!!*" – life guards from other stand have hopped down – sliding wooden boat – 'ACBP' bold on its sides – into water – hopping in, get paddling hard – and - "BLAAH!" – black and white milkshake and stuff – "BLERR!" - feel a stream burst out other end too – into shorts - ~not good~ as round two hits – "BLA!" - projectile - "AACH!" – everyone looking – a few guys swimming towards - peeing again – swim away from burger and fries – ~ah well, ocean can take it~ and away from swimming guard, advancing fast.

no swimming over into peopled area now – no blending in happening out here… - head for shore – guard sees, redirects – trying to cut me off – here, a massive wave – caught - shoots me at a fat guy with a mustache – see his eyes widen before barreling him over on my way down with pipeline - slam into jagged shells – dragged tumbling along, rise, turn, mustached guy, shaking fist - another, bigger – catch – superman position - right to sliding chest on shore - up and trotting – the blend-in eventually – under boardwalk, climb up other side, find a bench in sun, sit, dry, thaw a while, hungry again …

Pull anti-itch cream from back pocket… slather over the ~insane bumps~ …

Slouching...... ~why... go on~ .... ~what... to live for~ ... - thrusts me up to bumbling stroll on boardwalk ~Ok, have an objective here – we all need something to shoot for – keeps us going – fires the pistons, - beg twenty bucks, here we go...~

Ocean to right, casinos to left – one after next – SANDS, TROPICANA... CEASAR'S – here, a guy standing by a back door – smoking a cigar – frosted blond, her hands wrapped around his arm... they're laughing ...

"Hi... I'm trying to get to New York, would you happen to have 10 dollars - so I can buy a bus ticket there?"

The lady's expression goes serious (she's much older up close – makeup, cracking lines into leathery skin as her brows lower in examining me) – looks at him, gauging... He smiles – cigar protruding from center of teeth - for a while... it registers that he's shaking in silent laughter... "look at this kid" he says to himself – "what a *mess* – heh-heh III *love it* heh-heh..." – slips his hand in pocket - whisks out a wad of cash – "reminds me of me at your age aaaah-*god*" nodding head no "heh-heh" flipping through wad – "you're lucky I won today kid... – and 'm feeling generous heh (sigh)" – peels away a twenty – handing, looking in eyes – "don't turn out like I did kid... – run along now... – *here* – one for good measure." peels, hands – frosted blond spiking into ner-vous laughter, squeezing his arm, hissing a whisper as I leave – his "we're rich now honey... - gimme a cigarette wouldja?" hacking cough, spit ...

Joy surges though body - skip enters step – as pass, stop to take in, 'Korean War Monument': three poles flying military flags set around a sculpture – sol-emn (set atop shiny black stone walls – names of felled troops etched into it) of a soldier carrying a wounded comrade... – its backdrop: glossy black glass window grid – Darth Vaderesque -leading up to sign – glowing orange: HAR-RAHS... – and, next building over, huge letters: BALLY'S ...

Ask for directions to bus station from a Russian guy – lounging, hands behind head, reclined in his padded, canopied three-seater bike – casino adds covering outer shell – his feet up, crossed on handlebars – he points to the multi-colored onion-shape domes of the Taj Mahal, "go through... to street... go left... go two blocks..."

Electronic doors hover open – AC air sweeps over, step in... dim... blinking lights, mirrors, loud sounds... – vast, elaborately patterned red rug... row after row of blinking slot machines... booping, clanging, whirly noises - layered – poppy music mixed in... – here a white-haired lady wearing rose-colored glasses hits jackpot – 3 peaches aligned on flashing machine – red siren spin-ning on top... She's... frowning as she scoops coins into red plastic cup – grabbing one up from the pile – feeding machine – cranks lever, resumes scooping …

Here, a rows of people – mostly old – sit, vacant eyes agaze at whirling fruit… – feed coin, pull lever, feed coin, pull lever …

big black security guard in a suit, lil' microphone attached to ear, approaches …

"Sorry sir – gotta have shoes on to be in here."

"The street's this way right?" pointing across room. -

he points antenna of walkie-talkie he's holding across sea of blinking lights –

"it is that way but I'm sorry I'm gonna have to ask you to leave through the doors you just came in through – not allowed on the main floor with no shoes or shirt…"

Standing, it, registering, look over at heavy solid, brass, spinning, mesmerizing, roulette wheel – as the ball clacks, bounces, settles, round and round …

"Sir, we *don't* allow bare feet in here…"

look over at craps table – a crowd watching… guy (crazed look in eye, sweat on brow) throws die – skip to result – man scrunches face to grimace, clenched fist to touching chin… response waves over crowd… employee in red shoots a look at me while, using thin wooden rod, pulls heaps of blue and red chips sliding over green felt table to himself, his mouth muttering words mechanically into headset mic …

"excuse me *sir*…" he touches arm, notices poison ivy, pulls away, says something into walkie-talkie …

look over at blackjack table – cards in dealer's hands – whir in controlled blurs …

about-face, head for doors… passing through threshold – here, a guy, pacing back and forth, sweat, beaded on face, eyes, bugged, looking down, cell phone to ear - "you *will* – that's the thing – *you will*… no-no-no-no-no you will… yes you have to understand that – I *need* you to do this… – *no-no*…"

Walk past the 'Ripley's Believe it or Not' museum – its huge sculpture of an earth blasting through front of it right above entrance – and it strikes in… – that… by prolonging silence I'm ~feeding worry in others~ - see a payphone… grabbing receiver ~make this quick…" coins in, dial… ~Mom'll answer – give a quick reassuring head's-up…~ and it - ~Oh, beautiful day~ - goes straight to voicemail – "*beeep*"

"Hi Zach here – yes, made it through the shipwreck there – tragedy about Craig – saw it in the paper… I'm uh, gonna be traveling for a little while, -

thinking things through, – calling to say I'm ok - walking and talking and don't worry everything's fine - I'll look to call in a week or so - thanks for understanding as I deal with some things…" ~how do I end this one?~ "Bye…" 'click'.

Depressing scene inside the bus station – down-and-outers to right, left, awaiting Greyhounds… many carrying shopping bags full of stuff… huddled together in line - the poem – written on the scroll held in hand by the Statue of Liberty - flutters to mind… "Send me your *huddled masses*…"… - *"wretched refuse"* is in there too… – who gave us that again? – a gift to the U.S. (if I recall correctly from History class) from… – ~aaahh yeeeah - those *Frenchies!*~

Take a back seat on bus… us tired, hunkered souls… Sky a deep, sulfurous glow as we pull off… Stare out on the passing bay marshes… factories… stretches of trees… patches of strip malls, franchises… ~what're Mom and Dad thinking?… - Shannon – what's *she* thinking?… what can I say… – it's a 'new lease'… – total switch-flipper – reset button, hit… *resurrection*… ought I to drum up a new name to fit new persona… say… 'Michael Cando'? – but 'Michael' – too many experiencing life under this… tag… - Zach Barr has its flare… could drop the 'ch' – make it a 'k'… – drop that extra 'r'… - 'elimination of the inessential' – crack to core…~

Wake up to a twinkling Manhattan, sailing into view… a… hostile thing, this city – from the brief encounters I've had – from what I've read… ~will have to be… *made subject*… – or freedom looses – and freedom must win… - or the design is all wrong – flawed…~

Port Authority bustles with people - all looking like they're trying to escape from it – and, yes, here, huddled masses representing too: boarding or awaiting boarding… the no-shoes-no-shirt attracts stares… – I spring up escalators – blend right into sidewalk traffic – the night crowd, rustling along a crackling, razzley yet gloomy 43rd street, 8th Avenue… on bus I'd thought through heading up to Central Park (lying huddled in a blue haze behind a bush – pile of leaves for a pillow)… Stride north to ~perchance realize this~ and it's hot and I wipe sweat from face with Blimpee napkin, which blew down from above and stuck to chest… – here, brown broken beer bottle bits on sidewalk, carefully steer round – in clear, picture in mind had I cut foot, pulling along trail of blood over these black gum dots… -

"OOONNE PENNY FOLKS!!!" booms straight in ear "that's aaall we're asking – spare a penny *HELP* New York City's homeless…" – hefty white guy, dirty blond beard, stained Kansas City Chiefs hoodie, hands in pouch, standing behind small table with an overturned blue transparent water cooler jug - half-full with coinage and bills …

look into his blank eyes …

"Where's a place to stay around here?"

mechanical: "Down on 23rd between 6 and 7 – church there – they're the only ones taking anyone this late…"

About face, take off south - almost bump into guy in a tux leaving a theatre – in his thirties – jumps backwards, hands in air like I'm a cop with a gun "*Jesus H!*" …

- his date – gorgeous – dangling diamond earrings, blazing grey eyes – snaps red lips into a frown …

"sorry about that." – thought springs to mind of self breaking into sudden caveman movements – arching back, waving arms around ~"OO-OO-OOO!"~ -

they slink into open door of gleaming black limo which purrs right off… and I imagine the inside of the limo – wax vicarious on their night ahead – its unfolding – and if all goes well… – shake it out of head, quickening pace for 23rd …

An exhausting distance… – and left foot *is* bloodied now – who know how – nothing gushing, just… toe wrapped in a Wendy's napkin …

Four bums are huddled on the front steps of church, grumbling, laughing, one sucking at a roach, coughing smoke on my head as I descend stairs towards door (in an alley with yellow-painted brick walls)….

Swing in… sad vibes thick in air… a counter – sad, heavy, (though, an edge) black lady at it …

"Any more beds here tonight?"

she points at a clipboard on counter… "sign your name."

take up bic pen, tied to clipboard with shoelace, scrawl *Zak Bar*

"is there any food?"

"dinner got done a while ago…" turns head to kitchen - other side of a lounge area, leans back in chair, "Harold!"

thin light-skin black guy with bugged-out eyes wearing white apron and hair net darts head into view.

"There any food lef for this young man here?"

"I could heat somethin' up."

"Go over to him."

Walk through the living room area – dim - rows of chairs filled with slouched homeless, - blue light flickering on them – from a few TVs mounted up by ceiling, some of them watching a 'Touched by an Angel' re-run …

Harold's pulling a pot from fridge, setting it on blue flame on stove, pulls plastic off top, stirs – grabs, spins open a bag of six hamburger buns… "you lucky we got leftovers."

A stooped grey haired Native American woman has silently appeared next to me – moving her lips, making a noise like "maw-rawr-rawr-awr"

"Oh you want some too eh? heh-heh – now Milly *you* just ate – this here's for this young man her y'see?"

she lets a low groan… turns, shuffles away …

"There we go, that's about enough" lifting lid – steam puffing out, stirs… – opens bun with other hand, ladles a heap of tomato-sauced meat into it – "sloppy Joe night tonight…" puts it on paper plate – "I'll give you a little extra" – ladles another load on - flips another bun open – another big ladle – closes buns… handing in an intense eye contact moment – "there you are buddy, enjoy…" – "and here," swinging open fridge – grabbing jug of lime green Hawaiian Punch – pours a styrofoam cup… "there y'are…"

"Thanks." sip it… – tastes just like the red… smell the sloppy Joes as carry plate over to common area… settle in, look up at TV… "Wheel! Of! Fortu-uune!"… lifting sloppy Sloppy Joe to mouth, clamp teeth in - feel it burning tongue, savoring… – the lady on TV about to solve puzzle – "Six of one, half a dozen of the other!" calls someone from behind… lady on TV happily calls it… sloppy joe mix dripping from chin… "I knew that." grumbles long-bearded guy slumped in chair next to me, "just didn't say it." Access Hollywood starts – "Ginger Freehan – after a string of romances – is love life in Malibu *sizzling* again? - and Danny Dietch – *at it again* – a night of partying ends up with his Hummer full of buddies *flipped* upside down on his front lawn – only to have them *round out the night* at *Club Techi!*"… chewing, ~what does anybody in here care about Ginger Freehan's love life?~ looking to left, black guy in blue cotton winter hat, giggling to self, nodding head in disbelief – "boy done went and *flipped* that Hummer heh-heh-heh."

Long time sitting… digesting, watching… walk to counter… assigned a room …

open to darkness, smell of B.O… a big-bellied guy snoring on far bed… I put the change of clothes (just scrounged from donation bin in common room) on bed and head for shower (bar of soap, given at counter, and towel [from bin] in hand) …

Use towel to scrub crusty black blood off left toe …

in room, pull on the soft pair of sweatpants (red - 'UCSD' - in yellow - up one leg) and shirt (white - navy 'Citibank', small, on left breast) - man violently clears throat – worked – snoring ceased …

Lay back atop sleeping bag (given at counter)… feels like ~absolute Heaven on Earth~

~like on a cloud…~

CHAPTER 2

Eyes open to sun-filled room... ... ~all this sunlight through one iron-bar-caged window...~

judging by light... somewhere between 10 and 11... hear a snort, look over at other bed... sitting on its edge – black, buddha build, no shirt, bald, graying beard, yellow eyes - pupils jiggling back and forth as they stare at my face, "mornin'" he rasps ...

Go downstairs... see on (old school, beige) wall clock that it's 10:45... into main room –residents hunkered in folding chairs, watching Montel on TVs ...

"There any breakfast?"

"lunch is served at one..." ... she leans back in chair, cups hand to mouth to yell – but leaves off – "go ask Harold, he might have somethin'"

en route over see a fresh pair of yellow flip-flops in donation bin... slip them on... match yellow UCSD on leg - ~a bit big but, hey...~ Harold is finishing clean-up – wiping a towel at table – looks up, faking mad: "*you* again, heh-heh..."

"Yeeah better late than never – any vittles around?"

"I'll give ya some vittles heh-heh." – whirling open fridge – "let's see here..."

pulls out a gallon of whole milk, plants it down on plastic table "have a seat"... I sit... grabs a box of Froot Loops off top of fridge... styrofoam bowl... styrofoam cup... from fridge - a plastic jug – an orange liquid in it – tilts it in pouring – on label: 'COSCO ORANGE DRINK'... plastic spoon – "thereya go buddy, have at it..."

crunch a bowl down... feel sugar crash walking for exit ...

Dig through the donations bin... find a dark blue shirt - printed in yellow across chest: 'SPARTICUS.'

Pull it over white one, head out into bright summer's day, in search of more breakfast... fingers feel at ten dollar bill in pocket as flip-flop past bums smoking, coughing, leaning on walls, sitting on stairs ...

Half a block away is a blue awning - "CHESTER FRIED" on it... walking in, to left two Mexican guys in aprons behind a grill fry up chicken, further in - to right it opens up into a space with two rows of cheap tables – occupied by either blind (walking sticks hugged to chest, chewing food, blabbing out to each other- "I remember when... - do you remember that Jimmy?" ~must be a blind person's shelter close by~, homeless, or down-on-luck-looking folk. Passing see-through deli case on left – few logs of salami and bologna in it – cut to varying lengths, wrapped in plastic – here a chunk of yellow cheese half wrapped in foil... – here a big plastic jar of JIF – butter knife sticking out it – next it, big glass Welch's jar - knife in it too... One of the Mexicans leaves the chicken, walking over, zings pen out from behind ear, points it at me, then readies it on pad on counter... "Bacon-egg-and-cheese... on a roll."

by time I return from freezers, Tropicana OJ in hand, it's done, wrapt in foil, being handed over – pen pointing at next down-and-outer: "gimme a *buttered roll.*"

Asians cashiers – feisty wife, running show – elderly husband(?), assisting, squinting through unfashionable, large-lense glasses – wearing – sitting high atop head – baseball cap - brim (unbent) thrusts forward authoritatively – bold patch: cobalt blue, white and yellow, the black word 'HOFSTRA' – in a heated debate with thin black guy here – "*breff mints* – you got breff mints here? you know *mint* – spear-a-mint" – eating hand motions – "*mints*" – it clicks and he grabs, sticks a roll of Certs on counter as customer mumbles "slap you upside the head..." – the lady snatches ten from my hand – change zipt back – "next-*hello-hello*".

Sit at a front table, facing door, watch customers stagger in, wobble out.... unwrapping foil, taking bites, ~what are... next moves? What does... wisdom dictate here?~

Notice a TV's playing to my right – sits atop square trashcan lid... screen has Chinese television flickering on it – a soap opera – handsome Chinese guy about-facing before a pretty Chinese girl – walks quickly off – camera zooms quick in at her face – eyes bulge, well up – she bursts out crying... paper plate half protrudes from trashcan's flap lid... like a tongue... big circular sticker add below it: 'LUCKY STRIKE'.

Seated to right: thin, old Puerto Rican guy grumbling curses as he blurs a penny over "Crazy Eightz" cards – "you son of a…" scatches *you damn piece of…"* – blows, sweeps scrapings off table… next card… watching his hand, realize I'm scratching hard at poison ivy on nape of neck, – here little cherries and bells manifesting themselves in the blur… as he's softly, delicately, blowing scrapings away …

To left: a fat blind lady – frizzy curly black hair – walking stick propped on chest… with white plastic spoon she shovels mounds of pasty white mac and cheese from cylindrical see-through plastic container in between large open-mouthed chews – mayo, around mouth, spots on cheeks… -

~it's time to call Shannon…~

think through conversation, chewing on eggs and sausage… ~tasty sandwich~ – best part being heat of it – ~home-cooked feel~ …

Pick up pay phone receiver out front Chester Fried, roll in two quarters… dial… stare at red sticker – white letters 'YOU'RE DOPE' on it - as it rings …

"Hello?"

"Shannon, it's Zak…"

"where are you?"

"I'm fine… kinda going incognito a while… – examining things… – calling to say I'm fine, don't worry about me, all that…"

"When are you coming home?"

"I'm thinking things over – things have changed – in my thinking – outlook on things y'know… – I'll be re-examining things a while - plumbing depths, planning next moves – new moves – drumming up, hashing out new objectives – directions – other than Yale – you know how I'm into art right?"

"yeah"

"That's the course I'm going here on out – straight on – full on –cutting to chase – these are the prime years y'know - energywise – put that energy into building – *now* rather that 4 years down the line – 8 years more likely it would've been – with grad school – I'll bypass all that – straight into the school of life – real experiences over textbooks and lectures – so, yeah," ~gone too long…~ "just, give me time – if you're up for dating others or whatever feel free."

"what? when can I see you?"

"in time." ~("in time(?))"~

"Where are you? we can pick you up."

"Like I said, let me just think things through a while, sorting things out – I'm in a real planning mode – it's pretty exciting actually…"

"have you called your family yet?"

"Yeah, just left a message on the machine.... - Ok well was just calling to say I'm alright and please - go ahead and.. move on – move forward - I'll be fine."

"*what?*"

"Ok, Shannon, bye." Clank down receiver, deep breath... roll in two quarters... dial home... ringing... answering machine clicks on again, clunk down receiver ...

Shannon, having depressed silver key with illumined orange hung-up-phone icon on it, thumbs 9-1-1 – asks operator to trace call – a series of transfers – she has time, it's Sunday... "we see here it's... on 23rd Street... in Manhattan." – depresses hang-up button again... dials 9-1-1 again – files a missing person report... calls Mrs. Barr, relates the conversation... hangs up... sits at computer, finds photos of her and Zach at prom – crops, his head, enlarges, clicks print... writes MISSING with sharpie above picture, below: 'Zach Barr 6ft, blond, blue eyes, 160-170, contact police if you see him REWARD.'

~hm, she probably traced that call... should have called from another location~ heading towards Times Square ...

She walks to the train station – stops in at Kinkos – 50 copies... catches train and... four hours and eleven minutes after the call, here, stands at the pay phone in front of Chester Fried... pulls copies and new tape dispenser from bag, posts the first on side of phone casing ...

Approach the blinking lights... in flow here with the masses... stop in tracks, in central-most point of it all... just... *being*... this... new sight... revealing every detail, clear... do a slow, full rotation... it occurring that I'm... freer than I've ever been to date – ~there is *nothing* tying me down – I have no responsibilities whatsoever today – there are no hoops to jump through...~ looking at all the blinking lights... ~what is this here?~

~so... *impersonal*... – people (who knows who?) rushing by... – cold (love-wise) – *chilly*... – what if some homeless dude (what if *I*) dropped dead on the corner here – how many would charge on by to their appointments... – perhaps some Tennessee Christian group in town would descend upon – prop up head, dial 9-1-1... – ambulance pulls up – haul body (impediment) into vehicle – away... to obscurity, forgotteness ...

Tourists – here, a family, licking ice cream cones – passing through – here, a pack of Asians, snapping pictures of each other – here, Black guy with head-banging dreads, pounds away on overturned five gallon buckets... here: a Native American band - sheeny black pony tails hanging down backs – blow into multi-flute instruments, strumming at amplified acoustic guitars... here, cops – proud-looking Puerto Ricans in sunglasses... looking again at it all... fishing for words to put to it... ~it's...'blinking-lights-I-don't-know-you-keep-it-that-way-pass-on-by' land.'... venture on... towards park... – vague notion in mind that there, amidst the trees, a revelation of 'next steps' (intuit set of instructions, whatever) awaits my discovery ...

Having posted all 50 in Chelsea, she hails a cab, to Penn Station... presently sits eating slice of pizza from box - got from Rays - reading Albert Camus' *The Stranger*....

Inside the park looks, feels great – ultra-green lawn stretching, radiating... – bodies laid out... – college students, tossing Frisbees... dogs meeting other dogs - here a Golden Retriever –shimmering coat – sniffs behind of pure bred Boxer – its stubby tail, jiggling as it sniffs – jutting an eye up at me, emitting a growl... – here a pug, glares intense at me, also growling – as owner crouches behind it, Ziploc bag and plastic fork in hand ...

Go in search of solitude... climbing over rocks – startle a couple making out... stun a guy in a nook, dabbing touches on easeled painting ...

a remote curvy path... people taper away... skyscarpers visible over tree-tops... seem to be watching me... climb down another cluster of boulders... to... by a small lake – little blond kid in sweater vest holding a remote control to his wooden sailboat in water... he looks over, writes me off, looks to his boat again... climb over to other side of boulder... another lake, no one around... pick up a smooth stone, wing it – skips upon surface – 'pit-pit-pit-pit-pit-*glump*...''

~5 skips... hm... anything to that?... 5 boroughs?~ pace edge of water... ~what's... next... move? where to go from here?... what's... quickest way to top~ - ~how does one go about *owning* art world – in palm of hand?~

more pacing... a nap on a rock... wondering in woods... no answers... present themselves... start for shelter again... here, flip-flopping south through Time Square... ~who cares what for who here... how about those 50 - 20 years ago who 'had power' here – where are they now – what are their names now? - what does their walking, thinking, here then mean now...~ - ~*and who pays for all this?*~... all the hours of planning that went into building these blinking structures – the drawings, phone calls – and here it is – who's acknowledged for it? – as African guy – in over-sized bright orange football jersey and hat (new, stiff, propped high on head), frowning, pulls stick of gum from pack with teeth, - tosses wrapper angrily on sidewalk – stabs a look at me …

~who cares for who here? …. is there any TLC? Where is it?~

Stop in at Macy's to cool off… - ~the largest department store in the world – or *was* or…~ wander the aisles, floors… here, in cologne section, bottle after bottle, set out to sample… "Contradiction"… "Euphoria"… pick up bottle of "Eternity" – two big spritzes on neck… take up bottle of Hugo Boss' "Selection" – spritz wrists …

Push through heavy revolving doors, stomach, yearning, ~for even a morsel~ – bacon egg and cheese long ago burned up… and yet… muscles keep legs moving ~for one reason or other…~… picture an invisible being moving the meat legs… closing an eye, with open one, look at nose, traveling along through space… – ~the soul within – an invisible life force - propelling the piece of meat forth… operates, drives the machine…~

study people going by in opposite direction – picture the invisible beings moving, animating them – some brighter than others - ~how come? – 'force' in this one exceeding 'force' in that one… – age plays its part (youth tending to be brighter) – as, here, this teen-aged girl passing – fresh from Michigan or wherever – radiance shooting forth from eyes - compared to… this beggar, leaned against wall, holding cardboard 'Homeless and UNDERAPPRECIATED' sign – clear plastic trashbag next him, full of bagels… – stop in tracks, pointing, "can I get one of those?" he gives me a long sad stare… "whadaya want one a them for?" – "hungry - staying at the shelter on 23rd…" - "go get your *own* damn food then…" turn to go – "aah go ahead, *what do I care…*" reach in, grab an everything… "thanks man" walk on, close eyes, bite, feel garlic's effect on tastebuds, onions, salt… ~there are exceptions though (to age factor) – that fitness guru – Jack LeLanne – swimming across the San Francisco bay towing 5 sailboats in teeth at age 70 – or that guy – 50-something - ran 50 marathons in 50 days - *in 50 states!*

and why's that? – this one having more energy than that one… who's calling these shots – who gets which amount of energy? and why? all ties in to wisdom, could say… - degrees of it – preserving those who have/abide by it – have more than others – than those getting dogged down for their lack of it… – so then how does one go about getting more of this wisdom – seeing that it enhances, enriches, extends life… – well there're the answers rote off top of head – 'reading, going to classes, being mentored... – then the vague 'meditation, praying' cloud'~ finishing bagel, rounding 23rd ~then again you can't go and say every energetic person is wise... – there are those runners who have their issues – heard of one lady – avid runner - claimed she *couldn't* stop running – so, on a run one day, she just, got up, and jumped off a bridge... – right when you think you have something pegged – on along comes an exception – blows it up in your face...~

eyes catch, latch-on to MISSING poster taped to pay phone – prom night zaps to mind – mostly a blur – the spat with Shannon in the morning– Phil Green was there – next bed over – lifted his head up – told us to 'shut up and get lost – take it elsewhere' – her leaving in a huff... my searching an hour for a shoe – walking home – miles – wearing one... - forking over $50 at the tux place ...

I still look exactly like the picture – just... more scruff on face... pull 99 cent sunglasses from sweatpants pocket, put them on... ~gotta get a hat...~ - recall seeing one in donation bin... descend stairs... through alley... into shelter door ...

receptionist's eyes widen at sight of me... ~she knows~

bypass bin, a few others looking over at me - big, bugged, eyes... smell fried chicken - dinner about to be served, head straight for room ...

entering, fat black guy pulls a sit-up, scoots back – to leaning on wall, feet crossed, arms crossed... a 6 o'clock semi-darkness outside the window, in the room... ~he knows~

go to window, look out, see an NYPD car pull up... "*great*"

"Everything alright there?" he rasps ...

"I gotta get outta here." dash out door – down stairs – two officers stand at receptionist – there goes that exit... – turn to run back – "there he go! – right *dere!*" hollers one of the residents from TV area – up one flight – turn into bathroom – one guy – standing under gushing nozel, hair plastered down over eyes, lathering an armpit – whisk by – fling open window – blasting a pigeon to fluttering away – an egg rolling from its nest - falling, cracking at feet... push nest to floating down through air, get squeezing through window ~that's too far a drop... but maybe if I hang from ledge, drop into that pile of trashbags there...~ -

"Are you Zach Barr?" - I leave off, flip-flops touching down on tiles... they approach slow – two lady cops – the guy with plastered hair, covering himself "hey, what's going on here?"

"Are you Zach Barr?" repeats the tough-looking blond – hat brim low, pulling a leather glove on tighter. The other hangs back, near door. – here, the blond, approaching – intense, open-wide blue eyes - "Just remaain calm, it's gonna be aaalright."

the days of tackle football in Clark Park flash to mind – the dodging and weaving of punt returns ~gotta pull off some fancy footwork here~ - snap into a jog - she readies – bending legs into a wrestler's stance, gritting teeth – I bob head hard left – she doesn't bite – jut right – she commits – spring (all might) left – flip-flop flying off in process – and she's toast - but the guy showering (who's caught on – crazed face – lunging at me, arms spread *"AARR!"*) – but I whip a spin maneuver – feel his slippery body sliding across back "RAAAHR!" – hear his elbows hitting tiles – feel hot water from shower raining on me – spin move slowed me a second - enough for blond to recoup – dives at me – snags back of t-shirt collar – loud tear – loosing footing – see yelling black lady cop fast approaching – a square-on bump-tackle – to the three of us going over – through gushing shower water - land on naked guy – who overreacts – screaming, flailing – and we're tangled and all moving and clutching – growling, slipping, pushing, pulling - hear one of their CBs crackle a message - scramble to feet - naked guy's got my ankle *"hold it right there you!"*– kick it free - black cop leaps up – runs ahead of me - turns around to facing me at the door, trying to get billyclub from belt - *"Stop right there!"*- straightarm her to back pedaling – slams into wall, caving in plaster - shift into sprint down hall for exit – down the flight – get rounding turn, eyeing door – when one of those 'silent-types' – 'been-through-the-ringer' types – tattooed, short, lean, mean, graying Puerto Rican mixes – launches from a folding chair - feel his arms slither around my right ankle like snakes – they constrict like Boa's – catch a whiff of fried chicken as I go over – break fall crushing a folding chair… get up to one knee, look down, assess, he's burrowed in… raise arm to administer a punch – cue for one of his cronies to dive in – hooking arm, cursing – slams a knee into my face – grabs both sides of my head – rushes his Hispanic/black face towards – landing headbutt – explosion of stars – come to as falling back – hit head on floor – cops enter view as he clamps on a chokehold …

CHAPTER 3

The walls in the police station are a soothing pale green color …

"Officer Morely" (as black plastic name tag reads) shakes in laughter, talking quietly with another cop… I sit in chair, overhearing Latino receptionist lady asking my Mom questions on the phone - she points the receiver at me …

"Hi Mom."

"Hi Zach, are you ok?"

"Yeah."

"Dad's leaving work to pick you up."

"I'd rather stay here in New York."

"Zach you need some time to recoup, readjust - you've been through a lot."

"Guess I don't have a choice then." ~ah, don't be pissy.~ "Ok, well, I'll sit tight till Dad gets here."

"Why didn't you call us?"

"yeah I left that voicemail - I've been thinking things through – was waiting for the right timing…"

"You called Shannon – she called here…"

"Yeah – she had that call traced – cops came and nabbed me up – now I'm sitting in a police station – could have been handled better."

The Latino lady is staring at me, arms crossed, chewing gum.

"We just want to make sure you're ok –"

"I'm fine –I was doing fine – things are blown out of proportion – should iron out soon enough though – I'll wait here for Dad and see you in a few hours ok…"

Latino's eyes widen

"Ok Zach, see you soon."

She snags the phone – "hello-hello" hangs up, rolling eyes back into head, picks up, taps buttons with long fingernail… "Hello Mrs. Barr, we still have some questions for you, we have to fill out this paperwork." I stroll out of ear-shot, take seat …

Whole atmosphere changes as a tall Irish cop - together with a short Dominican cop – burst through swinging doors - shoving a black youth in hoodie (hood on – covering eyes – just large lips, open mouth, visible), baggy pants falling down, untied pair of hightops… And they're struggling now – very serious - but it looks… comical to me - stomach shakes, even, in a giggle – "nice one" hear self say between laughter. aaaand they're gone – deep into the innards of the station – like that… mind unwittingly unravels what the kid's scenario might be – probably a highschool student (education foisted on him) – no job – some misdemeanor - now this crazy situation - no money to bail him out… – who to care for him – who to come to his aid? caught, trapped, on to being thrust about like a pinball by and within the system – and for how long …

~well, it is what it is… – till unravels into 't'was what it t'was' and that'll (have) be(een) that (for one reason or other)~ … get cleaning fingernails with a pencil …

Dad walks in, looking (despite business attire) like an oversized kid, befuddled.

Smile curls on, awkward moment – puts hand on shoulder, gentle squeeze, "Hey Zach, everything alright?"

"Yeah, quite an experience."

"Glad you pulled through." – peers a concerned, probing look into eyes, gauging sanity …

"The car's right out here." –

"Mr. Barr?" – receptionist –"we have some forms here to fill out."

Officer Morely steps in – a "report" in hand – "would you step this way Mr. Barr?"

a half-hour question-and-paperwork-filled span transpires …

Drive up 95 in Audi is a tense one - despite classical CD playing – now jazz….

"Craig's funeral's on Saturday…"

"hm. yeah I'll… be ready for it…"

"Jerry's leaving for the Air Force base in September – out in Arizona…"

"Oh yeah…"

"Ruth's plugging away at school – got honors in math again…"

"Good to hear…"

the questions begin… I'm on the defensive (short-answer mode) – how it all happened: "storm blew in – knocked out by a mast – next thing I come to on shore…" – "what have you been doing all this time?": "wandering around – went to Atlantic City – on up to New York." - "Why New York?" - "Figure that's where it's at…" - "What's *it*?" - "Art – the art scene – highest energy there…" "Art scene?" "yeah"… "You want to be an artist now?" "It fascinates me."… "What about Yale in the fall?" "That's out." "Out?" "No longer an option." "Because you want to pursue art in New York?" ""want" isn't the word… – have an interest in… 'desire' to do this…" ~why steer into word usage?~ "This happened because of the shipwreck? – this… change in thinking." "You could say…" "We have an appointment set up with a counselor – tomorrow – just to… gauge things y'know – as you re-acclimate…" "That's fine…" - cessation of words… drawn silence – music unraveling. . . ~probably thinks this is all a phase – some kind of post-traumatic symptom – that'll fizzle as head clears… - perhaps it is, will after all… - time'll… 'tell' I suppose~ …

Things turning suburban – here, Dad waves to a mom in a minivan full of kids in soccer uniforms – bumpersticker on front fender – yellow with black letters, smiley face next the words: 'SMILE. Your mother CHOSE LIFE.'… Pulling into suburban driveway – everything looking idyllic (in a suburban 'togetherness; things-in-place' sense). . . Stepping out the car… smell of flowers in air… pleasantness ~'peaceville' here – safetyville~ – animal spirits inside, urging imminent departure …

In through kitchen door – Mom, walking towards, arms outstretched - looking older – stressed smile – masking woe, weariness. . . The embrace. . . Cold about it all though – a ~so what? all this~ vibe – sentence – surfacing, reciting in mind – ~even this – if in the end it all goes anyway…~ Jerry appears – crew cut – neck thicker than a few weeks ago – "Zaaach – *survivor*…" firm handshake – radiating hazel eyes studying what's inside mine… – charging an edginess inside – as I see in his – all the recent influence of Air Force buddies and bar scene antics – seen bare, clear as a bell – sticking him on edge now …

Ruth appears – looking somewhat dazed… - in her eyes: numbers, vast amounts of equations - potential for so many more to come – infinite – or, not infinite – likely when she dies, Isaac Newton will have had more ~'in number'~

Stand awkwardly, nodding head saying "yep" a few times – "well guess I'll head up to room, change the clothes…"

Everything is arranged as it was in highschool - down to the gleaming, lined lacrosse trophies (~boy, are they ever that they are(?))~... – yet all the stuff taking on an ultra-clean aspect now – a preservative kind of... *polish* – *ethereal*...
... - occurs I've been standing, staring, an unusually long period of time ...

Open top drawer of dresser: stuffed to capacity with shining white brand new t-shirts, underpants, cotton socks ...

"I guess you'll be wanting to take a shower then?" I hear Dad say, standing at doorway. . .

~ wanting to take a shower(?) ~

"Uh, yeah... I'll uh, take one in just a bit here..." - ~"take one"? ...– ~"bit"?~ ~"here"? – (where else?)~ ...

"We'll have dinner on the table when you're done... Glad you're back." And he goes ...

~ "back"? ~

Pull brand new underclothes from drawer, open next drawer down, pull laundry-detergent-scented bright colored shirt from it, and a pair of preppyish light tan GAP shorts ...

Into the sky blue bathroom – sparkling – late afternoon sun pouring in ...

Place puffy pile on closed toilet lid. Shed shirt... Catch - for first time in a long time – full-on reflection in full-length mirror ahang on closed door... curls instant smile on - ~*pirate*~... – scraggly bleached-blond-looking, semi-curly, dirty, dready, locks, hang down over tan, freckly face – whites of eyes, teeth beam forth... – the shorts – faded red mesh things – stripped of: tan line, stark. . .

recall electric clippers – under in cabinet... open drawer, here it is... click on # 2 clip, plug it in, flick on – 'BKZZZZZZZZZZ..." – put to mid-forehead – slide a clear plow over – locks tumbling down - to back of head... again and again... whole head... re-look in full-length mirror... ~convey forth an entirely *other* vibe altogether now – than five minutes ago... - into people's eyes – to registering in their brain – to eliciting judgment calls, influencing their treatment of me...~

standing in hot, long shower, imagine it washing – cleansing away – New York City filth - eyes gaze down at orangish-brown water, transporting grime from feet to... swirling down drain... ~revolutionary~ ...

~who to hang out with now... who from the crew is in town ... There's Don – off at Brown... Steve, Tristan, Greg – UMASS, Gene and Evan – NYU, Tyler – New York Film Academy... Paul and Jeff – Columbia... Gary – Upenn... Kent Merril and Dave Furl – BU - and Sam... Andy and Kurt – U of B... - Adrian –

Harvard... - Alisa and Shirley: Brown. Susan and Joyce: Wesley, Jess and Breanne: BU... Tara, Amy, Eileen: UConn... Laura – Yale... on and on... Who's around... – Jesse is taking the year off – traveling through Europe... Brad and Ben – working a year at a farm on Martha's Vineyard... Dan... – Dan Eggars... – said he was going to work for his Dad a year – before applying anywhere... – guess I'll give him a call at some point... – and Pete Hess – he's probably cutting his many lawns... employing a fleet of high school students... Heather is probably still working there at the mall... and Emily – she's probably working at the café... pay a visit to her soon enough... she'll know more what's going on... – will see plenty of them and more at Craig's funeral Saturday ...

Sling shower curtain open... – stark late-day sun beams through window... bizarro vibes ...

Pull on all the fresh, warm clothes... look again in mirror... ~skinhead brawler gone clean...~

Fresh socks descending wall-to-wall beige carpet. - memories flooding in – most vivid: – walking down these stairs – Christmas morning – to behold – there – glistening – reflections of Christmas tree lights splashed across - - - brand new Yamaha YZ80... – the smell of the glossy black rubber tires... - and how's that bike now? – still at uncle Earl's farm in New Jersey - tarped in storage shed. . .

walking in kitchen, smell of chicken fills nose,– like Mom used to make it – same scent ...

Pulling chair out, sitting... – strange, orangey lighting... Dad (sitting now – tie streams onto plate as plants down – grabs it off, clears throat). . . Mom sets down steaming casserole dish, center of table – carrot coins and onions surrounding a chunk of browned chicken. . . Sits... Tension high. . . memories appear: Thanksgiving days from times past – cooked bird on table like this – heads would bow – as Dad would rote a Catholic "Bless us O Lord, for these Thy gifts, which we are about to receive..." prayer – but that's with a big turkey - - - this here, just... sections of a chicken... He picks up knife, fork... – saws through to chalk scratch on plate, up it goes – the piece of chicken, on the fork, to where my eyes catch Dad's - irritated suspicious bolts zap therefrom – commanding I get eating, less staring at his eating – 'get in line' vibes – 'straighten up and fly right' vibes – 'and fast'. . .

Mom, half-sad looking, "Zach we arranged for an appointment for you tomorrow... - with a counselor... – Dr. Cohen... - just to help with adjustment... after the whole thing..."

~ 'whole 'thing'? ~ . . .

CHAPTER 4

Dr. Cohen's office is in the center of Boston. . .

Drive with Mom is a long one - - - few words spoken …

Yellow sponge-painted walls, big Winslow Homer painting, heavy black secretary. . . Musak plays overhead… – a gangsta rap song enters into thoughts – a string of lyrics repeats over and over again against my will – ~why did I subject myself to that then – here, it's dug in, pulling sway now – having its own way – ain't gettin' rid of it – and there's… no going back to 'unlisten' to it… had I known then - woulda foregone listening to it… and where's the control of the mind at times like this – c'mon – just quit it already - or when you get thinking of that girl you like – that girl who's already taken - entrenched in a relationship – even so, the mind slings into replay loop – and you're like "uh, stop" - - - and it's like "ha Ha! Fat chance! You're mine – I OWN you!"~

"Ryan." – the secretary… A look to Mom - sad, scared expression… proceed towards his office, down hall – towards opening door - from where a girl – presumably another patient – emerges, looking shell-shocked, walks by – zapping watery eyes up last second… ~of aaall places on earth I could be now – here I am… in a psychiatrist's office… - of aaall things I could be doing… – *this*… - this is what I'm doing… and why is this?! – think of all these others having such fun this second! *what gives?*~

Dr. Cohen is tall… beak nose… thick glasses, light khakis, sky blue polo. . . disarming smile. . . holding clipboard, yellow legal pad, clamped in it….

The 'nice to meet you's' – shaking hands, as culture silently dictates… "Call me Barry." He says through smiling toothy mouth. . .

"Now Zach, I offer the options of either the couch – to lye on – or, the chair – your choice entirely."

I recline slow – feeling muscles ooze soreness …

"So, the shipwreck…" sitting "how do you… *feel* about this?"

~he gets paid for this?~

"It happened…"

"More…"

"The future excites me more than dwelling on the past…"

"One must deal with the past before moving effectively into future…"

"Well, says you…"

"Let's put it this way, what do you hope to achieve in the future?"

"Where are we going with this?"

"You'll see."

"See what?"

"I've dealt with thousands of people over the years. I speak from experience. I know where I'm going with all this." -

"Where?"

"In time, Ryan, it's a process – cooperating with the questions helps to expedite progress in the journey." –

"Journey to where?"

"Is it ok if I ask the questions here – just for a little while – to get the ball rolling?"

"So you're asking my future aspirations…"

"Right."

"It's foggy… Who knows… what's worth doing? - Has been a recurring question in head. – so you're… positing… that the fog will clear as the past gets resolved?"

"You could say – now, future aspirations, what are they? – fog aside…"

~to be a top artist – live in total freedom - but who's this guy? – why share it – what does it mean to him… meeting him here for the first time…~

sooo, evade around (which he easily picks up on, notes on pad) …

"I understand you were on your way to Yale… – good school – very good school… – would you still like to go there?"

~'still?'~ "that idea – concept – framework – tradition - was foisted on me – schools of fish – go-with-flow type deal - 'fall in line' – cue-taking - I'm more up for cutting to chase – real life experience, growing from that… – and no monster debt to pay off later – and skip having to get up to speed after four years in Uni-bubble…"

"You feel you'll learn more in… 'real life' than in a college setting?"

"Utilizing echo technique I see."

"…Ryan, you're suffering" –

~ 'suffering?'~

- "from what's know as 'post-traumatic stress dis-order'. – this is perfectly, ok – perfectly understandable – given what you've been through… I'm here to help you… Help you… re-acclimate to a normal functioning society" ~?!~ "and would like to see if we can make more headway at our next session, ok?… think about it…"

walk out to sad mom, waiting in lobby. . . the sad, quiet car ride… to house - where it dawns ~I have no real schedule at all for the rest of the day…– all friends away at school or working… Shannon's left for Brown… - it's me and 'the options, possibilities are endless'… – well, more like 'limited' though, 'given present circumstances.' …

Dad stops mid-chew…. "So… your wallet gone, guess you'll have to go for a new license – and was your social security card in there?"

"Yep."

"Well you'll have to get that too…"

~hm, pieces off plastic and paper…~ "yeah… guess I can look into it tomorrow…" -

spooning clump of mashed potatoes from bowl to 'clank' down on plate - "Tomorrow is Saturday. – the funeral… can look into on Monday…"

Craig was a childhood friend… Constantly popping up at our house… went on vacations with us – and I with his parents… – yet I can't quite gauge whether my parents are going to funeral or not… – I'd rather they didn't… just… they probably should… an uneasiness in air… "do you two plan to go?"

Dad, stops chewing piece of beef… "do you think we should go?"

"He was here at the house a lot over the years…"

"We'll go…"

"It's up to you."

"We knew Craig – didn't know his family that well – but yeah, it's fine, we'll go… Get your suit all ready to go… – we can leave here around 9 – it starts at 10…" no sign of dessert, I open freezer, find a gallon of Breyers Vanilla Bean – freezer burn, encrusted on… "how old is this?"

"Ice cream doesn't go bad…" says Mom.

See the expiration date… tomorrow… rock hard… stick it in microwave… spins… 'ding'… two big scoops… slice a chunk of supermarket-brand banana bread, lay it on top the mounds… into den… click on TV… News… spoonful after spoonful – here, a "shootout at a convenience store" in the ghetto… a "fire in a factory"… a "dolphin found swimming in a river" – helicopter view of it – "experts say it is either sick or disoriented – the last sighting of a dolphin in the Jones River was *nine years ago* – no account of what happened to that one" …

~exciting, scooping ice cream in bowl there… felt deserving, shoveling it in mouth… now just… feel like a slob…~ lift shirt… ~can afford it… lean 'rib look' going…~… fade off in puffy sectional couch pillows …

Morning… don't feel like going to funeral …

mechanical pulling on of the suit – last worn at high school lacrosse banquet… fits ok… – looks good in mirror – which it has to – considering I'll be the 'star' at the funeral …

And all eyes *are* on me… handshakes, hugs, pats on back… Ryan – a closer friend than Craig a while there senior year, wearing a fake, crazy smile "hey I don't know what to say man – glad you're alright." – Tom, Kurt, and Adrian too – all with these sad smiles… no one knowing what exactly to say to me – beyond 'good to see you' and 'you doin' alright?'… - parents seeming all to have happyface masks in place… – turning glum at start of, and through the ceremony… Andy: "anything I can do, man, just let me know…" squeezing hand in a shake – which has me stifling laughter… – just Sandra and Chris – two of the more 'arty' friends of Craig's really carry a sense of frankness – sad-faced, not wanting to be there, hoping it's over as fast as possible …

Shannon appears – looking slim, sophisticated in black dress with rectangular black bag - held in black gloves… Her eyes widen at sight of me …

~it's the shaved head~ we hug, and she - with Eileen Fields right with her – stays by me through the ceremony …

a sea of black around the burial plot… Craig's family has money on all sides… the tension between the relatives, for one reason or other, lingers, gnaws in air …

Feel an edginess leave - realizing I won't be called upon to give a speech …

Shiny Cadillac hearse pulls up… his Dad, brothers, uncle(?) slide the glossy black coffin out the rear… lower it into plot …

~who knows what's gonna happen here far as religion goes…~ Craig rejected any form of organized religion… ~what to do about a funeral in such a case?~ A guy in a blue and red – Episcopalian-looking - robe steps forward (from the "Unitarian Church" Andy whispers back to my "who's this guy?") and delivers a neutral message – no mention of Christ – 'God' sprinkled in a few times) - all given in a quick, smiling, friendly way – a few sniffles heard round… tissues to noses under designer black sunglasses… – no mention of the afterlife… which seems to open a void – for everyone's mind to go there –

even moreso than if the guy was pointing with open Bible the need of salvation from the fires of hell through the redeeming blood of Christ… it's evident these questions of the aftermath are stirring – and now everyone – relatives and all – want the ceremony over as soon as possible – this guy, checking his watch – over here, a discreet scrolling on a Blackberry… – the preacher perceives his neutral message backfiring -speeds it up, starts improvising… – the one wail of the day lets loose, women converge, console… he's shaken at it, wraps it up – no prayer… Craig's Dad steps in, hands raised, making calming up and down motions "Thank you all for coming, thank you for your prayers" ~'prayers? This batch?'~ "Craig is going to be missed dearly – but I'm sure he'd want us all to move on… We can thank the Lord for the time we had here with him as long as it lasted – I speak for my family in saying thank you very much for coming out here today to pay respects to Craig and the life he lived." – hands waving – "Thank you for coming. God bless you, Thank you…"

more handshakes, hugs, tension, eye-darting… men charging off, cellphones to ears, SUVs fire up, vying for the gates – this one, rolling right tires up on grass to weave round a Benz –'th-thunk!' – shocks bounce over a nubby gravestone… The younger crew – high school, college students, lots of us, mill about… pretty low key, catching up… Ryan has a distant vibe to him – signed up with some frat – "don't you gotta pay money to get in a frat?"

"yeah, well, dues – it's all good… - it's been pretty much party nuttiness since day one… – I do whatever I want at school – it's hilarious - you'd think my grades would suffer but it's so hand's off – I'm pulling A's… - whacky… no sleep, no rules… lost in it… – but man, this thing with Craig – what a shocker… – but yeah, it's like his Dad said – gotta put it behind you…" – pulls buzzing phone from pocket, clicks button, returns to pocket – "feel free to cruise up anytime… – so you've scrapped Yale – getting your bearings a while, or…"

"Yeah, thinking it all over… This whole thing changed me bigtime…" My Parents aren't talking to anyone – sense it's time to go… "Well, I'm gonna roll – I'll shoot you an e-mail…"

"Do… See –ya bro… Be well…"

Hug Shannon good-bye –

"Sooo, are you going to come visit me at school *Zach?*"

"Uuuuuuh, give me time, ok"

"How much time?"

"I can let you know, ok"

long eye contact… ~love that shock of green on hazel in left one…~

"ok, bye Zach, good seeing you, call me soon."

"bye."

See Emily en route to car… "heeey…" hug… "you still over at Lit Café?…"

"Yeah, - you're staying in town a while I think I heard?"

"Yeah…"

"Stop by – I'm there during the week…"

"Sounds good – gotta roll – see ya there… soon enough…"

CHAPTER 5

Sunny Monday drive, sitting in car, Mom at wheel, cruising to Boston …

She has errands to run… I'm to go in search for a new social security card…
– meet at Quincy Market afterwards …

Open the folder on lap, look over a few questions on the 'SS-5' form…
Notice 2 blank lines: "Parent's social security numbers"… take pen from breast
pocket, click it open …

"Mom, what's your social security number?"

Eyes on the road, "190… 58… 2880…"

"How about Dad's?"

"190 …77… 6540…"

'SS-5' form, completely filled out, in hand here, walking towards big rectangular government building… – a lady – Malaysian – Thai – or whatever –
wears one of those circular pointy hats - looks in a daze – like, shell-shocked –
I half-bump into her – spinning her a bit – press on – determined with mission… the rectangular building is… fenced off with a rent-a-fence – yellow-
hatted construction workers within… moving piles of rubble about… big drill
thing on tank wheels, hammering away… walk along fence… here, ten foot
white box, glass panes – on one, in red, the words "DO NOT DISTURB
GUARD" – Hispanic man inside, wearing Magnum P.I. glasses, chewing gum,
his hand on a button… see a line of slouching foreigners ahead, standing at a
roped-off section… close now – a short Mexican or Puerto Rican woman with
long shiny black hair says something in Spanish to another guard, who turns
head, looks at me …

"this the social security office?"

"you have to go to the *other* side of the building"

I start walking –

"no – you'll walk longer – you'd be better off going around *this* way."

~ 'better off'? ~

walking… – machinery going ballistic, other side of rent-a-fence 'BLAM-TAT-TAT-TAT!….'" – passing a car entrance – shiny Lincoln pulls up – Hispanic guard in brown outfit approaches - German Shepherd on leash… it sniffs at the wheel wells …

just beyond is a fenced-in playground – plastic jumbly structures – sliding boards… overturned Tonka truck… red, round Fisher Price car… walking towards door… above it – stark white letters on glass – all caps: "THIS ENTRANCE FOR FEDERAL EMPLOYEES WITH SMART CARDS ONLY"… stocky, tough-looking Hispanic lady, standing guard –

"social security office?"

she points to the other side of the playground …

Older black man, graying hair, bored expression – eyes half open behind glasses, light brown uniform, stands guard here – "can I help you?" -

"social security office?" – he points in …

a line zig-zags through ropes …

In line behind an old Korean guy – talking gruffly to daughter – dressed like a (hipster) boy - smart eyes though… Indian in front of them – extreme bed-head… looks he's worked 5 days straight… girl behind me: tiny Hispanic, hoop earrings, G-UNIT shirt… behind her, white woman with long, graying black hair, carrying briefcase, frowningly thumbing numbers on cellphone…. speaks into - ~first time I've heard this language in my entire life…~… behind her, another small Hispanic, with a stroller, earplugs in, booping at a black video ipod …

My turn for the metal detector… "Wallets, coins, keys!" calls the security guy, shuffling trays… bag conveyers through… – "you got a laptop in there?" – I nod - "gotta take it out – run it through again – so I can see through it…" send it through again… pocket stuff from tray… take up bag, laptop… sailing upwards in elevator… crouched, shoving laptop in bag… walk into office - "SOCIAL SECURITY OFFICE" printed above doorway… – thin black security guard – "what county are you from?"

"Irving"

he presses a button… small beige box chitters out a ticket… "take a seat, wait for your number."

The guy (who's number is before mine) steps up to glass-encased counter… – tall black guy ~blackest guy I've ever seen…~ – clean… – wearing a large K-

Mart button-up shirt (green plaid on yellow), new jeans, shiny dress shoes... hung on wall next to me is a big American flag - yellow outer fringe... closer, are two framed pictures, hung... a smiling President Bush on left, Vice President Cheney on right... The tall African leaves... I step up... Guy behind glass: prematurely gray hair... sweatshirt with

N A U T I C A

COMPETITION

on it... he receives my filled-out SS-5 application in slot under bullet-proof glass... and passport... clickers on PC... as my mind plays out all that ~would 'have had to have happened' 'had I had' my passport 'on that boat'~ - ~all the hoops *that* would've entailed~ - ~phone calls, government buildings, paperwork, waiting in lines, getting picture taken, mail, on and on...~ - ~spared~... ~spared(?) – what does this *reeeally* mean – *mean*? – why '*mean*'? – it has that other meaning – *definition* – of being base, lowly, common, inferior...~ - the guy is asking me to sign a paper... another... speaks into microphone: "it will be mailed to you in about 2 weeks."

Elevator down, walk towards a clearing in the ropes – signpost: "THIS IS NOT AN EXIT" ... – to right, another opening – swirl through, out the revolving doors... head for Quincy Market ...

Sitting across from Mom, finishing our bowls of chowder inside bustling market. –

"So in two weeks, when the social security card arrives," she says somewhat robotically "we can go get the driver's license..."

The two weeks crawl - fly by at the same time... Shannon visits on Saturday... – her eyes search mine, studying – trying to look inside... just an hour-long stay.... leaves after a long silence... in which I just... nod my head yes - saying "yep" about every ten seconds... – no call that night.... just... me and my thoughts... in bedroom – gazing up at ceiling, dreaming up possible futures – how many can one 'go do' in this brief number of years of heart beating on this here spinning planet – thought recurs – read somewhere - paraphrase: ~'in the beginning, the possibilities are many. when maturity comes, they are few.'~... what to do – what... *worth* doing... mind starts reeling through the possibilities – 'teacher' – well, summer's off are cool – but so much... 'puffing something up as important' in it – how fast would that get old... – sure – could switch subjects – but then it's puffing that topic up... cheerleading... be a doctor? hm, that 'holding people to the earth' aspect... such high emphasis on the physical... – like this all round here is so *it* ...

Business person? – hyping things up - which won't mean that much in long haul – pushing things on people – 'getting paycheck' to pad 'bank account' and book vacations – stuffing mouth, having drinks at this, that tropical location… lawyer? – needless to say - a joke… – meddling over earthly issues – has its place at times – but spare me the aggravation – the fleecing… – strikes in - ~ am I… hardening into a cynic heh-heh… - maybe this is all just a phase – and I do have to just… 'acclimate' and everything will be… 'ok'~ … - only thing that appears to make any sense – after reeling mind down countless roads… – is to become a non-sensical artist… – in a sensical way – *very* – shining-light-on-things… – and not in a dummy angry way – so prevalent these days with artists – pity-party angryville – pissy venting - flipping bird at the world, raging against the machine, 'slam' poetry, vitriolic - audiences, seal-clapping their rants… -

~so what is it then…~ lying here… staring up at ceiling – leaf shadows cast across it… listen to breaths… ~what is the thing then to… – to continue to breathe for… - has to be this 'turning-goofball-system-masking-itself-to-be-legit-system-on-its-ear-via-art' route…. how else – what else could fire pistons more than this… - what could be funner - regardless of how challenging… – and what's life more than having fun. . . – if it's not about experiencing fun – then what's God but a big grouch above the clouds, wielding knotty wooden club, eager bash some heads. . . – fun – with challenges in it – growing elements, aspects, dynamics to it – i.e. not fun just in a 'lounging on a cushion, being fed grapes' way (which can be fine at times) - more fun in a sense of really digging(?) significance – doing it to it – to life – living life abundant – overflow spilling – feeling all the SENSES – through and through… doing something that's *worth doing* – despiting (in the face of) phoniness… form right hand into fist… knock it against head a few times… sounds like someone… knocking on a door… -

"Zaach!" – muffled… "dinneerr!"

trot down stairs …

clinking silverware, mid-meal… Dad stops chewing, turns, "So, the driver's license is to be taken care of tomorrow?" loosened tie, red face, resumes chewing piece of beef.

"first I gotta get my social security card…" chewing – "have to have a social security card in order to get a driver's license… - already went and filled the forms out– should be here any day now…"

"That's good."

week ebbs along… soon I'm laying on leather couch in Boston again …

"So… you have a better idea this time… – of where you're going and why… – aspirations-wise… – action steps - realizing them…"

~ for what? … – and this guy gets paid for this – puts his kids through college on this? – hm, could go one way or other – a total lack of respect for (pulling this gig off) – or tremendous respect for… pulling this gig off… – leaning towards the latter – as he leans over, inserts pencil into electronic sharpener – 'bzzzznt' – examines tip – blows away residue… - "now… – any thoughts here?"

"I feel my head's been clearing, Barry."

"That's good… – in what sense?"

"In the sense that… it's occurring more and more that… one has to follow certain rules to be accepted into society these days."

"ok… aaand so…"

"On all sides the message is clear: 'fall in line' – 'conform'… – to me though – where's the fun in that – the excitement – the purpose?"

…"Where would be the fun in… not-conforming?"

"Freedom… – freedom to fight in forging a new and better way… – better in the sense of more style – less stodginess – more fluidity – over wooden mechanicalism – I actually think it's possible – that we've all just been living in fear of change far too long and things continue dragging on in this humdrum, stodgemuffin way – no one really stepping up – save a few artists over the years – but they tend to get snuffed out quick by those in power – those with the money and/or political strings…"

Barry appears to hold a question in his mind - like a happy cat with a bird in its mouth – one that will change the course of the entire discussion …

"What if I told you to resubmit your application to school?"

"Ah… told you before – loans – system…"

"You're fully aware that future employers will weigh education as a very significant factor in the hiring process" - midway through the question, a tinge of regret (at saying it) grew apparent …

"What are we even talking for? Humans are talk-talk-talk… – I think what helps me most in this season is a healthy dose of solitude - reflection, and planning, strategizing for the future – veeery… intently… – yet here I am talking – encouraged to just… blab out what's on mind… - what aim? – blah-blah-blah-blah-blah, y'know heh-heh…"

Barry scratches a few strokes on yellow pad …

"What is the alternative to college – 'again' – remind me."

"it's in the works… – like I said, I've been experiencing these solitary days… – I used to be on the internet hours and hours – downloading songs – listening to them, walking around – reading books, magazines – movies – on and on – constant stream of distractions… these days… it's been like… me and God – direct connection – many of these heavy-hitters through the ages have had their times of solitude before smashing the doors wide open – look at Jesus and the forty days in the wilderness… – I think I've surpassed forty days… The gears are turning… Things are surfacing."

~('things'(?))~

"Things?"

~went too far there… got blurting…~ "it's growing, building… – this vision of what's worthy to go do… – can't rush this – 'can't rush genius' saying goes…"

"I heard you went and got your social security card the other day… there's a step in the right direction…"

"I went and filled out paper work… – they said they'll mail it in two weeks…. it's been two and a half – which raises the question - - - who's watching them – who are they accountable to?"

"You're making progress…" . . . and on and on it goes – his sensitive, packed-with-experience - yet subtle questions, Zach's dreamy answers – as unique sounding as ever entered in through Dr. Cohen's ears to date… which he savors - he suddenly considers writing a case study on it all - to submit to top psychology publications across the country – or even a novel …

"Do you tape record these sessions, doctor?"

Tension grips in body of Dr. Barry Cohen - his mind pictures the delicate spinning reels in the mini Sony recorder in his pant's pocket. – he brought it today – first time he's ever brought one to a session… – and now hearing the first ever question about whether he tapes the sessions …

"Yes." Zach, too pure – too clairvoyant to lie to …

"figured as much…"

~('as much'(?))~

CHAPTER 6

On transpire the weeks …

Start working behind counter at (old hangout) Lit café… -

mixed reactions from old crew, turning up time to time – most on edge …

B.U. or Harvard parties weekend after weekend – till they trail off… – initiating the trail-off: sitting at one, keg taps flowing, youth standing crampt - plastic cups in hands, 'keeping conversation light' for hours – on prowl for a make-out session – or heading off to dormroom or frat house for more… – I positioned full cup of beer – handed me by slurring host Evan - over trash can, let it go… – turn, to Jenna, "see all this" - motion with hand to whole party… look straight in her eyes – "you know what it is?" she doesn't know what to say… stands, wry smile… "it's exactly what it is… that's what it is… – all it is…"

"golly, profound." she says, looking somewhat spooked, darting eyes… "you're not like, having a meltdown are you – saw you drop that full beer - dramatically - into the trash there…"

"ah, well… is what it is babe…" head for door …

"roger wilco" hear her say, walking out – skipping metro – clear home …

Still, go out with friends here, there – very intentional though – selective – more and more believing in notion that, ~each second, in a sense, one's either advancing or regressing from this, that, the next goal(s)…~

Read in room, nights… - and the countless hours on myspace ~so insightful – people making so clear their personalities – their minds~ - like an article read a while ago – about the… facades of museums – how they inform people what the contents are on the inside – how this ties into people and what they wear – fashion so telling; clothes communicating what's happening on inside – reflections of inner workings – revealing degrees of togetherness or out-of-control-ness – look at the clothes - what do they say? - ~I read shoes – I see your shoes I got you pegged...~ - here, 12:31am, mind wandering, trying to glean enter-tainment from the rustling leafy shadows on ceiling... in and out of sleep... reading, thinking... morning... sit staring bored at add – upper right of mys-pace page: a cartoon guy back to back with a gorilla – who squats – clouds poofing from rear end, again, again – arrow pointing to a red button – urging I click it - blinking white headline: "Outfart the Gorilla, Win a Free Ringtone!" - switches to new add – skinny monkeys running by – wearing hats - red targets on them – "shoot ten monkeys and win a nano!" – pick off 3... 4 – then it strikes in -

Open new page, google "social security card Boston"... find phone num-ber... dial... automated machine: "We offer this service in Spanish and English... if you would like to continue in English, press one," 'beeep'... rattles on about 'medicare' and 'if your calling to obtain help with your medicare expenses...' and 'if you have questions regarding social security benefits'... ~what is this?... how does this count?... as the seconds just... go by... heart, beating, here, within ribcage... as... this... goes... on... and on... can this... be... serious? worth... anything? all these... unnecessary... options~ "to talk to a representative, press 6" 'beeep'... - "due to heavy call volume, we can not transfer your call at this time. Please try your call later, thank you... click, boooooooooop."

Call later... the meandering options... beeping... "your estimated wait time is... 4 minutes"

"Social Security how can I help you?" mumbles disgruntled lady on other end – as if expecting a fight from me ...

"Yeah, I uh, filled out a form a while ago – they said two weeks it's been over two weeks..." she gets my social, address, mother's maiden name ~(?)~ ...

"You have to give it two to four weeks... Give it another week... and if you don't get it, you'll have to come in again and fill out another form..."

"I already filled out a form – will you look it up on the computer – see how it's going..."

heated up: "I *can't do that* sir... you have to go and fill out an applica-tion..."

"Yeah, I filled out the application – it's been over four weeks so..."

"like *I said* – give it another week and if it doesn't show up you'll have to come in and fill out another application."

"It's all filled out and sent in – is it ok to just mail the card straight to me – seeing as I filled out the application and all the information is in…"

"We *can't do that* sir… Like I *said*…."

hang up the phone …

Week later, walk into house - at sunset, after a hike through close-by woods …

Envelope on kitchen table …

The return address:

OFFICE OF SOCIAL SECURITY CARD ADMINISTRATION

gently tear it open. . .

gently (whispering '*yes-yes-yes-yes*' under breath) rip perforations… slide crisp Social Security Card from envelope… pull new wallet from back pocket – a velcro one – recent gift from Mom… – rippy velcro noise… insert card in hidden pocket… slide wallet back in back pocket with a pat… ~tomorrow morning: driver's license~

walk up carpeted stairs… – reaching top - ~look at time passing here – while doing what? – walking up carpeted stairs, walking down carpeted hall-way of parent's house~ - "heh-heh – aaaah my, my, my."

open mini-fridge in room… remove bottle of red wine… pour to brim of wine glass… sink into puffy circular, pocket of a chair… take up Dostoevsky's 'Ann Karenina' and commence speed-reading. . .

wake, book atent on chest… happy, bright morning… ~'cool' way to wake up…~ – ~vibey -could be in a novel or something… – yet, here I am, no one to witness, appreciate, care about… how cool I am heh… – or just even how I'm doing in general – because it all ties in with what you're thinking about – and who can relate – to this vision – to these… *envisionings* – these levels - these realms explored in solitude….~ ~kind of a rough call…~ – surfacing the whole ~'what's the use?'~ line, which gets unraveling en route to bathroom…. on auto-repeat… – but I chase it off, stepping into shower – for, there *is* a *purpose* today – going to get this driver's license - ~another 'card'~ - strikes fascinating a few seconds - ~if it *kills* me…~ ~aaah the current system – a physical plastic thing – that causes doors to open or close before the one carrying (or not car-rying) it~ - scene ebbs to mind – as step into shower, getting scrubbing – of walking though the campus of University of Pennsylvania a few years ago... – and thinking, there, as I walked, about how, here, in this 'free' country – how if you were, say, 27 or 30 – and tried to walk into the freshman dorms - - - you would be flat out *denied* access... - barred entrance... You would simply *not be allowed* to go inside... If you tried dropping a "it's a free country, I can go where I please" comment - and persist walking in past guard. . – I picture a thirty-year-old lanky white guy with beard and glasses being tackled by guard, struggles to keep going in, other guards run onto scene - beating him now with billyclubs... dragged to paddy wagon... driven to jail... behind bars... "what are you in for?" grizzly inmate asks ...

"I... tried walking into a college dormitory..."

Step out... feel cool, Spring-blossom-laden breeze wisp in through open, sunny window... Towel off... trying to rid image from mind – the blows continuously dropping - falling on poor skinny bearded white guy ...

Pour a tall glass of Tropicana orange juice... ~any plastic cups?~ grab a red one from cabinet... pour OJ from glass to brim of a SOLO ...

Head out front screen door... step from cement stairs to paddy green lawn, head for bus stop (5 blocks yonder), sipping at OJ in plastic red SOLO ...

A strange pressure tightens inside... – rooted in a kind of... 'not-wanting-to-be-seenness'... like... High School was highschool... being seen now by any of the neighbors would be ~awkward tension - mutually~ - ~Oh no... can it be? - Mrs. Robinson's car, 12 o'clock...~ - no use jumping in bushes – she's already spotted... – picture her eyes dilating in keen interest behind those shades – as maroon beemer hovers on my way – picture Brett (her son, my longtime [now estranged] buddy). . . ~don't-stop-don't-stop-don't-stop~ - see the brake lights flash on – time to take action – shoot up an arm in an I'm-in-a-real-rush-here-but-hey-good-seeing-you wave – raise SOLO in a kind of 'cheers-hey-you-have-a-good-one' fashion. . . her smile shifts to an uncertain haze – and it's too late to stop now – she's just about by – hear a double toot of high-quality-engineering horn – and engine propel her off... ~why this... pressure – shame(?) is it(?)~.... comes down to ~chalk it up to~ 'fall in line' culture – here you are – you've not gone on to college like the rest – you're 'not in line' – you're 'out of line' - you've unsettled the waters – rocking boats – you ought to be else where – like the others – away. . . ~ No. Not Mr. Menker's convertible Cadillac – anything but...~ - it rumbles to a stop – looong, gleaming white classic 70's boat... – piercing blue eyes - through cloud of cigar smoke – laser-beam through mine – through back of skull... "well, well. here we are, look at this guy heh-heh..." Mr. Menker was my high school gym teacher –

head coach of the football team – for one reason or other took a strong attachment to me – even though I only played freshman year… – a known character
about town – think he played a year for the Indianapolis Colts back in his
day… "am I seeing a celebrity here or what!"

"heey Mr. Menker…"

"Quite an experience you went through there – read all about it in the
papers…"

"Yeah… things are going much better now though…"

his eyes say he wants to ask more – wants to probe - why I'm not away at
school… – what my plans are – but thoughts of Craig appear to be entering his
mind – and he doesn't want to go there… and now - by the way he sort of
smiles, nods his head and squints his eyes, seems he's trying to… ascertain my
inner state… (just hear idle of massive V8 'dub-dub-dub')… ~bye conversation…~ "Well I'll letcha on your way then…" pointing a finger, slowly rumbling forwards "hey it was good seein' ya. You take care of yourself y'hear…"

hand up in wave "Good seeing you Mr. Menker…" - VRRrrrooooomm….

in little magazine shop, few minutes to spare before next train, paging
through photography mag… – the feature: an artist who shoots celebs 'make-
upless'… hear… ripping sounds as I leaf through… look over… a young (20?
30?) Indian employee blank-facedly tearing magazines in half – one after the
next… – slices razor across it, tears down the center – into trash bag – next. . .
~how about sending these to unlearned nations or something? *aaaany*way…~
Pick up this month's New Yorker… – in some way, this cash - slid presently on
counter towards dark Indian guy – will go towards feeding New York writers –
'every little bit counts' as they say ~('they'?)~…. how many others are… pur-
chasing a copy – this second - around the globe – how will this compare to last
month's numbers - I didn't buy one last month… How many are currently
penning in blanks on a new subscription? 100? 1000? More? No way of knowing, really – an impossibility …

On train, amidst the Bostonians – each, sitting… with their own set of sto-
ries – all seeming… pensive… today… – just a few of us – it, past rush hour…
slide mag from back pocket, kick back next window - blurry-trees whizzing
quietly outside – and enter into world of article… – ~people being… paid to
write - what a concept! - paid for… eliciting pleasure – or this or that – in
readers… – putting groceries on table for family as a result of inspiring others
with words – by stringing words together just so – giving them an experience –
if they so choose to read it that is – if not – if it's overlooked: no paycheck…

baffles me... - people *getting paid* for 'creating' – or 'bubbling up' thoughts,
emotions in others... – an extreme case - painting perhaps the clearest picture
of point here: stand up comedians... - what else are they doing up there? - sole
objective: make people laugh... make people laugh: get paycheck... harder you
make them laugh, the higher amount written under the "Pay amount to:" line.
-

   branches into thoughts on the media – is it all just them scrambling around
– hyping 'news' up – to get themselves paid? ... – what if we all – or a large
number – just stopped buying papers – quit watching TV – turned to the internet for info... – no one tuning in to, say, the Monday Night Football game...
what would they do – the media giants – what would they do about the whole
'getting paid' thing? Engine would begin to sputter, bog... break down... As it
is we're feeding it, them – fueling, rolling it, them right along – they keep on
getting their paychecks – certainly pouring plenty of it back into the hyping
machine – pushing forward this and that – and so many words in it - words,
words, *words!!!* – how many words in a day – compare it to amounts of words
spoken on another day – gauge progress – ~see, study, learn from connections
between communication and progress...~
   the article's about Harper Mansfeld – snippets from her memoirs – ~days
long gone by~ – Paris in its prime – her, here, flying off pages, young and overflowing excitement over it all – relates account of how, night after night – middle of night – famous drunken artists and writers would stumble back and
forth across the street – from café to café.... – they'd be up next day – make it
to a favorite café at 1pm - - - there till 7 - - - go out to eat with friends – return
to café – there till 2am. . . she looks back on it all fondly. . . so - 'caught up' she
was in it... – then the... *exiting* of that scene - the return to the States - the fail-
ure to duplicate it – not even a chance – aaaaand the years... gone by... and...
that's that... she pours it on again with another memoir excerpt... here, reading pure enthusiamos recorded on paper – a flurry in the prime of life, hopping off page now - acharge, crackle-zapper. . . – well, at least she had a rich
prime – will hand her that – not to call their bumbling around drunk 'rich' –
but the vibe in air, I'm sure, was quite fun... – if only she had the energy to
drum it up in the U.S. afterwards ~ah well, what's that to me...~ – that was her
generation's flurry – ~now it's our time~ Seems then artists *had* a *real* scene -
were... chummier about hanging out and batting around ideas – more of a
community feel... – artists these days seem more on the go – more of a... ger-
bil-spinning-wheel type of an existence. . . – and rivalry – a looking-out-for-

one's-self type thing winning out over a looking out for, supporting, others kind of atmosphere. . .

Mind reels back to summer in Cambridge last year... the long nights in Harvard Square... that – *that* probably being closest I've been to this Paris vibe... – the long nights – the bamboozley friendships – hazy – tight at times – drama at times – romance at times – so much music about – those songs - now ever enlatched to that summer – a draaawn out summer – a *deep* summer – high energy – we were exploding with ideas - potential – to point of... at times a, just, taxed, state of... laying on some campus lawn, catching breath – or copping a few z's – then up and at it again... recollect a 'typical' night (which none were) ...

We'd (Brett, Evan, Shannon, Alisa, Tyler, Emily... Jeff, whoever else) drift - after this, that, the next outing, adventure, meandering – to Danny's Diner... – that *mystical* walk to apartment afterwards – with friends – or solo – and the solo times – how the mind *soared*... – how the night *spoke* to me then – how the doors of *everything* slammed opened to me then – and more than doors – imaginary extravaganza ...

"Sooouuth station!" snaps me out of it... shove mag in bag, rustle from seat – 75% of men and women in filing-out line – ~wearing facial expressions sending 'sad sack' messages...~ ...

Onto thick-vibe train to New York... – whatever's in air: close to palpable... scene from high school springs to mind – one of those summers – working construction – on the Vineyard – two of the co-workers – Russian kids – one a Jew – he, exaggeratedly, sniffs in through nose – "I smell something..." he says - more sniffs - "yep, definitely smell something..." "what's that?" I ask... another sniff... big smile – Russian accent: "I smell an American." Bigger smile "you know what that smell is?..." "what's that" I asked ...

"fear." biggest sniff of all – "yep, definitely an American around."

New Yorker magazine, 'grown old' that fast – toss it... pull Breakfast at Tiffany's (just getting around to reading it now) from bag and resume plowing through it (halfway through already) with a goal to finish it by time we pull into Grand Central ...

snapping it shut as people rise – scurry bags from overhead luggage racks... the vast Grand Central atrium is high intensity - a mixture of working man anxiety ("gotta get there by 9" – or "gotta seal that deal today") and tourist anxiety ("gotta get everything in – gotta see it all – just *4 hours*") ...

roll a quarter into a payphone, dial up Tyler's cell... "hello?" – music in background –

"Tyler – yeah this is Zach…"

"hello?

"Hey Tyler – this is Zach."

"Hey bro – oh yeah - you're coming today right?"

"Yeah, I'm here at Grand Central."

"Really? Ok… Yeah, I'm in Brooklyn now… – there's a rooftop film party thing going on here – open bar – food - the works - can you get over here – is that cool?"

"I have to get my driver's license… - It alright if I swing by and drop my stuff off first?"

"hm… dude, Spanish Harlem's a long way off man… – you got a lot of stuff or what?"

"nah, not really – backpack – that's about it – I should be fine… – ok, I'll give you a call after I sort out this driver's license thing - see if the party's still going on – maybe cruise over – meet up with you there…"

"yeah man – it'll be all day – gimme a buzz…"

The DMV is closed.

I stand at the locked doors for some time… People passing by… in the oppressive vibe strangling in air… as I gaze at Penn Station across the street …

Roll a quarter into a payphone …

"yeah turns out the DMV place is closed."

"bummer man."

"yeah well, what can you do… - anyways, guess I'll head over there…"

he gives directions – repeating at times – music and laughter in background interfering …

L train… walk up stairs into sunny Williamsburg… Bedford Avenue - aswarm with hipsters… – here, on corner, in front of Salvation Army: stuff laid out on ground for sale… – junk – but… imbued by the sun – lending salability at points… – framed colored pencil drawings, pairs of used shoes, shirts… a tennis trophy, VHS tapes, books – here: 'Dog Training for Dummines', and 'You Can Be Happy *No Matter What*'… toy robots, roller skates, toaster, camouflaged hat, IBM electronic typewriter, frames, wigs – on white styrofoam heads, old golf clubs in PING bag, a blender… old skateboard… the guy selling a lot of it, shirtless, red-nosed, thick glasses, brown furry hat - orange fishing lures stuck in it… next blanket over: a pair of spacey blue boots – 'MOON BOOTS' writ in futuristic font around heels… walk on… records, belts, old Atari games – here: 'GORF'… outdated software cds – 'ACROBAT Pro 7'… 'QUARK 5' …

Stroll past lil' Thai restaurant… past the 'mini-mall' – 'Verb' café… right on North 5th… long stroll – industrial, factoryish feel… beat-up fences… row houses… – to by the water… hear music coming from roof – in sight now - see people (just their heads) – laughing, some taking sips from yellow SOLO cups …

a group lingers at open front door… climb stairs – opens up into big stretch of loft… - bachelor furniture scattered about - big expressionist paintings on wall… up another flight – through traffic flowing down – to out into sun again – more intense, here on silver-painted tar roof… lots of people… loud chatting… at far end stands a twenty-foot tall inflated movie screen – a muted film in action on it – Anime – as it sways a little in the wind… Eyes scan for Tyler… there, by the DJ table – big mounds of speakers, pumping out bizarre, experimental… ~whatever-you'd-call-this…~ – catchy though… – techno – electro… guitar in there… his arm around a cute, arty-looking chick, sipping from her SOLO, giggling at whatever he's whispering in her ear… his eyes light up – mouth extends its grin - "Ladies and gentleman, I give you Zzaach *Baar-rrrrrr*… - what is *up!*" clamps hand, pulls me into a back-patting hug …

"Tyler, definitely good seeing you…"

"You're all set to move into Spanish Harlem or what's going on?" – he points to arty girl "We talk soon, gotta catch up with an old friend here…" she giggles off… –

"Yeah, ready to couch-it tonight – do the whole DMV thing tomorrow – then hit the rails for Boston – but yeah, in a few weeks when I have the license and everything – will be looking for a place to move in, so…"

"so yeah, would love to have you bro… You'd have a room to yourself – rock bottom rent – it'd slice my rent up for me – win win all around – here, get a cup – my treat – I work with the guy running this gig – real champ… – and wait'll you see the featured artist – *genius*…" – he hands a SOLO, pointing – "kegs are over there – go with the apricot lager – very fresh – you can taste the apricot… – chat around, mingle, we'll catch the feature piece and" – looks at watch – "jet after that, cool?"

"yeah" stroll, observing, towards kegs – electronic music - playing loud - sounds like laser beams firing… just about everyone looks arty… or fabulous… or a combo… - this guy, big afro, sunglasses, SOLO in hand, swaying, gesticulating as a steady stream of words flows from mouth – to orange-haired girl with black-rimmed glasses - popcorn bits shooting from her laughing mouth, and shaking-in-giggles thin Asian guy with a Beatles haircut …

Fill up and head over to where a sportier bunch of guys (arty-sporty) are congregated... They're tinkering with a kind of... canon... alongside one of the four-foot high roof walls ...

From its crudely-bolted-to-the-roof base, a shaft extends up to a... what looks like a... fire extinguisher tank, which is attached to a metal, spinnable sphere – two handles welded on each side... from sphere, extends a long barrel... –

A guy comes walking over in flip flops, white trashbag slug over shoulders... sets it down... full of small, jiggling, multi-colored water balloons... he opens the back of the sphere, puts a yellow water balloon gently in the chamber, shuts it... – "oo-oo – here we go – here we go" says one kid – pointing down the street at an oncoming Acura Legend... – gleaming white – rims, glaring in sun, windows down – loud bass of a rap tune bumping... guy in flip-flops spins the gun towards it – one eye closed, tongue creeping out – Acura - traveling at a good speed – passing now - "FOOMP!" puff of smoke as balloon rockets forth – yellow streak - directly into driver's-side window - transforms Puerto Rican's gelled head into an explosion of water - thousands of sparkling droplets – spray flying out passenger window – rear lights flash on – tires chirp a screech... –

laughs and high fives are going all round by the canon... I - way more sober than the celebrants, feel a knot in stomach, heart going out to the poor guy – viscous-looking now – out of his car – shaking fist and cursing – about five foot tall - in a tight white tank top – gold chain asparkle in sun... giving the finger - demanding the shooter come down like a "*reeeal* man"... finally, with a pointing "you *watch!*" he's gets in car again – front tires squeak smoke puffs as he zooms off... From far, we hear... see a fire truck approaching – "oo – the *attachment – hurry!*" – he's given a big funnel thing – connects to sphere... he wobbly hoists up the trash bag, empties half the balloons into funnel – a few missing, falling over edge, popping on people lingering below at front door... "alright-alright-alright" throwing attachment aside, swinging barrel into aim as truck roars onto block – sirens blazing, lights swirling – see finger pull trigger: 'FOOMP-FOO-FOO-FOO-FOO-FOO-FOO' – on and on – blurry strings of colors – "Wham!Wh-Wham!Wham!Wham!Wham!" – direct hits - every one - various points... a firefighter standing at the rear - grasps a back rail with one hand, shakes an ax high in air with other, hollering curses as horn drowns him out – '*WWEEEEEERRRRRRRRRRNT!!!*' piercing ears... – rig, leaning round corner now, hardly letting off gas, races on... contented, nodding afro guy with shades, slow-golf-clapping – SOLO tucked between inner forearm

and belly: 'yeeeah man, right *on* man… right… *on…*" - then ~the timing~ –
hear the jingle… – Mister Softie gently rolls into view – "c-mon – c-mon – my
turn man," says the one, pushing flip-flop guy aside (he exaggerates response –
falls down, rolls around… feigns an epileptic fit) – 'FOOMF! –FOO-FOO-
FOO-FOOMf!' – 'BOW-BOW-BOW-BOW-BOW!' – a thin black boy running
after it – runs for cover – "get 'im – get 'im - get 'im" – gunner swivels head,
eyes half shut, five o'clock shadow, fat nub of cigar, clamped in side teeth,
"whataya take me for? some kind a *sicko*?" – aims – 'F-FOO-FOOMPF!…-
FOOMPF!…' misses… misses… hits kid square in back – hear the scream… –
takes aim at, here, a partygoer - leaving on a bike – FOOMF!-FOOMFT!-
FOOMPF! click-click-click…' - two burst just shy, one explodes in back spokes
– hear scream – last is a direct hit - back of head – shooting her wet locks forward – wrap round face - hard leer left – front tire hitting curb, the topple onto
grass island… laughs howl… she stands, flips bird, rides off… –

"Ok…" – someone on mic – "ok… – I have sound? – testing-testing… –
Okaaay we're going to… go ahead and… get started here… - play a short film
by Elliot Frank – here with us tonight – Elliot, wave… aaaand we'll be starting
the film in about fiiive minutes – so if you'd like to gather round, find a seat,
that'd be faaantastic…"

Everyone… milling around… leery, dreamy, dramatic, intoxicated, giddy
sort of way - arranging, finding seats, plunking down in them – film guy –
Elliot – stepping to mic – "so I've been creating this over a span of about a year
– just down the street here" (pointing) "it's a bunch of segments – core bits of
my favorite films, other clips I found – I… hope you will enjoy it -" – pointing
to rear – a guy standing at video projector – "Jim."

big, blue, lighted square… – and on into the car chase scene from Bullit –
cheers going up - guy at wheel, noticing Mustang in rear view mirror… pulling
on driver's gloves, buckling seat belt… light goes green – engine flares – diagonal launch of car left-upwards - wheels screeching burnout – smoke trailing–
'Stang, roaring after – '*BRRAAAAAAA!!!*' - cars bouncing airborne over wavey
streets… – Steve, not quite making that right turn… – thrown in reverse –
white smoke billowing from bouncing shrieking reversing tires… – slammed
in gear – engine thunders - screaming wheels, shot into pursuit again… – skips
to: scene of goons firing shotgun through shattering window at McQueen –
skip to - their loss of control – into gas station - mushroom explosion – shot of
their sizzling heads… - right into film 'Run Lola Run' – her sprinting full speed
to electro music – right into Rocky – sprinting all out there through 1970's
Philly streets to 'Eye of the Tiger' – on up stairs – jumping around – thrusting

arms up - into Jap Animation – huge robots – crushing a city under feet as they shoot laser beams at, punch, throw each other – cut to 'Akira' - slanting into skid on red futuristic motorcycle – ball of fire shimmering at gun barrel as he unloads – mouth open – screaming - rounds of lasers at shattering robots… - to (high energy electronic music kicking in loud) 'Transformers' - charging into battle with Decepticons – lasers machine-gunning yellow, pink, blue, orange… – flash to pro bike racers – zooming through Parisian streets – leaning into curved downhill juts left, right – standing up, turning it on – amazing cam angles – bright sun – see shadow of pick-up truck – silhouette of camera man in rear - - - flash to bike crashes – cartwheeling jumbles of bikes – flash to formula one racing – to European car racing – tricked-out classic Ferrari's - Masaradi's - Alfa Rameos - Volvo's – Mercedes - Porsches - to tumbling crashes – flash to Motocross – launching off massive dirt mound ramps (music real high, fast – electric guitar now) – insane mid-air stunts – flow into other mound - to cigarette boat – peaking top speed – hear the engines through music – vibrating whole roof – aerial angle – to side view – reflection of copter in water – to hockey fight – flutter punches to square blow – the reel – to laid out spin on ice - to football – handoff to running back – dive over pile – one diving from other side – the clash mid-air – the spin of running back – the rewind – the play again – and again – to wide receiver (Seahawks) – jumping high – catching ball (semi-slomo) with fingertips – defensive end (Philadelphia Eagle) swoops in – takes out legs – receiver full flipage to landing on head – rewind – again – regular speed – and again – flash to boxing highlights (heavy speed metal gunning now) clobber after clobber – bell after bell rung, clock after clock - explosions of sweat – flying mouth pieces – falls to slidings on backs – here one knockt clear through ropes to - dropping down the five feet – boxer victory leaps – gloves high – to music cutting off – scene from 'The Doors' movie plays – young Morrison on LA beach… - flash to 70's rock concert footage (music kicking in again) – long haired guy on drums bashing cymbals in dreamy Californian outdoor concert at dusk – flash to 90s metal concert – tall thin shirtless long haired guys head banging. . . – flash to judo tournament – fighter throws opponent - rewind-forward-rewind-forward – to Thai boxing (boxing/kickboxing) – lean competitors - lightning fast – to Hawaiian surf footage – huge waves – surfers carving thin lines top to bottom – this guy – disappears behind pipe wall… - – shooting forth from it… - flash to Bruce Lee – him in top form – popping foes – clenching into poise – to scene - battling Chuck Norris – to close-up – exiting plane in those 70's sunglasses – flash to a tiger sprinting after gazelle – swiping paw - trips it up – to tumbling – to clamp-on – to lockjaw – flash to (music cutting off) 'Planet of the Apes' – in Spanish (no subtitles) - drama – one throwing rocks at another – skip to main-character ape administering stern lecture to young female ape – a big group of enemies charging at them – a spaceship taking off (music resumes) – cheetah in full sprint after zebra - to scenes from movie 'Baraka' – blurry-fast traffic – aerial views – egg factory – machinery – robotics – crayon factory –melted colors – red, blue, yellow - pour from cauldrons into lil' vats – conveyor belts - flash to a rodeo – broncos hurling riders – to crazed bull running through Spanish streets – leering into – smashing to bits – running over café table…. (music cutting off) black preacher – "they don't need condemnation – don't be givin' them a ticket to hell – they already *got that* – you gotta be givin' them a ticket to *heaven!*" – to scene form movie 'Moonstruck' - Cher, firecracker-slapping woman - declaring "*snap out of it!*" – rewind, play "*snap out of it*" rewind, play "*snap out of-*" – again – again – back and forth the hand goes –"*snap*" – rwnd – "*snap*" – rwnd-"*sna-*" rwd- "*snap out of it!*" – "*snap out of it!*" - screen fades out - tiki torches light up – guys, migrating to kegs, sun, setting. . .

~man…~ ~all taken together - energy conveyed – sent off by that piece… pretty much higher than any I've seen to date…. '*floored*'… '*blown away*'… – ~*must* meet this artist.~

Elliot – a, like, aura to him – seems to be… awaiting my greeting… – shaking hands it's… reading minds through eyes – messages sent – registered, replied to - many levels – all in seconds – a… *reckoning* – bringing-up-to-speed(s) – impartations of understandings – exchanges, gauging, and an unspoken certainty that collaborations will occur in near future …

"really enjoyable piece there – have you a business card?" ~("have you"(?))~ extracting from wallet, handing "Here you are… You know Tyler?"

"Yeah, how'd you know?"

"He knows so may people."

"Yeah -"

Old guy steps right in front of me – one hand to clutching Elliot's shoulder, other hand vigorous in handshake …

Slip card in pocket, heading over to keg… Tyler, arm around a different laughing girl – "hey man, ready to jet?"

"are you serious…" reaching in pocket… – "here're the keys – I'm gonna chill here – go drop your stuff off – cruise back if you feel like – this is gonna be goin' on all night -"

"Ah, I'm gonna call it a day – gotta get ready for this DMV mission first thing in the morning…"

"Alright man – you're on the futon – if I wake you up – my apologies ahead of time…"

stick keys in pocket… decide on an apricot lager refill… discuss the film at keg with a girl – smart eyes – in city for summer – heading to Dartmouth in fall …

"jury's still out… – kinda found it a bit too… testoste*rony*"

"hey do they serve that as a topping on pizza?" - tikis dim again - mc steps to mic – starts announcing next film "a collection of shorts all the way from Oslo." – everyone migrating to seats again… finish cup, turn to gauge - see if I can spot subway entrance from up here – eyes met by a tabby cat, perched on ledge, staring silvery green eyes with vertical black slits at mine, intently… tap a few pats on its head… a scratch under chin, (brick factory building blocking view of subway stop) …

bag strap foisted up on shoulder, other bag, taken up, waddle down the stairs - managing bags easily - ~feel the youthstrength… – or is it the 2 beers on empty stomach?~

turns to stupor, sitting on slow 6 train up to East Harlem …

'lowlight' being homeless man falling on me… - push him off and he falls into a roll on the black rubber floor, "I'm suein'!" he slurs - people looking at me like I'm a brute… "ya hear dat – I'm *suein!*" - two stops of him rolling around, cursing… before rising ~for what?… what hope, - really? – say he goes and gets cleaned up – then what… - really?…~… he's bent over, picking up the change - spilt from his white Domino's Pizza cup when he went over… – automated voice overhead: "Ladies and gentleman it is illegal to solicit money on the train – we ask that you please refrain from giving and help us to maintain an orderly ride – for a complete list of subway rules, visit our website at www…" he rises, slow, holding lower back, grimacing… brown, hairy, glistening, blotched skin… eyes swollen nearly shut… salt and pepper afro protrudes either side 'ACE Hardware' hat… and I try to imagine what it must be like to be in his head… like, if you were to transfer and reside inside his body – even for just a minute – experienced what he experiences on a second to second basis – there in his head – to see through his eyeballs - experience all the thoughts and inner-workings - experience his outlook for a few minutes – how *intense* that would be!! – the flashes of lights, colors, the voices - such *charge* – probably buzzing - constant battiness… doors open, he bumbles out …

shift into thinking what it'd be like to enter into - experience the existence (*reside inside* – see through their eyeballs – see, feel, their thoughts, conscious-nesses) of the highest ranking judge in, say, Britain – or a world renown profes-sor of physics… – a top philosophy prof… – ~who else is super-revered for their clear-thinking abilities?….~

wooziness turns to outrage for whatever reason - - - - ~who's respected!!!! WHY DOES ONE HAVE MORE RESPECT THAN ANOTHER!!! IS IT BECAUSE OF THE STUFF THEY DO!!!! THINK ABOUT IT – THIS ONE HAS MORE RESPECT THAN THAT ONE BECAUSE THE STUFF HE DOES IS CONSIDERED MORE IMPORTANT THAN THE STUFF THE OTHER GUY IS DOING!!!~ - automated voice chimes in: "Ladies and gentlemen riding on the outside of the subway cars is dangerous – always remain on the *inside* of the cars…."

- and it all thought through not in a fist-shaking way… more in a slumpy, sad-faced… resignation… – ~like that Robert Frost quote - "all men lead lives of…" – and how do we go about cracking that code?…~ -

a beautiful young woman – tight-fitting top, denim skirt, high brown leather boots - enters scene, stands, grasping pole near door, tapping toe… sit-ting in seat across from me, staring on wide-eyed: a short, bespecled old guy, wearing tired suit… looks her up, down… up again, down… bemused smile melds on face… - distant look sets in – looks he's… gone off… somewhere else – thinking… what… could have been… –

automated voice: "Ladies and gentleman, *back packs* and other large con-tainers are subject to *random search* by police… Thank you. Remain alert and have a safe day."

116th Street and I'm calling on all strength to lug bags up grimy steps… here, passing under feet as I ascend, a yellow Wendy's container, crushed, red chili, splattered from it…. stop at top, hunched, hand on railing, catching breath… ~all that laying around in room staring up at ceiling~ press on into darkness, Latino music, playing from open windows above to right and left… here, a… band of guys, sitting in a circle, beating on bongos, congos, singing loudly out front of Tyler's apartment building… black guy sitting on front stairs in grey hoodie looks over his sunglasses at me, 'honkey-tonkey, honkey-honkey tonkey." he mutters as I jiggle, re-jiggle key – two small Hispanic kids burst door open giggling and I jumble in… to lobby hallway - where a tall His-panic guy, leaning on wall… new pair of hunk boots, black leather jacket, sun-glasses, scar across cheek – smiles – gold front tooth glistens… – black baseball hat - bulky yellow Sony Sport wireless walkman headphones on ears, playing loud Latino music... pulls roll of cash from pocket, gets flip-counting twenties ...

frequent stops, dragging bags up the five flights... dim, grimey worn, chipt marble stairs, passing under nose... key clicks deadbolt open... into small kitchen... need water... tall plastic cup from cabinet... full-blast-from-tap fill... looking at water though... a yellowish tinge... swirling specks of green... bring to lips... can't... bring self to drink it... look in fridge... two gallons of spring water... both half empty... jog down the flights... buy a gallon at corner store... up, up... up again – up, up... up... sit on futon... catching breath... drink from one – 'Great Bear' brand... recline... head, aspin, stomach, hungry ...

Eyes open, brain, kicks in, - registers freezing temperature of room – the big window, wide open – gusty early Fall wind, blowing curtains toward me - ~wind... can't see it... yet it's there... no stopping, no grasping, wherever it goes, that's where it goes... *wind... what...* - is wind?~ hair on arms standing straight up – body in like... survival-caveman mode... sit up, swivel head around in search of a blanket... camo sleeping bag, sticking out from behind bookshelf... unfurl... get in, zip up... lay, stare out wild window, feel insides warming up - ~what a machine the body is~... – some clouds roll in before my eyes – 5am lighting – tinged through with orange glow... waxing many a vibe poetic – urgency in the scene – apocalyptic... ~and I here, to witness? - in cozy camo womb – inner heater abuzz~ ... line of thought branches in mind - a... realization... that... things... - reality as we know it... – the structures of how things go... that all this doesn't have to stay as it is... it doesn't all have to remain locked into the long, ongoing unfolding traditionalisms... – realization that so much stuff seems so cemented in place – but who says it has to remain as such – no one – just a sort of invisible intimidation factor – passed down from one generation to the next - hollering its 'don't rock the boat!' messages – be they audible or silent... - realization grips in – further and further – even beginning to compel – waking me more and more up by the second... – change can happen – that the boats are there for the rocking... – change possibilities by my volition – possibilities, countless possibilities – day to day... – that I can be the maker of it – in that, this, or another shape, form, degree or other... very basic concept really – just, seemingly mind-blowing at present, standing here, pissing into toilet... ~yet, a catch(?) (is there(?) in form of green rectangular paper bills~ - body shakes in little laughter to self... at how... in our current system – 'the way things go' these days - money – actual *paper bills* – cut off certain possibilities – preventing them from happening... – like, say, now (within context of the current system as we know it here early into the 21st century) – it is impossible for me to walk into an airport today and fly over to Europe... – *~to think*, lack of paper bills *prevents* me from doing so – absurd! heh-heh – or is it more outrageous that we've let the system carry on this long... – and one could really run with this - could expand to – paper bills 'preventing relationships' – say I'm in love with a girl in London - paper bills *bar* me from getting over there to visit, cuddle with her – weeks go by – her eye, caught by another guy.... – ah the current system – is there no one smart enough, brave enough to stand up and fix it – or start fixing it... Ah, that we – our generation – would be about rectifying – about ushering in newness – about betterment – about expansion of freedom across boards...~

Speedreading novel – pluckt from Tyler's bookshelf – *Herzog* – ~what a first 20 pages~ - on 6 train – transfer to E at 51st – to 34th.... a bustling (bizarro, bile-in-belly, dark, foreign, confused, little-to-no-love vibe weighing down in air) Penn Station... escalatoring up... – automated lady: "Be careful while riding the escalator... Have a safe day." -

Emerging – people bustling, scrambling to a fro coming into view and 'POK!!!' – eyes hone in, brain registers: small Dominos Pizza Toyota pick-up truck has just smacked into the back of a new, dark gray, large BMW... guy at wheel of the beemer, short, fat, massive bald head, frizzy gray hair around ears, big nose, bushy, frowning eyebrows, crooked glasses, has both hands up (one with gleaming gold watch round wrist), clinging back of neck, face, scrunched, grimacing in agony - stubby fingers, rubbing at nape ...

The guy in Dominos truck is very dark – Kenyan or Ghanaian – looks straight from the bush to – given a Dominos collared shirt - to behind wheel of this deliver pick-up truck – now with its hood arched – headlights, slanted down and in - like angry eyes – its bumper bent in a U – all forming a cartoon-ish face ...

Sweat, sheens on his face - eyes abug wide, hands still white-knuckled on wheel ...

Walking onwards – ~guess his life in the States is pretty much shot through... well, it is what it is... one way or another...~ – as all these suits are rushing by me – everyone looking so grim, pissy – here, one of the business men steps on a random 'Head and Shoulders' bottle – sending it into a spin - helicoptering diagonal across sidewalk – to where a homeless man's shoddy sneaker happens to come planting square down on it – making a loud farting noise as a straight white stream and dotty spray splat onto pant leg of hard-charging business man – head leaned into Blackberry at ear - - juts head – taking in the white design on pant leg "Oh for the… – you've *got* to be…." - giggles bubble up in my belly… till, seeing the line standing out front the DMV …

swiveling into place. I picture Domino's guy going back to his Queens or Bronx apartment tonight… Telling his wife and kids about the accident, what's to come …

pull *Herzog* from pocket – ~try to distance mind from present reality of time being consumed in this fashion…~ doors must have opened, as, we're filing in… – just before door, head enters into a swarming cloud of gnats – two stinging into left eye – one in right – everything going blurry –blinking, tweaking at eyelids with fingers entering into revolving door - hear guy behind me - "*Sheeezus H…*"

big black security guard lady – seen through liquid jelly eyes – wavering amoeba-like -pointing this way and that, calling for everyone to "gimme another line here! – right here sir – *stay the line* everyone! – right this way!"

after a few minutes in line, blinking, picking at eyelids, tears rolling down cheeks, realization strikes in that ~perhaps I'm… not in the right… line~ – picture being in it half an hour, getting to counter, the grim discovery… decide to leave bag on bench – tell angry guy behind me – also picking at an eye - that I'm "just checkin' on something real fast at the counter – I'll be right back."… – whisk over to black lady guard – sitting at info table - see now that she has dyed blond dreadlocks… – I wait for her to finish with the guy she's talking to – to just… slip in the question (one small enough to justify a cut-in: 'is that the line I'm supposed to be in?', holding up form) – but the dark Indian (Arab?) guy is really dragging it out…. his skin is dry, flakey - looks he hasn't slept in months, wears a GUY AND GULLIARD hat, dandruff flakes on shoulder… – one blank-faced, heavily-accented question after the next – infuriating blond-dread security guard (now desk woman) more and more – each met with a sharp, angry reply, baffling him, "get your *S-55* form over there, fill it out, and get in line again – it ain't so hard to understaand" – circling in place, "is there a pen?" he asks –

leaning over desk, thrusting finger forth - "you have a pen *in your pocket.*" pointing at Bic sticking out his breast pocket - as he drops an envelope to a slow flutter towards floor… bending over, more papers spill from folder tucked under arm – to splashing across floor… –"I'm in the right line right?" I slip in, pointing to where I came from –

"lemme see your form"

hold it up to her squint/frown - "yes, *next!*"

Three "REMINDER" signs hang in a row on wall: "Complete your application <u>Before</u> coming to the counter." round a bend in the partition ropes… see they're administering on-site eye tests… – chart on wall – person standing five feet away, hand over one eye… rubbing at eyes – feel tear stream on cheek… - ~maybe should go find a bathroom - flush these stupid bugs out…~ turning, look at line of mad and sad people, wound back and forth amidst partition ropes behind me - ~and loose my place in line, *fat* chance~ – lady at counter – to kid ahead of me: "read me line number eight…"

"S-I-E-K-D-F-V-E-O-U"… steps to counter to fill out a form… I'm blinking hard – whipe at open eyeballs with t-shirt… –

"step down…"

walking towards her …

she's pointing through me "step back to the wall…"

"Um, a couple of bugs just… flew into my eyes, so…" -

"*stand with your back to the wall please…*" pumping pointing glittered-design-painted-on fingernail at the maroon wall …

"I'm having trouble seeing – three bugs just flew into my eyeballs - right outside the front door -"

"Well are you gonna *take the test* or *aren't you* – there's a line *waiting* behind you…"

almost ask "what if I fail?" – but ~the gratification she'd take at telling me I'd have to take it all over again…~ so I refrain, and it's, I suppose, one of these 'crisis points' we experience time to time here in life…– where 'decisiveness' is called for… another look at the waiting line – the woman behind the guy still picking at eye - looks to be early forties - business woman - big hair, make up… she's… ~out and out~ grinding her teeth at me - hear her growling… - guy even stops picking at eye, swivels head, frowns in disgust, observing …

Assume back-to-the-wall position ~C'mon clarity, - *clarity now! help me here…*~

"Read line number nine for me."

~c'moooon~

Eyes feel like battery acid coats them as the letters waver – swim… little black blobs… I see a large solid black semi-circle down in the bottom left of my view – ~damn dead gnat~ - no time to try picking it out now… get blinking - finding flashes of clarity between each blink – have to speak the letters out fast – as they register in short term memory before eyes blur again "F-Z-X-U-(~are they playing tricks though – *God*, this *pressure~*)-T-D-no wait-O-yeah-O-S-G"

"do you wear contacts?"

"no"

She angrily swirls a few circles on form – points to maroon wall again – "stand *back* at the wall." She clicks a few buttons on the big PC – connected to a mounted, government-looking, beige camera… "stand between the lines on the wall…" on the maroon wall, are two vertical beige lines… "look at the smiley face…" – a sticker – yellow circle with dot eyes and a smile line – tongue sticking out – red and black hat on – like a baseball hat –sideways-backwards… try a smile – feeling so awkward though – thoughts appear in mind of primitive peoples – their tight-knit communities - ~everyone knowing everyone… and here's what we've come to, eh… 'progress' got us here, or…~ - ~and will this uncomfortableness – here, now, - this feeling – will it convey forth from eventual photo – *into* any future viewer… probably so, guessing…~

Sit around waiting for number to be called… ~"story of my life"~ watch a young black guy - donning new (cheap) dress shirt – bit large, puffed out, cheap black pants – K-mart-looking… pair of Pay Less dress shoes – black – faugh-alligator-skin – with silver buckles… a mixture of fear and befuddlement on face, talking on his silver flippy cellphone, glaring at application form: in thick accent: "they say I need a valid, New York State…" – see my number – blink on screen… I pay forty-five dollars… she prints out a sturdy piece of paper – rips it at the perforations – tiredly, "this is a temporary license – your permanent one should arrive at your place in 2-4 weeks…"

I'm smiling huge, receive it – she's smiling too now – like a girl in a fastfood commercial – a driver-through-window girl in headset – handing off bag of burgers and fries …

walking away "yes!" pumping fist "*Yes!*" people in line, staring glumly …

burst out revolving door – duck cloud of gnats, pull rolled mag from back pocket, start beating at the cloud "Yyyyy*eeeeeeeeaaaah*" – swoosh-swoosh-Swoosh! – people, looking on, concerned… "*yyyyyeaaaaaaaah*-hahaaa!" Swosh!-Swoosh! – "ya lil' *buggers! haheee*" Swoosh!-Swoosh!-*Swoosh!-Swoosh!* "*ha-haaaaaa! Howya like it! Howya like me nowww*" Whoosh! WHooSh WhoooSH!

CHAPTER 7

Train up to Boston …

resume work at Lit… Increase number of poems, read at mic – trying with all might (nights, in room, at desk, pacing) - to push language (communication) beyond - into new realms – construct new structures - dynamics - in listener's minds – what else is poetry other than creating scenes in other's heads – like a construction worker builds a building – piece by piece – brick by brick… – word by word leading to this, that – building, building, forms, scenes, characters, feelings, on and on… ~realm to realm – and *beyond these~* – and ah, the expressions on faces at Lit as it all enters in - clicks! – the looks, one to another….

A letter appears on kitchen table – return address: Tyler's …
Rip into… another envelope inside – from the DMV…
Tear …

"We regret to inform you that, due to a technical malfunction in our camera, we are not able to process your license at this time. Please arrange for a photo retake at your earliest possibly convenience. Thank you."

– crumple in hand – "*rrrrrr!*" – hurl in trashcan – "*rrrrrr!*" - bounces off plastic milk gallon and out – as I'm falling, twist in air – butt hits floor – back to wall, where, body, deflates… Mom, walking in, head, atilt, face, befuddled "Are you ok? Zach?"

in room, call Emily – she agrees to cover my shift tomorrow… –

"and Zach – there's a uh, 'W-2' form still here for you."
"Ah, yeah, right, well… ok, I'll uh, - yeah, that's fine, ok, bye."

The setting of alarm… the long stretch of no sleep…
The early rising… wild dawn walk to train station… the sailing, sleeping, sailing on rails….

Sitting at Seattle Coffee in Penn Station… – eating a no-fat-mixed-berry-oat-bran-muffin, sipping at a coffee – Mariah Carrie, playing loud overhead – "you got me feeling *emotional* baby – higher thaaan the heavens abooove!…" muffin is good – heavy though, - ~how is it (as advertised) "97% Fat Free?"~

Here, the long, sad line… walking by it… passing a shiny steel breakfast cart, craving another coffee, – but ~the pee factor – what with this long line…~ - second's eye contact with a guy - finishing off his ice coffee - up through slurping straw – spaced out eyes… his hand rattles see-through cup of ice …

Last in line is a young Indian guy – perhaps the most intense ~glower~ I've seen to date… – oily sweat glistening off furrowed, frowning brow… ~has his face irreparably melded to this by now?~ K—Mart shirt, faded cargo pants, dark leather sandals, a tong looping over just big toe on each foot… he suddenly walks away… bends over, picks up a free newspaper from a pile… returns …I resume reading book – Susan Sontag's 'On Photography'- as he opens paper, slowly edging back in front of me… let right in – with that face (after whatever he's seen, been through) who's gonna give him any more grief… Notice over his shoulder the article he's glaring at: headline: "No Peace, No Contract" - has pictured a bunch of plump MTA workers wielding picket signs, shouting with wide open mouths, behind them sways an enormous, inflated rat, big buck teeth protruding …

Line gets moving… as filing, lady, in front of Indian guy, into cellphone pinched to ear by shoulder, while rummaging in purse: "I should be out… no later than 9:30…" we pass by a poster in restaurant window: 'Prime Rib' (pict under it: a rack: asparkle) printed above: 'You Deserve the Best'… press through revolving door – ~no gnats today~ – soon as step foot in: female automated voice: "now serving ticket number 400, at window number 9…"

Here, the blond dread lady - wait - *red* now – ~must've dyed it~ – is yelling out "*Sir*" – she's making pushing motions "*this way* sir – *curve* the line around…" we curve, linked, snakelike – triggers memories - National Geographic TV show – seen years ago - as a kid (seems had… so much… time…

then – sitting round watching shows at leisure... – the cartoons Saturday mornings... – was like a little business man, there, taking them in) ...

cellphone lady ahead of me is rummaging through bag again – produces a pen - frantically scratches at a form – it dawns – ~I have to fill out the "M-44" form~ – dig it out of bag... scribble in the rote answers... as line crawls zigzag in ropes... Dread guard stands front and center - holds a piece of paper high in air "Anyone have this photo retake form? – Anyone with this photo retake form, *step off the line*, step off the line, and follow me." Me... and a pretty girl - rockstar shades on, glossy lips, humongous fashion bag hanging – break free from the line, follow dread guard... – as automated voice chimes in "Now serving ticket number 600, at window number seven."

"stand back at the wall" different camera lady than before mumbles ...

~here, looking at the smiley face sticker again – it's tongue sticking out - ~thought I'd never see this smiley face again while on this planet... yet here I am... it's ok... – actually don't quite recall – who's to say 'never' – could be that it did cross mind – who can remember...~ trying to smile... ~why smile? – Oh, this must look *pained*...~ - ~and this... all... just... seeming... 'beyond my realm of jurisdiction' – all 'out of my hands'... - and what is within my realm of jurisdiction? – is there such a thing – seeing as everything must be generated from a source – where is this power coming from – I don't make it... - are my thoughts even from that source – whatever it be - hence not from my own volition – what's this 'free-will' people so like to think and express that they have if something (the source) grants its freedom (i.e. no freedom unless given by the source – who could ever 'generate' freedom in and of themselves – other than an all powerful source?) – and can a thought happen without the source making it happen... - even in the head of one that happily affirms itself it's free - has a 'will of its own' to 'exercise'...~

Handing me a ticket, "wait for your number to be called - *next*."

~and what am I *doing* here – here in a place I'd rather *not* be at... – chalk it up to another hoop – all these dummy hoops – some of them flaming... – rooted in there having to be *such* order - because things are so botched up – botched due to... the scientists have their explanations – the Christians say Adam... - hoops due to bad a apple? or is it 'forbidden fruit' – could sinking teeth into a juicy peach wreck stuff for countless generations – could slicing canines into (spattering its juice) a grape be the reason for the bomb's detonation that day in Hiroshima... – or is it metaphoric or symbolic or...~

sit on bench... "stay on the line!" shouts dread guard ~'stay on'(?)~ ...

A guy in middle of the line asks her something... I notice she's wearing lots of gold jewelry... – she looks at his paperwork, and "you got the *wrong* place honey... you gotta go two blocks down" pointing "to Herald Square"... the mans shoulders slump, cartoon-like, as he lets out a hissing sound – first sounding like a cat – then snakelike, finally (stretching long now) like air escaping a bike tire... room packed more than ever here now – she turns, taps a guy on the arm – guides him to the middle area – "this gentleman is starting a *new* line – all y'all over here *line up* behind him..." then, pointing, "do *not* move this line past this line." flowing, snaky movementation... – everyone sticking close... "here, make another line – here – *here* - yes I'm pointing at you..." – they adjust accordingly, as one sad-faced creature (comprised of sad-faced creatures) – here, an Asian couple – not understanding the directives – as evinced by their scared faces – just... going with flow, anyway, though, darty-eyedly....

Slide book from bag... quote from Schopenhauer: "Photography . . . offers the most complete satisfaction to our curiosity." – and my number blinks... –

standing at desk... black lady looks over forms just handed... slides them in a folder, files it away:

"It'll be mailed to you within 2 weeks" ...

"this is my second time here, are you *sure* it's going to go through ok..."

"We just put it in and hope it do what it's supposed to do..."

Walking through Penn Station – sign out front Seattle Coffee reads "Citizen's Bank Free Coffee Day." Go in, get another muffin... chuck a dollar tip in jar (even with bank account being $57 in the negative)... trot down subway stairs, chewing muffin, sticking ipod ear plugs in ears... press play - walking on platform... behind a college girl (looks to be from some Mid-West school) wearing pink tank top cut high (skin around waist, exposed)... printed (in white) across her plump jiggling bum: 'PRIDE' ...

CHAPTER 8

Supplement 'income' by helping Pete Hess (on edges of cool crowd during high school – would just exchange a few words with at parties – was in the... level 3 classes – always a clever wit to him though) cut lawns – he and his 50-60 lawns and troop of junior-high kids... and we joke and laugh – rumbling through town in dented, back-firing Chevy pick-up – guzzling big iced tea gallons - - - and how thoughts would delve, soar - surprisingly deep, high - during long spans walking behind five bladed roaring 'SCAG' mower ...

reading more books – a pile accruing in room now... and much jotting of notes in notebooks – attempting (as writ on cover of notebooks) "sheer originality" ~what pretension(?)~ - ~'pretension'(?)~ add, under it: "total frankness."

Saving up a bundle – literally – stowed under bed – a mass of bills (put some in account – about... 30%) – experimenting with this system – this notion of seeing the bills – ~actual stacks~ – to better gauge - ~grasp a better understanding of~ money ...

The stacks grow... thoughts stir... ~entertain~ returning to New York... time frames ...
See Tyler online... Skype call him.... "yeah..."
"yeah I'm heading to city tomorrow..."
"ok..."

Exit Penn Station ~get some air before subway up to Tyler's~
Sunny, hot... waiting to cross street... automated: "signal is green to cross 6th Avenue, 6th Avenue..." as I cross... guy walking opposite direction: Yankees

shirt: 'Got Rings?' printed on chest. Cloud of smoke from chicken sizzling on vendor's grill whooshes in face... Three steps - gust of roasting chestnuts smoke blows in face... - Bus roars by – black fog exhaust - hits face... – here, parked - a tar truck - caked black glossy tar holder whafts smoke... - the bull dozer – Mex guy sitting at wheel (resembling a... bug) – mashes asphalt down tight... pass a Ray's Pizza – doors open – Mex cook whirls spinning floppy dough disk up (blink-eye-photo-capture) – cheese/oregano/garlic/pepperoni fill nose... – little further - open Subway – vinegar/Italian dressing/their usual assortment of meats – enters nose... – as ambulance wails by... followed by fire truck, laying on horn *"EEEEERRRNT-EEEEEEEEERRRRNT!!!"* – flower merchant stand now – colors passing – scents tickling at brain... – another construction site – Mex guy, drearily rattling at jackhammer –*'B-R-R-R-R-R-R-R-R!!!!!!'* heading into subway – guy coming up, lighting up a cig, blows smoke right in my face... – yellow-eyed homeless black guy, drags a slow hit from a roach – stench of weed, sparking memories - casting them from head, swiping card, through turnstile... walk along platform... guy, pressed against wall, looking over shoulder... puddle lining out, branching, to edge, trickling over... whiff caught... board 6 train – people, huddled in... stand with nose next to underarm of fat guy in tank top holding top rail – b.o. hitting hard as we all sway northward ...

Key in door to note on table: *'working late – see you in morning   Ty'*

Eyes opening to: Tyler, standing, staring down, bowl of cereal in hand, mouth, chewing ...
"Ey..."
"Mornin'" ...
pull sit up, rub face ...
"ever wonder about that..." he says "the same word we use to start the day with – also means to grieve – y'know... *mourn*..."
"yes."
"So what'd you say you were gonna do for work again?"
"What time is it?"
crunch-crunch-crunch "one..."
"thinking of walking around downtown – see if any stores... catch fancy – inquire within sort of deal..."
"y'know I cater right..."
nod no ...

"Yeah, gotta do something... – anyway – there's a gig tonight – they're looking for more workers – what do you say?"

... "what do I wear?"

"this way" pointing ...

slides open closet in room... amid colorful shirts, four white ones... "here," unhanging, handing it, black pants inside - "we're the same size pretty much... there, covered – and here – I got two pairs of dress shoes..." Scene flashes in head of me walking around with a tray of sushi – people nabbing up the rolls ...

"twenty an hour – easy money – whataya say – two, three gigs a week pays rent and then some..."

"Ok..."

"Good, let's get crackin' – we gotta be there at 2:30..." – he pulls a shirt from hanger, examines collar... yellow ring around it... crumples it into ball, "that's it for that one" presses it into little trashcan next desk ...

shower, shave, forty minutes on 6 train, dress clothes in black zip-up sleeves ...

Show at Soho venue – a bunch of actors and models stand or sit about in black dress pants, white t-shirts - some know each other, chat, catching up... regulars looking bored, newbies looking nervous ...

To curly-haired girl sitting with clipboard wearing headphones-mic:
"name?"

"Bar... – Zach"

"don't see..."

striding over from talking with some manager-looking guy - "he's with me" says Tyler – "write 'im in – just got the ok from Eric..." she scrawls name – slashes through it, points at a pile of white fluffy things on floor – "put on a pair of booties before going into the main room." pull them on – made of a, like, fabric softener material – over shoes – all the caterers milling about inside have them on – adding a dynamic... must be fifty of us ...

A huge space – nine chandeliers hanging down – covered in white flowers... in center of room, a square pond... grand piano right by it... a pair of workers hurriedly shift a ladder around in spurts – adjusting spotlights overhead ...

Thirty-something guy dressed like a college kid - hat on backwards and ripped jeans - charges into room with a clipboard – "Hi everyone, I'm Joe, I'll be the captain for tonight..." eyes scanning clipboard - "this is going to be a *huge* event – a wedding... – Leanne and Justin – we're here to make it a special time for them – let me give you the quick rundown - we'll kick things off by rolling the round tables out – Oscar's bringing in the table clothes – four go on each – keep an ear out as we go along – he'll tell you the order of them…"

we roll out the big tables – actions all… working together – adjustings… ~like… ants… building an anthill…~ - the four sets of clothes go on each… – carry out crates of plates – set on – silverware: 3 spoons, 2 forks, 3 knives – three glasses "red, white, water"… glass bowls full of yellow-white flowers – tall centerpiece vases - white flowers shooting high… candles… a group of girls, sitting at far table, folding napkins …

a curtain runs along one side – other side is the dance floor – where dj's testing sound – multi-colored strobe lights blinking, swirling …

two bars set up out in hallway – hundreds of glasses aligned – built into pyramids – on it… bottles, somehow illumined from below, aligned, displayed along front… cases of beer, soda, wine, vodka, behind table cloth …

chairs are hauled in from back room… eight per table… "Ok good work – that's the lion share – let's taper off… – we'll all gather soon for a role call…" we sit around the pond, – a few (assigned the task) chuck white roses in, to floating on the surface… - "good distance" kid sitting next to me comments at one toss… floating candles set in, lit …

Cake is wheeled in… – has sculpted figurines on each of its five tiers – mainly of the bride – here, playing tennis – here skiing… riding a horse… in a boat… sun-bathing… running a marathon …

Joe calls the staff meeting… us all sitting around in booties as Joe says into headset mic "right-right-right-right-right no yeah listen it's totally cool yea-yea-yea-yea-yea…"

turns to us …

"Great job, we're ahead of schedule" –

"Ice is here!" someone calls in'

"Ice is here, excellent." Scratches check on clipboard …

He calls out duties for each caterer – "Zach Barr - bussing – then pass hor dourves – then final breakdown."

"Tyler - VIP table, shadow the bride and groom – make sure they have everything they need…" ~well, quite the seasoned caterer…~

"Ok so, people arrive, cocktails in lobby an hour, we pull everyone inside, open bar ready - special note to the servers – right off the bat we're gonna flank the doors with tray drinks – take the brunt off the bartenders." referring to clipboard… "toast by Leanne and Justin… two course meal… band kicks in… cut the cake-" "wine's here!" someone calls from lobby – "great, wine's here, ok… Ok, cut the cake… dessert buffet, dance floor opens up, people will be hitting it – we'll pull some people to help with sparklers at that point... – figure on staying to one or so – they're a partying crowd."

"also no clustering in groups – doesn't look professional... – and no booze – we've had problems in the past, believe me, please, no booze... - Ok, break for staff dinner... Everyone be ready at 6:15 - wine stewards come with me..."

we line up in back kitchen area, fork sauced chicken and pasta from aluminum cooking trays onto plastic plates... sit at one the three round tables or stand, eating... chefs, off to the side, intense – the older one pumping pointing finger at dish he's stirring, spouting directives at two assistants – other helpers sprinkle bits of seaweed from tupperware onto hundreds if little dishes set out on adjoined tables – others following along behind them, laying on cucumber slices... a type of hierarchy forms – 'cooler' caterers huddling - the others, with the new ones, watching... not much love going round, ~survivalist lifestyle vibe in air...~ table I'm at seems we're... all not wanting to say anything to each other - ~ hmm, - all dressed alike... can't quite gauge where each stands on the 'coolness ladder'... - don't want to say anything stupid – or, if already cool, don't want to waste breath...~

go for seconds... bits of small talk chime in - shoo off thickening (turning awkward) silence ...

Guests start arriving – can tell they have money ~well fed over the years – tanned – lots of wrinkles from all the smiling – jewelry...~ – and they're thirsty and hungry – grabbing champagne off trays (sip at it, schmoozing, - some, pinkies, fully extended) – and picking at hor dourve trays – which circulate about in steady flow... - whisking behind curtain, empty tray in hand – replaced with stocked one (mini grilled cheeses, mini hamburgers, sushi, on and on) – emerge from another curtain – weaving through – explanations given at points ("yes, here we have caviar and cucumber on a wheat cracker") – till it's back to kitchen again... - here, a tall caterer, advances forth from behind curtain - carrying five tiered tray - pigs in a blanket – cut in the shape of pigs - toothpicks, driven through chests... I walk about, silver tray in hand, gathering empty champagne glasses, beer bottles, napkins... bringing it to the 'sanitation room' where a thin, spunky, wise-cracking old guy commands what (glasses, plates, silverware, etc.) goes into which bins ...

~got packed quick~ - and ~people are seriously getting their drink on~ - heads, thrown back in laughter... chubby guy to lady: "the meatballs'll knock you over – much better than that-" juts thumb behind him to tray leaving – "whatever that was."

Oscar (a higher-up caterer – wearing headphone mic) points out a quicker route – "you go in here (into main room) walk a ways, then come out - right across from the sanitation room – bypass a good chunk of the jam-packed-ness." – I give it a go… about to head through curtain – "no-no-no-*no-no!*" – turning, it's Joe –"that's where the cake is man – right out those curtains." – picture myself knocking the huge, figurine-laden cake onto a fat old rich lady – her falling to the floor, her legs, covered in cake – "use another curtain man thanks" – his eyes space out – sticks a finger to earplug, shifts mic stem closer to mouth – "what was that?"

weaving through, observing – the ladies – here, a group of frosted blonds… make up loaded on… happiness seeming… too off charts – exaggerated… going in through a curtain - following one of the few girl caterers - her foot snags drapery – silver tray with contents floats through air – sliding clattering glass breakage as she breaks into stomping run to prevent rolling on to it all… -

bartender waves me over - "fill in a while – I gotta go grab another case of wine." –

here, tall celeb-looking blond "I'll have a half-Coke-half-Diet-Coke." . . .

Beat-looking bartender returns eventually, replaces me without a word… – on into sanitation room – where spunky old guy points to bins of half-melted ice… "would you empty these?" – lug them out - into brisk, wild Soho night – dump it to splashing in sewer grate… inside again, other caterers sit round here, behind scenes, pour plastic jugs of spring water into tall glass Evian bottles, pour quarter full bottles of red wine into half full ones, chucking empties… – over here, scraping leftover food into trash bag – one caterer to other "man, all this stuff gets thrown out… – can you imagine how many poor people you could feed… – and it's all because of that law – some homeless guy a while ago - ate leftovers from some party – got food poisoned or something – sewed the company – all kinds of money – now they just throw all the stuff out – so they don't get sewed by anyone, it's ridiculous…"

In main room, lights are cut – lone spotlight on cake - pianist, playing softly… couple of speeches… cake, cut… section of curtains open to dance floor… people streaming in – live band belting a tune "*burn* baby *burn* – disco *inferno!*" - Joe waves me over – stabbing sparklers into cork tops of champagne bottles – hands me one, hands others – gives us lil' lighters… "start of next song – light 'em up – walk around – make it festive." - band shifts into Def Leopard's "Pour some sugar on me" flick, hold flame to grey sparkler tip a while… – bursts to sparks, weave about packed dance floor – here, an old lady with died light brown hair – executing full-fledge running man dance to "*That's* the way ah-huh-ah-huh *I liiike it!*"... Oscar calls me over – "new batch of trays in the kitchen" walk around with tray after tray – mini cheesecakes, blueberry cobbler, plates of cake, cotton candy, mini sherbet cones, popsicles... which staggering, reeling dancers pinch, scarf... ~dance fuel~ here and there are geometric, orange couches - people lounging on them... off to the side, a long bar – poured glasses lined thereon for easy grabbage... - here, guy in corner, dancing by himself to "At the *Carwash... Carwash...*"

We're given glowstrings to distribute – people tying them around heads, whirling, throwing them... dance circles form, fill, form - as time stretches way beyond 1am... Joe lets a few caterers go - stride smiling to changing room... Tyler and I remain clear to here, loading truck... In back kitchen: black plastic bin - full of figurines from cake (tennis player, skier...) – icing still on stakes... unthinkingly ask an assistant chef if they're getting thrown out – if I can have the one with the girl riding the horse ...

"that's probably for the couple - as a keepsake, I'd imagine."

We arrive, haggard, at apartment... 4:01am... brushing teeth, looking at reflection of myself – seen moving on the black pupil of eye in mirror... mind branches into ~what to wear?~ tomorrow - to ~go looking for a job~ in... ~one's understanding (demonstration) of fashion – communicates the degree to which that person is... *in control*... your hold (or 'grasp') on fashion tells how in control you are...~ – think extremes – the mega rich – wearing authoritative designer suits – sharp, powerful - loud messages sent, ears perk up at his entering the room - it's clear he's calling shots... – as for homeless guy – raggy, shaggy, dirty, dumpy – i.e. *not* in control of situation at all – hands over ears at his walking onto scene – no one wants what he's selling – i.e. what ever you're doing (or selling) is going to make me more like you (i.e. undesirable) ...

~fashion shows others the degree of control you wield/(can) exercise over self and others... similar to how it is with art as well – when you grasp/have life pretty nailed down – you can (you 'have time to') branch into artistic pursuits – you're 'freed up' – wriggled out from under heel of (d)oppression... you've control beyond the grind now – to call greater amounts of shots – to experience 'artistic endeavors; pursuits'- be it creating - crafting that sculpture or painting – or collecting - buying million dollar pieces at auctions... ~brushing teeth a while now...~

turn round – Tyler, handing a rectangular piece of paper – red and white:
JURY DUTY SUMMONS
"*man*, I *just* got here."

CHAPTER 9

Days flow by ...

Saturday morning... drop off dirty laundry at Mexican Laundrymatte... walk over to Associated Supermarket, pick up a few groceries... round corner - pass local store 'Magical Party Land' – two Puerto Rican guys setting stuff up out front – here, taping a long plastic pink pole to a parking meter... – up at the top: an inflatable Tweety Bird – a small Puerto Rican flag, taped to its hand, fluttering,... tape makes a loud noise as round and round they go, fastening... smiling, conversing... ~like their cartoon characters around here – seems a... type of... *connection* they have... – some kind of... meaning in it(?)...~

halfway down the block, here, an 80's model Chevy Caprice... looking in... on back seat... a mini-dirtbike... white # 7 on its lil' yellow front tire mudguard ...

A long time folding laundry in room, listening to NPR... take a break, finish Fitzgerald's "This Side of Paradise" ~Ok... though – that arrogance heh-heh...~ - core being ok though – Princeton living intrigues well enough... these others – recent reads - ~miss mark locationwise – and how key is location!~ – there's 'On the Road' (Middle America, Denver – being a goal?) – Faulkner's 'The Sound and the Fury' – do I feel like being transported to the deep south of old? – (only made it a few pages in...)... – anyway it's fiction - who can impose rules on fiction.... ~why do I read them though?... – why continue reading them – what's their worth?~ in their... consolidation... I suppose... is their value – crystallization of experiences, thoughts... - weeding out sleepy day to day hum drum spans of time... – novels can align the potent highlights – right there – which readers can dose in – liven up the mind, stimulate possibilities... – we're all looking for that buzz one way, shape, form or other. . . escapes to higher realms… – some requiring more than others… guessing it stakes on how much you value, require, pleasure – how much you… go for it, what your understanding of it, experience with/of it is… standards crop up over the years… goal-setting sessions… determination to meet, surpass set standards grows and grows…~

Open sock drawer… the summons… ~oh yeah… that's tomorrow…~

Step in subway car filled with people from the Bronx… have to stand… pull AM New York paper from back pocket, open to article: 'Getting that job'… bullet points:

*Do a lot of research …

*Adjust your portfolio to fit the work of companies you apply to …

~heh-heh – could I be further out of this loop… - *hoop*…~

pull out ipod, latch on ear phones – ~time to 'grease the skids' of this, scene, here, presently finding myself in…~ press play - ~is that not an aspect of what art's for - like, 'functionalitywise' – lightening the load(s) of life…~ – the silly Basement Jaxx song adds an instant light – slant – angle – hilarity - to the ride… looking into these faces… this… ~present reality I'm existing in~… seeing it for what it is… 51st Street – large influx presses in - sad, foreign faces, avoiding eye contact, pressing in closer, closer to me… here, a quiet Dominican lady – pregnant – cleavage-revealing tank top – being pushed into my lower chest – the music is growing steadily zanier as things apparently start getting heated by the door – a taller black guy – wearing a new Chicago Bulls hat, is pushing to get in – I watch mouth of a round black lady, head leaned back, eyes closed, - it moves fast - like a puppet… – thin junior high kid next to her grimaces in pain, a white business man in suit has his Blackberry up three inches from his face, thumb-scrolling downwards… - another thrust - feel the pregnant belly press into my crotch – the nervous, embarrassed look of the lady - the music synching perfect as a tall guy wearing a construction hat with a Puerto Rican flag sticker on it – tries squeezing in closing doors – scrunching his face – hear him yelling over the music – start chuckling – as Asian guy grimaces in foreground… belly shakes against the Dominican lady – who's unwinding the earplug cord from around her ipod …

Reflect on past weeks - so packed with variety and new experiences - soaking in this, that from happenings and conversations - fascinating people, books, magazines, dvds… - crazy moments, situations – too many to describe – which ties into article, reading here, standing in line for the metal detectors, to get in Supreme Court Building... – 'New Yorker' – about what makes for a great novelist... - the writer relating how he once recommended a thick novel to a friend – calling it a 'first-rate second-rate-novel'... whereupon the friend – an older man – replied that 'at this point in my life, I haven't the time to spend reading such books – my time is running out...' mm – and how this concept relates to other pursuits... ~who has time to deal with, allow mediocrity in...~ think of exercising prevention of – finding ways around – ~time-wasting stuff... – eyes just – bringing in the better scenes – letting them do their better work inside...~ - at *this* stage – while young ...– such vast spans of time ahead – that'd be fizzled off (if not... vigilant) – spent on (in light of grand scheme) tedium... – we see how vital that capability to know what is vain and what is worthy (i.e. worth the doing) is – see the utter idiocy of perversion or sloth here – cheating so glaringly clearly *off* (moronic) - when taken at that angle - that in long run – it doesn't just go away... – the wrong - eventually comes around ~ah *consequences* - caressing, biting, stinging, goring – one way or other, showing up in the lives of any thinking they can pull off cheating the laws of the very universe...~

Through marble-pillared corridor... to elevators... up to 4th floor - over to room 452... – large space – a desk, central, up front... A short guy – thinning reddish hair, nasal voice, glasses, mustache, steps to mic, begins mono-toning instructions "If everyone would take out their summons form like you see here..." holding it up... "you'll see there are four sections – looking at section A, make sure it says '60 Centre Street' - if it has another address you're in the wrong place – take your form and proceed to the location printed there..." two people leave... I tune out ...

...tuning in again: "Anyone who falls into the following categories can not serve... If you are not a U.S. citizen..." tune out ...

..."We're now going to watch a 20 minute video about serving on a jury..." he points a remote at a big TV mounted up on wall – screen turns blue... – scene of people walking in white robes – like they'd wear in Jesus' day – and they're pushing a convict-looking guy, yelling at him, over-acting... narrator describes how in ancient times they dealt with crime in a "trail by ordeal" fashion... - they'd plunge the accused's hand into a pot of boiling water – if it healed within a given time – they were innocent, cleared... they'd throw the accused (hands tied) into water (here, actors hurl tied up convict into a lake) if they floated: innocent, if sank: guilty (video shows convict bobbing to surface – family grabbing him up, rejoicing) ...

Next scene is Ed Bradley, of 60 Minutes, grey hair, earring, walking along, hand in pocket, elaborating further... "That's how they did it then... Times... have changed."

Old etchings of robed philosophers flashes up – "Greece made strides – with Aristotle setting in place a system where the accused was given the right to *argue his case* before a group of peers... The Romans came along and threw this out..." tune out ...

..."In England the jury comes into play – the rights of the accused to a fair trial before citizens of the community... the system worked - though not without its share of bumps in the road – when William Penn was arrested for disturbing the peace, for instance, - the jury ruled him innocent – the court pressed for another decision – and when they refused to give a guilty verdict – the entire jury was thrown into jail... Soon a law passed to prevent this from happening again..."

switch of narrator's voice - female - as clips from black and white Perry Mason episodes play... – "we've seen our share of courtroom scenes on television – which, while giving an idea – tend *exaggerate*" (court officers rip a fake mustache, wig, off a panicking, bug-eyed guy) "and use their dramatic license." – clip of woman at witness stand, rising from seat, pulling small gun out from bobbed hair – "It was *him!* – points, shoots, hits, fat bald guy, teeth grit, clutching belly, hunches over ...

Diane Sawyer appears on screen "in real life, things just don't happen that way..."

She describes litigation as "a dispute between two parties which comes to a final showdown before a jury of peers..." - shows actors in a court room setting, each playing their parts as Diane describes their function "we have the judge": (a black woman with high hair, wearing black robe, takes seat at upraised desk)... "there's the court officer": bulky light-skinned black guy crosses arms, gives an eye scan over the room... "the court clerk": guy speed-typing on tiny computer... "the prosecuting attorney – the attorney for the plaintiff" guy in suit, straightening a stack of manilla folders on table, camera pans over to plaintiff, sitting at same table, looking serious... "and the attorney for the defendant": guy, leaning towards, whispering in ear of defendant... – "now all the characters are here – except for one vital part – the jury, *your* role... The jury is chosen according to whom would best suit the case... – If you're dismissed it is in no way a reflection on your intelligence or personality..." ... "Most people come away with a more favorable opinion of our legal system."

Lady wearing pink blazer, high hair: "I'm Judith Kay, Chief Judge of New York. Diversity is a great strength to our society..." on and on... concluding that the system is working to improve so that there will be "fewer calls" to jury duty and "shorter terms." her face turns serious "you see, you are extremely valuable to the system – and the system is extremely valuable to you." – a giggle bubbles up, I'm shaking in chair – a few heads swivel – like this petrified-looking Asian lady sitting in front of me... - "certainly it's the best system the world has seen, and I believe we have the best system there is." credits roll ...

Orange-mustached guy returns to mic, – more casual - holding a coffee mug... "Please put away all reading and writing material as we have the Honorable Mark Bearclay come and address us..."

A squat Disney-looking character steps up – graying red hair, beard:

"Prospective jurors! Welcome. You are performing a valuable service to the community... One that *no one* is exempt from - judges, doctors, lawyers, taxi drivers, engineers – *no one*..." on and on... light applause ...

nasal-voiced coffee mug man returns to mic... holding up a paper... monotone: "pleease keep your summons in tact, don't tear it apart... You'll be expected to be here from 9:30-5 each day, lunch is from 1 – 2... if you have for any reason to postpone due to an emergency, the number to call – you'll wan t to write this down – is 212-386-5999... please do not be handing that number around and use it in emergency cases only, we don't take personal messages..."

"Now, should you be picked, during your jury service you'll be expected to sit silently and hear the case out – you can not make unsolicited remarks... Making prejudicial remarks will cause the entire jury to be disbanded – you'll have wasted a lot of people's time - *most importantly* your own time - so you'll want to be mindful of that..."

"Finally (pointing) we have the lunchroom there beyond the... statue of liberty, em, sculpture... If you want to take a break – go downstairs for a cigarette or the... coffee bar downstairs or outside you'll have to sign out at this clipboard and we ask that you make it no longer than a fifteen minute break..."... zone out, looking around at the murals painted on the walls – George-Washington-types, looking austere, august... fade in again... "There is internet access on the computers lining the back walls there... And if you have your own laptop, there is wireless internet..." holding up a form "you all received in the mail", he instructs us to rip a section off to keep – put the other two sections "filled out" in a wire basket, which he holds up, shakes ...

Standing in line I hear the stocky black lady in uniform - standing behind counter with the announcer – saying "next person please, good morning, next person please..." - thought surfaces to mind – line from art philosophy book read years ago: "repetition is the death of art..."..... think of her doing this job day in, day out... - what those words, repeating (without feeling in them) *do* to her over time - she does, I notice, break it up at times "Ok, look alive here, look aliiive people, here we go, thank you, next, good morning..."

I see people in line have their section ripped off – still haven't figured out which one – no time to ask as, here, I stand before frowning mic guy – "like this?" I say, acting about to tear a section – his eyebrows shoot up – then cut into frown as swipes form from hand – ripping square out – thrusts it back... walk away, "did he say go to another room after handing that in or..." – when a small Japanese woman steps to mic – starts reading – in thick accent – a list of names – "here"'s firing or moaning in response... "if you heard your name called, please report to courtroom number four."

the lunch room is pointed out again as an option to "make yourself comfortable in..." grab bookbag... stroll in... scan the magazine racks... remove an Amazing Spiderman comic, place it on shiny new particle-board table... – a TV, mounted up in corner, playing news – a school shooting – helicopter aerial view, serious-looking woman-news-caster's voice: "two schools in the Bristol Bay area are now *on lockdown*..." Another guy joins me at the table, unwraps a big corn muffin from plastic, uncaps a Snapple, gets eating, drinking, flipping through Sport's Illustrated ...

The squat black lady gets on the mic, starts calling names... "Christopher Lombardi..." delayed response – "Ok look alive – give me a nice response... *Work with me* now people..." I pull laptop from bag... open... hm, "Welcome to *Courtroom Online*" requires $6.95 - credit card info... – ~who gets the money?~ punch it in... pull card from wallet to get expiration date... connected... ~when is this city going wireless?~ - ~think of the spread of knowledge – a *more knowledgeable society* – answers at fingertips... - *who's* preventing this from happening? Big business? Are they banning us from connection to internet – to all these answers and communication – so that they can get bigger paychecks?~ ... computer is processing slow... ~time for an upgrade~ - faster computer – faster answers – quicker you know - faster communication – efficient use of time – one gets done *this* much in a given span – another (with better, faster computer, better programs - in that *same* amount of time) get done *this* much... – like, say, a distance competition - which society goes further – here, a village of people - all on bikes – vs. this village – all in sports cars – starting gun fires – twenty minutes later – who's covered more ground... ~a more knowledgeable society – better and better resources - more and more people getting on quicker and quicker wavelengths - progress sky rockets – exponential increase week to week – excitement acrackle in air... – which opens into – would pleasure increase in relation to such technological moves... - and does a happy people make a happy country – sounds safe to say... what's keeping me, others from acquiring speedier computers – yea *speedier progress...* $$$$$$$$...*" -

"Zach..." overhead speakers blare "*Barr?*" – closing laptop – "Is there a Zach in the house?" shoving it in bag – "Hel*llooooo*" jogging into room, waving hand, heads turning... "pick up a questionnaire at the door, fill it out, and bring it to room A18, - seat number 16" ...

Into A18 - full of glum faces – a few strange smiles – about 20 people... A tall Dominican guy in suit stands up front, next to a tall black lady in pants suit – next to her: a short, round, bright-white lady – intense, fiery blue eyes, bulging, bullfrog-like chin... The Dominican guy – maybe part Indian – a serious edge to him – slight accent – introduces himself (lawyer for the plaintiff) the two women introduce themselves (representing the "City Transportation Department"). We're asked to hand in our questionnaires – which strikes in that I forgot to grab one from the main room... I get permission to get the form, fill it out with quick scrawly strokes, hand it in ...

The judge from earlier shows up... Tall Dominican gives him the floor ...

booming voice, "You have been chosen to be a part of the community... What you're called to do is precisely what others have been called upon to do for centuries... The Latin word *vor deer* - means 'speak what you see – speak the truth of what you see.'..."... on and on... – gives a "quick rundown" of the case – "it's what we call a 'slip and fall' case..." on and on... elderly woman tripped on an upraised subway grate – owned by the city – fell, broke her elbow - sewing city for hospital bills, "pain and suffering..." wraps it up... pitter-patter of applause, leaves... tall Dominican stands, starts to pace ...

... "Unfortunately, everyone comes in here with his or her *baggage...* – what our job is - to do now, in this room – is to find out if you would have any biases against the parties represented in this case... We're going to look over the questionnaires that you filled out for the next..." looking at watch, looking at other two lawyers... "fifteen minutes?..." they nod... "So if we all reconvene promptly at... five till... We can continue with the proceedings here..." we file out as they divvy up, start leafing through, the papers – jotting notes in their yellow legal pads – looking very serious - ~they are *definitely* getting paid, these three. they're getting paid plenty...~

return to lunchroom... notice (set in Home-Depot-faux-antique frame) poster hanging on wall by table: a mountainscape – monochromatic orange – sunbeams bursted through clouds – onto evergreens below, curvy weaving river winds through... a lone eagle, floating in sky – bottom central: white font in black square:

<u>ESSENCE OF DESTINY</u>

Watch your thoughts
For they become words.
Choose your words
For they become actions.
Understand your actions, for they become habits.
Study your habits, for they will become your character.
Develop your character
For it becomes your destiny.

Snap a few emails, myspace responses ...

A18... chair 16... stare at the prettiest girl in the room – petite, tanned, blond, sitting front row, expressionless face gazing at Blackberry as thumbs busily press tiny buttons... I imagine the strings of words forming along in her brain – ~where does it spring from – why do the words... appear as they do – compel forth into, out from, individuals?~

Tall Dominican talks a while – another rundown – how plaintiff "smashed her elbow to pieces"... on and on... "now, if there's anything which would prevent you from making a fair and impartial decision, please raise your hand..." A guy sitting in front of me – frosted hair, faded black t-shirt – had a thick Chekhov book, opened in front of face earlier: "I... had an altercation with an MTA employee, so..."

"So you feel that incident might... taint your mind to where you would not be able to make a fair and impartial decision in this particular case..." long pause... "You feel you would not be able to make a fair and impartial decision?"

"No."

"Ok" a jot on yellow pad "anyone else?"

... the pretty blonde – feistier than I'd imagined –

"We live in a city where there are plenty of obstacles around –

you have to watch where you're going – I've fallen a couple of times on the subway" – I picture these falls – collectively (somehow) - in head - without trying – her cute little self - with those glisteny gold locks – tucking into tumbling, rolling on black (white-specked) subway floor… - "and, I mean, I just owned up to it – it was my fault…" –

"So you feel you would not be able to make a fair and impartial decision in this case?"

"No I would – it could go either way – I'm just telling you… - if she's looking for a substantial amount of money - beyond medical bills – I'd find it hard to approve that…"

"Thanks…" a jot "Anyone else?"

Guy's voice from behind: "I just want to understand the crux of it a little better – is it *gross negligence* or…"

…"At this time I can't really speak to that – we'll get into that more in the actual case…" –

guy again: "in my mind it should have been settled." –

"but do you feel you can be fair and impartial?"

"No"

"Thank you…" jot "Anyone else."

~I have to say something…~ - working to put together right words …

Looking at clipboard… "Jerry Hansman… – that's you… I see here that you… sat in a jury on a case which went to verdict… – was there anything about that case which would taint your mind with regards to this case – do you feel you could be fair and impartial?"

He's nodding his head yes …

"Won't effect you in any way at this point…"

nodding head no …

"You'll be open-minded, fair and impartial." Nodding head yes… – to everyone "these are the key words you'll hear pop up again and again 'open-minded', 'fair', 'impartial' - whoever is selected has to keep an open mind, hear the full testimonies through the trial and then make a determination together…"

raise hand.

Pointing, "Yes."

"I'm thinking it would be better if you picked, uh, six others – other than myself. – for this case… – I feel they'd be more… into it… than I would be…"

…his eyes go diagonally left and up… "Iiis there a reason why?"

"I think another six would be… – would be more… *into* the case than I would…"

... "Oookay." round white woman furiously jots at her yellow legal pad, her hair shaking... "Anyone else?..." - dramatic point of finger – stunning the lady with raised hand - "*Yes.*"

"ah, yes, I work as a physician here in the Manhattan – I know a *lot* of doctors in the city – is there a name of a doctor associated with this case at all..."

"Yes, leaning over, eyes scanning clipboard..." "Aaaa..." frowning hard "A Dr... *Fishman*... Out of the... Chelsea Medical Center... - does that name ring a bell?"

"Do you have a first name?"

"... We can get that... we can..."– looking over to black lady shuffling through a folder – "you're looking into that, yes, ok – yes, we can get you that name shortly... aaanyone else" – pointing – "yes."

Small Asian lady, thick accent: "did she get attendant after the accident?"

"...You mean, like an in-house nurse?"

nodding head yes ...

"No... her... husband, actually had to look after her – he's filing a loss of consortium claim in this case as well-"

"what's 'consortium' mean?" guy sitting next to me calls out ...

"Consortium is a legal term which deals with one having to take time off from work to attend to an injured spouse – that sort of thing – which we'll get more into in the actual case..." - the round white lady lights up – to Dominican "Harvey."

"Come again?"

"The doctor – Harvey is his first name" –

"Yes, yes, great" to juror, pointing at her, eyes wide "Dr. Harvey Fishman."... "Well ok... on that note, I'm going to hand the floor over to the defendant attorneys..."

Tall black lady, looking related to Condoleezza Rice, glares at the Chekhov frosted hair guy... "This... *altercation* with the MTA employee, was it... instigated by you?"

"Uuuhh, partially."

"Were the police called to the scene."

"Yes."

"Did it go to court."

"No."

She jots on legal pad, nods to round blue-eyed lady... who rises ...

"Does anyone here *hate* the City of New York?" - air in room, changed... "If anyone has issues with the Police department, Fire department, Parks department, if the Sanitation department dumps trash onto your sidewalk every Monday morning and it just has you shaking your fist at the city – we would *need* to know that... If you had a day where it was105 degrees and there were no working water fountains in Central Park – and you made a vow of some sort – *this* is the kind of stuff you would need to tell us now... – anyone have anything..." – but she doesn't really allow for much processing time – "thank you." and sits down... "now... with that..." she says "that brings us to..." squinting at legal pad... "y'know, I've reached that point..." wriggling something out of pocket "where I require reading glasses... – don't like to admit it..." putting glasses on – tip of nose - "trying to hold on to that last vestige of youth I suppose... Any other questions before we break for lunch?..."

feeling of liberation, pushing through revolving door – into sunny fall day, embark on longish walk – into Tribecca – café Pecan... recognize Karolina Kirkova – Chzech supermodel - right as I swing in door, sitting at table by self, wearing large tortoise shell sunglasses, chewing with big open mouth chomps at croissant... instinctive nod of head – she smiles – one cheek bulged with croissant – and resumes chewing... every other table has designer-looking or celeb-looking types – in groups or alone, gathering thoughts, reading, or on laptop... Order "half a tuna sandwich"... expensive... sit by sunny window eat, sip coffee, think, reply to e-mails, check myspace... – red 'New Messages!' blue 'New Comments!'... en route – quick pace - back to courthouse, text Shannon 'when visiting NY?'... one block... two blocks... think of her in class... reading text ...

feel phone buzz in pocket... 'soon... what's up?' – two more sent, received, and it's ...

A18, seat # 16 ...

Dominican, standing, "Judge Bearclay... has requested to see a number of you individually to... question you further... in relation to the case and your involvement..."

~refining stage~

"First we have... Miss... Wegman?" The cute blond – ~figures~ – ups from front row, heads out dutifully... ~ol' Bearclay knows what's up~ ...

some small talk about... - a 'what are we doing here' feel in air... "might as well get picked for it" overheard "otherwise it's coming back tomorrow – might get picked for a more boring case – although a slip and fall is just about as dull as it gets - a whip-lash case would be more interesting..."

She re-enters room – projecting an 'I don't want to be stared at' vibe, adjusting stray bang behind ear en route to chair - making it fall again, adjusting again …

The guy who asked for the meaning of 'the crux' of the case is next – he walks out, arms slightly spread away from his torso like a body builder… Returns, resigned… A few more… – all ones who spoke up earlier - ~guess they're 'weeding out' the aggressive ones…~ - except me ~written off as a lost cause?~… ~make it all work out just the way the system would like it to… – let it play right into the hand…~ O.J. Simpson case years ago flutters into mind – aerial scenes of the white Bronco… scenes on the 20/20, Nightline or some show – they placed cameras in college dormitory lounges – where students gathered to watch the decision together… the camera one in dormitory full of white kids – verdict delivered – grave, motionlessness, a visible sunkenness, shaking of heads… – this, played alongside footage of dormitory lounge at a black college –– their reaction causing camera to wobble – due hands thrown up all at once, clapping, jumping around, laughter, high fives …

…chit-chat behind me as I zone into New Yorker article: "yeah I've totally lost track of any sense of time heh-heh – what day are we in… I'm serious…"

twenty minutes later the air is waxing serious again - the three lawyers standing up front looking furrowed-browedly at their legal pads …

"We've chosen our six for the case…"

"If you do not hear your name called, we'll ask you to –

~we'll?~

-leave the room and return to the larger room - where you might be picked for another case - so don't go anywhere just yet heh-heh… Ok… Jay Rundazzo… Phil… Terkle, Jill Sanders… Dan Carp… Gary Shelly…. and Angella… Brackstone…"

feel tension leaving body… a… decompression – in the air too – a lightening occurs …

We file into big room… receive instructions - to "go to room 419 - to receive further instructions…" we're feeling better, ambling over in hall – I'm being pally with the blond from front row - 'Wegman' - who walks with the second prettiest girl (curly-haired brunette – physical trainer [overheard in A18]) - "I think we're all heading out to go play a big game of dodgeball" – cracks a smile on her face –

"yeah, welcome to high school."

"I wonder if they'll have a piece of cheese in room 419 for us…"

quick chuckle and serious edge surfaces – arm twitches towards bag - ~a half-threat to pull blackberry out~... –

"well rest assured - I did hear this is the 'best system.'"

Gone too far – yet –

"yes, clockwork."

~clockwork indeed~

In 419, a squat bald man with thick black-framed glasses is at the mic ...

Speaks in heavy-bass-yet-whiney-nasal voice – "Because the religious holiday yesterday-

~Yom Kippur~

there will be about one hundred and twenty people coming tomorrow – and so we will be discharging you all early today..." – hands thrust up - cheering breaks forth ...

"Listen for you name – when you hear it called, come pick up your 'proof of service' form and you're free to go."

Japanese lady from earlier steps to mic... "Christopher Lombardi..."

I get mine, fold it, slip it in back pocket, squeezing into elevator - happy bunch inside – "I'm just afraid they're going to call us back" says one... "O this is fabulous..." says another ...

placing on puffy headphones... press play, revolving-door out into blazing brisk October sunniness – as electronica soars me into boppy realm – trotting down stone stairs – cross street – dial up Tyler – leave voicemail – down into subway station – see physical fitness instructor girl, standing on platform, concentrating at punching a text – "hey no slipping and falling on subway." –

"I'll watch my step."

on over to 6 platform – right as train sails in... here, out way earlier than expected... – the phrase ~"possibilities are endless"~ on out-of-my-hands-auto-repeat-mode in head ...

CHAPTER 10

Swing in door to empty apartment… envelope on table …

~Ah, DEPARTMENT OF TRANSPORTATION, eh… let's see here…~ *rrip* …

says… they sent the new license to 231 E. 116 St, Apartment 6f – it's been returned and they're holding it till further notice ~how in the - *rrrrr*~… – can be re-mailed, or picked up directly from the DMV on 33rd… would have to bring a "valid form of identification" …

call the number …

"Hi yeah I just got a letter in the mail – my license was mailed to the wrong address and got returned there – to 33rd street – it says I can pick it up – you're open till like three right – is it ok if I come and pick it up – I could be there in like half an hour" –

"Wo-wo-wo-wo-wo – *hooooold up* now. You're gonna have to *slooow* down here. Now, what are you calling about?"

Go through it again… it's ok to come pick it up – just "you gotta bring a form of identification"

"passport ok?"

"passport's fine."

Dig through bag… find passport… unvelcro wallet… hm, doesn't… fit… see a blue rubber band on counter… stretch it around passport and wallet, bind them together, shove in pocket, jog for door, out, down, subway, up stairs, jog… 33rd… in through revolving door – dread lady - *"stay the line* people!" – show her paper – she points to a desk – "go straight to it – you ain't gotta be in line for that – go right on ahead…"

Lady at desk – same tired heavy, African American lady from weeks ago, looks over my passport… opens, closes filing cabinet drawers, pulls a paper out, sets on desk, checks a few checkboxes, circles a few words – ~rote~ – places it up on counter before me – ~this is… *so far from fun* – can words even describe?… – yet's gotta be done – but says who? … *Society* says who – *Societal Norms*… is this a form of taking (a) cue(s)?~ - points with pen "sign here, here, and here."

Scrawl Zak Bar thrice …

More opening and closing of file cabinets… stapling happens… pulls an envelope… slides on counter with passport… "here you are, thank you."

~O, the joy.~ walking away, tearing it open… remove glossy New York State License… – sure enough - eyes half-closed in picture - hair asunder – but ~*that's fine* - at this point – at this point in my history everything in the entire world is FINE – *beyond* fine – can any word fully express…~ – as walk for revolving door – imagine this surging joy - leaping up - bursting through top of head – through roof – ozone – orbiting planets – galaxies, universe(s?)… – raise arm – finger points to ceiling "YyyyyeeeeEEESS!!!" dread lady's eyes widen… – swoosh through door – raise both hands to sky – one grasping new license – other in fist – head back, eyes closed "YyyyyyyeeeeeEESSSSSS O Thank you God O Thank you-Thank you-Thank yooouuuu…"

Pull wallet out, remove rubber band, unvelcro, slide license in between Bank card and Social Security Card, seal it shut, - rubberband – double-wound-tight - passport to it, slide it in pocket with a pat ~O, yes, very, *very* good stuff.~

Trot down – as subway pulls in - swipe through turnstile – people pressing in full car – slip in – feel people pushing me from behind – 'scyuze me' growls a black kid chewing on a red straw - Yankees hat high on head, bubble head-phones playing loud rap as he pushes grimacing middle-aged Asian man into me – an Indian woman appears between us – she'd been bent over – she's grit-ting teeth as - 'scyuze me!'– see beads of sweat on Asian man's face – see his smart, rimless glasses – picture him in all his classes at Columbia – now gradu-ated – working at his firm – experiencing an uncomfortable moment now though – the kid's head is bobbing – he raps to the music "dealing death blows right and leff with my right-left combo yo"… I picture a rapper walking around just… punching people – them, falling – to their deaths… – ~what drove a person to write these lyrics – why – is there a root - could something be done to ameliorate the situation~ - "Aaattention ladies and gentleman" – as doors open and shut on a cursing Puerto Rican girl in puffy black coat – "there is another train di-*rectly* behind us – I *repeat…*"

Many flush out at the next stop – see a seat open up – head for it – three black kids suddenly jog on – one, boom box on shoulder – the front kid, looking back at buddies, runs right into me – "YO!" he shouts, frowning, jolting a quick shove – ~fierce lil' guy~ - and the others instantly surround me - and they're shoving – all lock hands – have me in a kind of hug – boombox somehow turns on - "*yup-yup! yup-yup!*" they yell – shoves, karate chops, punches - all in a dancing sort of fashion – sudden brake off, laughing – music cuts off - the one changing the big D batteries in boom box as he skips along – chucks packaging to floor… I plunk down on seat, as boom box cranks on again - they clap hands - 'Showtime y'aaall!" – train shifts into top speed they take turns dancing – this one spinning on floor, this one doing the worm – here, a backflip, here, a full split… these two, linking hands and feet, roll in a human wheel up, down the isle – over feet at times – hitting knees… hat's passed by the smallest one – tallest jamming door open with foot till hat makes full round – and they're gone – door closing – an arm shoots in '*clunk*' – old homeless guy squeezes in… dusty blue coat, black Pittsburg Steelers winter hat, sticking high on head… dragging trash bag behind him… stands in front of me - the odor kicking off - drives the guy next to me scurrying away, hand over nose… down on seat beside me he moans – right up against me… has draped over his arm two pairs of old sneakers (their shoe laces tied together - more are bailing – hands over noses… I pull magazine from pocket – ~c'mon article – bring me away – counting on you…~… he's rustling the shoes which press into my leg, mumbling gibberish… ~now here's a guy who, it's safe to say, does *not* have popularity as a high priority in life… – not knocking him – think he'd (if he's… *coherent?*) agree - here's someone who, think it's safe to say, does *not* have a cool myspace profile going on – not in that 'race' – 'not his bag'…~ – the door connecting cars clanks open – black kid comes striding in – toting taped-together candy boxes – "Ladies and gentlemen my name's Anton I'm sellin' candy – not for no basketball team - be honest just sellin' 'em for myself – help keep me off th' streets – at this time all I got lef' is M n' M *Peanut* – thank you, get home safe n' God *bless* – anybody like to buy some *candy?*"

Emerge from subway onto platform – give pocket a pat – ~no~ - tinge of panic flutters through spine – scene of the dancer kids shoving and hitting me on subway flashes to mind - another pat… ~don't seem to… feel it… heh-heh~ - panic strikes harder - scene of homeless guy rustling his hands at the old sneakers on my leg – by pocket - as, patting, re-patting, side, back, pockets, ~there's cellphone… - where's… *wallet~* - voice in head, furious… pull pockets out to bunny ears – hear change fall, bounce on along ground… ~no, *no, no~*"no, no, No, No, NO, *NO!*" – people watching, from across tracks, awaiting their train… - hear a "go easy buddy" from guy passing… - shove hands in jacket pockets - knowing I just checked them – (whiney voice) "no, no, *no, noooo.*" – occurs I'm… slumped over, hugging a cylindrical black trash can… "uuuuuu*uuuuuuuuhhh…*" – two peppy college students (NYU-looking) bop by – "woe – psycho man heh…" quips thin kid – launching girl into nervous giggles… "Ooooooooooonnoooooooooo-this-simply-can-*not*-be happening tooommeeeeeeeeeeeeeeeeeee" unwittingly I've walked a few paces – here, an Asian lady, serious-faced, holds a half-peeled, just-bit banana… jaws, teeth chewing mechanically the mush… "noooooooooooooooooooooo" feel tears slide down cheeks… ascend – not feeling legs moving me - stairway – to, emerging, make eye contact with a black poodle – instant, inexplicable, deep, connection – it's squatting - glaring now – bares teeth – growls - its tongue, half sticking out, it's… straining, muscles in legs contracted, quivering… owner, crouched, holding plastic bag under the dog's rear as, in periphery, tube drops into bag… – suddenly snapped out of it – here, a balding guy – tinted glasses - holding a stack of papers in one arm - thrusts one of them at me 'The Epoch Times'… just, robotically, proceed by… get… wandering streets… – face in hands at times, sobbing loudly …

Fourth or fifth outburst though… turns to… laughing… – ~here I am with these… levels of clarity… this *sight*… this… *mode* this… all-encompassing… '*go for it*' vibe… – I must go for it – yet what's this *it*?…."

An insane 2 or 3 hours transpire – repeating "well it, just… – *what's this "well"? – what's this "just"?* it *iiiis what it iiiis*… – aaall this… it… iiis what it iis… - no way around it… it… is… *indubitably what* it is – more or less in a nut shell – *no-no* – no 'more or less' – it *is* what it is – *has got* to be that – *is* that… nothing else, really…" followed by a few minutes of… plans… which… just… seem… to… appear… in… head… descend into subway… beg a swipe – the ride to 116… key in through door -

to Tyler, sitting on futon, watching a DVD, thumbing a lime into top of Corona –

squints, "what's with you man?"

"I'm heading up to Boson"

"Oh?"

into room.

"What's up?"

Grab stash of $80 from drawer ...

Heading for door, "something came up."

"When are you coming back?"

"see what happens... – can send you an e-mail..." close door, spiral down stairs, subway all the way down to Canal... – catch Fung Wah Bus. . . 40 minute walk into suburbia... key in house at 10:37pm – Dad, closing paper, swivels head round, "Zach."

"Yeah, hi Dad."

"Been away a while – had us wondering again..."

"Yeah, I picked up a few catering jobs" open fridge, get a yogurt "yeah, that was about a month."

"Hope you're ready to get on track with things."

~'get on track with things?'~

"Well, see what happens."

"See what happens?"

"Long day, think I'm gonna get some food and hit the sack."

"hey Zach." – Mom, in dim hallway, slowly approaching, concerned look on face ...

"Is everything ok?"

"Ah, I'm alive – there any food around?"

"Here let me cook up some leftovers..."

wolf down a salad, microwaved salmon, big steaming potato with butter... catching up with mom – a few interjections from Dad... No mention of stolen wallet ...

two scoops of ice cream into a mug... mash an oatmeal raisin cookie into it... "well, think I'm gonna turn in..." head to room ...

check on the ~now greatly diminished~ pile of cash under bed... count it ...

~should be $270~... yep ...

Still half a bottle of wine in mini-fridge, finish ice cream, start into, kick, bottle, myspacing at computer well into the new day ...

CHAPTER 11

Rise around noon... big breakfast... lounge around, thinking things through ...

3: shower... pull on t-shirt, long sleeve t-shirt, undies, cargo shorts... pull on, tie Vans... look out window... Dad, pulling Audi out... cash, into pockets... down steps... in kitchen Mom sees me heading for door – "Zach where are you off to?"

~should have snuck out window or~ - "just heading out..."

"Out where?"

"Uh, I'm heading to New York for a while."

Her facial expression drops – "Oh no you don't - are you *crazy?*" rushing to block me from door - ~hm, sudden drama~

"Jerry!" she yells – grabbing hold on my shirt -*"Jerry! Help!"* ~what on *earth*~ - "Mom get a hold on yourself." -

"*Me* get a hold – *you* get a hold of yourself – Jerry get up here *now!*"

hear Jerry's feet pounding up basement stairs – here, Ruth, enters scene, walking down the stairs – doe-caught-in-headlight's look on face – turns, rushes up - "Ruth call your father!" - scene flashes of Dad – on way to golf course – receiving call on cell – turning car around – racing for home - "now Zach you stop this foolishness *right now* – you're *not well* - you *need help!* - Jerry come here and help me – Zach is trying to leave – he's trying to go to New York."

Jerry locks my arm behind back – "stop... Zach, just, *stop*... listen to Mom – you're *not well*... just, stop... - we're not letting you go down there to be a homeless person – just, stop... Zach... *enough*..." - as air spikes in a kind of... insane panic moment – struggling – Ruth, padding down stairs again – "*Ruth call the police!*" snaps Mom – "*do it!* – here Jerry - bring him in the living room." – he growls a bearhug – takes my feet out – we land on glass coffee table – 'PSSHHT!!' – flying glass bits - ~can it be this crazy?~ - I crank a hard twist – Mom falls on us, crying – we knock over another table – shatter a vase – "*Now look what you did!*" Jerry snarls – "look what you're *doing!*" clamps in my other arm as I thrust up, rising to feet... – Jerry took Judo a year – maneuvers another trip move – succeeds – we crash down on antique wooden chair – hear it crunch, breaking under us – to its tumbling, sliding pieces... and now he has bearhug clampt on hard – ~incapacitation~ – "it's *aaalright* Zach" says Mom – "everything is going to be *ookayy*" – grabbing a wrist, pressing it to floor... – a deep growl - a sort of flip-over – make it up to one knee – push Jerry's face to get on other foot – punch his hand off wrist – scramble for door – Mom diving from behind – grasps collar of shirt – spins me around - as up it goes - over head – pulled off – crazy second of her weeping face - turning, heading for door - and here, Ruth – bug-eyed, barring way – "*Zach! Stop!*" – push her aside to banging off wall – frame slides down – glass shatters across floor – eyes hone in – make sure no blood – hear Jerry's feet rushing for tackle – spring for screen door – bust through - he latches on, passing through threshold – we fall down the three stairs – to rolling on front lawn - "you caused the family *enough pain* – now *quit the insanity!* – it stops here – just *chill* and *get in the house...*" – clamps on a headlock - another hard flail of a twist – sliding free – he falls - and I'm on my feet – dragging him (locked on right heel) along... - two tiny blond girls having a catch with a pink ball – both look over – the one disregards catching ball – it bounces away as they run, screaming, towards house "mommy-mommy-mommy!" – Jerry climbs up – throws a punch – hits square in face – quick recover and start throwing punches – we're windmilling a solid minute – landing, clobbering – here, blood from my nose on his fist – in periphery Audi bounces into driveway – hear door open, shut – Jerry swoosh-ing into, clamping on, a headlock, tightening – feel impact – of Dad (four years of football at Harvard) – and we're going over – feel his bear hug clamp on - both of us – hear all of us sucking air – "Zach *what's a matter with you* - this is *enough* – you've gone *way too far* now *quit it...*" – see an old woman – staring on in shock - walking her batch of short-hair Chihuahuas... - my eyes lock on one of the little dogs a second - cowering, quivering, eyes radiating fear... look up at old lady walking them – total bugged eyes too – mouth, open now... "get off!" I yell – tapping into some sort of reserves – thrusting a push up – to foot-ing - dragging Dad, Jerry... – here, Mom grasps arm, crying – Ruth, other arm - here, the new neighbor – fresh from Wisconsin – watering lawn – drops hose

– jogs over - in comfortable-looking, paddy running shoes - as I'm, somehow, breaking free – but he, keeps a distance – waving hand – "hey! – hey! easy now buddy it's ok!" – rip leg free from Dad's grip – punch down on Jerry's head – while jerking hard twist of ankle – popping free – shift into jog – Ruth, hanging on arm – thrown off – Mom – grabs on collar dragged along – "Zaach *stooop!*" collar constricts round neck - cuts off circulation – push forward – Jerry army crawls up – clasps heel in arms again – pop foot free – he keeps the shoe – lunge forward – *tschrrrriiiip!* – t-shirt rips down seam – full way - off - leave it – here - Shannon shows! – envision Ruth on phone with her moments ago - intense look on her face – hands go out in front of her - form a triangle – "stop right there Zach!" in crazy half-crying voice – but I reel towards - grab her shoulders – to hold me up from falling – feel her fingers cling to forearms – see tears stream from her squinty eyes - throw her aside – hear the bush crackle as she descends into it... shift into a run - towards street - here, Mr. Menker's Cadillac suddenly swoops in from nowhere - shocks-wobbling halt on curb – door flies open – Menker hits ground running - eyes set on goal – I break into sprint – he's hot on tail *"Barr! – you stop right there boy!"* - but I'm pulling away – a confidence flowing in – seeing a clearing – fed by sudden realization ~realization? rationalization?~ that ~there's just *no* other way – it *has* to happen – *has to happen* - that I go~ – sprinting into backyards - leaping fences like a track star – hear clinkling of dog collar – deep growl – dog slobber on leg - teeth ripping off a piece of shorts – grazing skin – sprint on – punching - hit its snout – explosion of moisture on fist - over another fence... up pace... full speed – yard after yard – vibe after vibe ~territory after territory~ getting dark... - hear a chopper overhead... ~*already?*~ -

here, an old speedboat - covered in blue tarp – dive, roll under – peer out from – see spotlights flash over yard, house, hear it fade away... out and jogging again... into plan (hatched, wandering around Manhattan yesterday) – heading for Uncle Earl's place... stop in at Shaw's Supermarket – buy a t-shirt – pair of cheap white imitation Vans ...

1am Boston South Station... bus bound for Atlantic City, rolling in at dawn ...

Gate 80 – no line – into dim garage - where bus is parked, engine running – painted on its side – in front of outstretched running greyhound: "LUCKY STREAK' – head for a back seat – a black guy swooshes bathroom door open, his hat has the words 'I'm rooting for you' on it – stench cloud hits – crinkles up the nose of an Indian lady, see lines cut through dot painted on forehead...

Sit, unwinding, bus, pulling out – and we're… cruising over bridges – through tunnels… things, just, fusing, themselves, together – ~what day it is? Where am I going? why?~ Notice girl across isle – window seat – ~fashionable-type~ blond in sunglasses – pretty face – head kinda big - ~body of a designer - or promo person…~… an elderly Japanese ~or Korean?~ lady enters scene points at the girl's red 'La Sporte' bag on seat… the girl grabs it off, shoves it under seat in front of her… Old lady sits, - has a… peach –polishing it carefully with bright white napkin… starts eating… seat behind her: fat light-skinned black lady, purple leotards, hoop earrings… next her – window seat - behind fashion girl – her small child – light-skinned - big curls… – high voice – filling bus – "mommy-mommy-mommy" over and over – "eeeeyyyaaeeeyyyyaaeeeeeeeee… ayyaayaaa… mommy-mommy we going – we gooo… motorcycle eeeyyaaaaayyeeeeeeeeee" - fashion girl bangs her head into head rest – bottom teeth jutting out - rolling eyes up into back of head - lets off a hissing noise… as I stick earplugs in ears… press play on nano - Daft Punk beats in loud – here, a commotion in periphery – look over as lady smacks the kid on his arm – all happening right to beat with tune - crumbs spray from his yellow muffin – a second's eye contact with mine – a confused daze, processing life – as lady frowns a sip from super-sized orange soda… – work hard at suppressing laugh – start into a cough – clear throat… – as Asian lady rises – steps wooden sandal on my two smaller toes– "*Arrrrrrgh!*" - swiveling heads…. attempt eye contact with fashion girl but ~given context~ she juts head away… open Boston Globe - got from bench in station… here, "Weekend Style" section… find a big open grey section in an add… get drawing lines (with CAESERS pen, found in crack between seats) ~must be *new*… lines – arrangement of lines like never before…~ but, 'finishing' it up… it… it's… shrouded in 'cheapness' – ~bic pen on newspaper eh… what did I expect… – is it all about materials? – Le Trech did pastel drawings on pieces of cardboard… – they were probably high qual-ity pastels… – materials do factor in… 'to a degree…' 'there are degrees' 'there are factors and degrees…'~

In bus station, find men's restroom (the sign by door [with silhouette of filled-out standing stickman] reads 'men restroom' …

At counter: "Yeah looking to buy a ticket out to Colt's Neck New Jersey."

"We got a bus going out to Monmouth County at 12:06 – it's right by Colt's Neck – you could get a bus there from there."

~a chunk of time to burn~ decide to go for a stroll …

deep breath of salt air "aaaaah Atlantic City…"… walking up Michigan Avenue – line of casinos to left: Bally's, Sands, Caeser's, Trump Plaza, Harrah's,

Showboat, Tropicana… To right: outlets: Tommy Hilfiger, Ralph Lauren, Banana Republic, American Eagle, H&M, Izod, Nautica, Aeropostate, Gap, Guess…. – looking left again: huge, upraised movie screens, running advertisements for upcoming events – Caesar's screen has a scroll on the screen, which unravels to announce Barbara Streisand's Nov. 5th concert… screen just across street: "Motocross Beach Jump!" – shows clips – highlights - close-ups - guys on dirtbikes launching off ramps - mid-air stunts – this one doing a 'superman' – straightening body out to flying horizontal above bike at highest point of trajectory - fists soaring a few seconds – camera flash explosions in background – grabbing grips again… – this guy pulling a slow dirtbike back flip… – triggers thoughts of my cycle – sitting in shed at Earl's – anticipate riding it soon – visualize ascending mountain full throttle… here, a guy, sitting in shade of dwarf tree - on lil' curved hill of grass between sidewalk and a gas station parking lot… tanned, leathery skin, graying beard… worn clothes, worn blue duffle bag… drinking from a 2-liter bottle of Coke… eyes me suspiciously… turn around and head for bus… quick stroll through inside of Polo outlet store – ~now here's a guy *making money*~ – shirts churned out in… Turkey or wherever – sold here - $160 a pop in States – 'marked down' to $69 in outlet stores… hat-tip to the simplicity… – but… lil' guy on a horse – c'mon… - has grown a… 'bit much' eh – what relevancy does this sport (i.e. trotting about on a horse, thwacking at balls) have to me?~ hm, 4 minutes till bus – out door - up pace… no bus in sight… - to tall old black guy – high, prominent cheekbones (though, cheeks, sunken-in) standing by his cart: "hot dog with sour kraut, spicey mustard, relish… and a water…" - he gets putting it all together – hands, shaking… – fished with tongs from soupy steaming water, wobbling dog goes in bun - as, here, bus, pulling up – grab handful of change from pocket… count out three dollars… – he ladles on the mustard, tongs pull steamy strings of kraut up - tucks it in… the line at bus disappearing inside… – "that's fine – the water" – he reaches for cooler – I dash over – look in at driver - "you're going to Monmouth right?" – dash to hotdog guy again – who hands the water - holds out a shaking, cupped hand – drop change in it – a bunch missing – clanging, rolling on sidewalk – "sorry about that" – bang on pulling-away bus door – stops - opens - hand ticket – lunge – driver, taking off, laying on horn …

Bus is a quarter full… ~quite the assortment of characters~ – most of them sending off 'Jersey local' vibes… here, two Mexicans… – exit out front a diner – tye on aprons walking towards it as we pull off …

Looking out spotty window at sunny day, play out in head Earl's possible reactions at seeing me... – ~of course he'll be happy – no worries of him... 'turning me in' or anything... what he a... certifiable 'rebel-from-the-old-school' type and all...~

Monmouth is the last stop – at a gas station... I look on map, taped to wall – calling on memory - the three weeks spent here last summer... finger tracing... roads... to... Meadowbrook Lane ...

A wild walk... – such open land – lines of vegetation on either side stretching yonder... the occasional hubcapless pick-up rolling by... left on Meadowbrook... dirt road ...

Winds... to, here, on left, lone house of road, Earl's ...

Wooden front door is open... rattley metallic knock at white metal frame of screen door... dark inside – shades pulled down... Earl appears "Well, well, look who we have here heh-*heeh*"... opening door, exaggerated handshake "how-are-ya-buddy, good seein' ya – *c'moon* in... – Greta look who's here – nephew Zach has turned up on the doorstep." – she's standing in a dark corner, arms crossed, eyes set on me, forces a smile... – recall her... 'personality'... last summer – seemed to resent Earl and I being out so much – her, cooped in house – recall the... ~dinner table brooding...~

"Hi Greta"

"What brings you here?"

"Well, on my way up to New York, figured I'd visit, say Hi, stay a little while – if that's ok" -

"Of *cooourse!*" booms Earl – "here, I wanna show you something" - follow him through small dim living room – he jolts a stop - "Ah, fancy a beer? – fresh variety of Belgium Ales in fridge."

"Yeah."

Squatted down, clinking bottles – "here, this one, very smooth..." pulls two tall clear mugs from cabinet... head out on deck, mugs, bottles clink on glass-topped white-metal-framed deck table – "we'll have a beer, catch up a bit – then get to what I have to show you..."

Special wire and cork tops on bottles... they last a long time - sun sinking in sky as we bat back and forth this, that... – Earl holding forth longest on "the law of diminishing returns – you've heard it right?"

"Yeah"

"What is it?"

~it is what it is~ - "the more you... press in to something – the less satisfaction it gives... pretty much..."

decompressing, leaning back in chair... "I found this to be the case with traveling... – after experiencing what you are *convinced* is the ultimate destination – open cracks another void - demanding to be filled with another option – someplace *else*... – with one overriding prerequisite: that it top the place – the *experience* of the place – you were just at... – and, so, if you give in – you go forth – and – get this - filled with *less* juice than you had in you before those past places, past experiences – that juice which fueled you through them – the physical wears down on us after a certain age you know – wears away – so with this lesser, more-drained self, one... slodges on - for the bigger, better..." sip from ale... – "whoever's tied to this law... – and it's very prevalent these days – many, many-many are full on in the throes of it – wittingly or unwittingly – rapid acceleration of drain... - So anyway, years ago, I gave *imagination* the top spot – seeing its... unlimited style, resources – countless possibilities... – and – as for its... sturdiness – vigor... - just gets better with use... – if you treat it right..."... finishes beer... – "but that's neither here nor there - or is it? heh... – iiin any case, here, let's go see this... – in the shed."

rise, walk through thick grass... – big back yard – acres stretch – blend into neighbor's farmland... dim inside shed – old printing-press-looking machines – know them well – working at them last summer – an entire summer a few years ago... – the intricate pieces, polished gears – the *exactness* - ~exactitude~ of them... made in Germany... – ~*precision cut*~... – each having its *presence* to it... – the older ones, like... exuding ancient wisdom... – Uncle Earl works in here through the week - crafting pieces for historic guns – Lugars and such – old rifles, custom guns too...- – makes a living at it... "let's seeee here – *ah*, here we are."... turns around – rifle in hands... - wiping it with cheese clothe ...

"German 1927, beauty eh?"

"my-my" taking in hands "definitely..."

"what say let's give it a shot..."

Heading out, recall the many shooting sessions over the years... – Earl's accuracy – my... aching shoulder from all the kicks of guns..."

Cans are already aligned on wooden fence about fifty feet away ...

I give him the gun... ~hm, feeling that Belgian ale...~

He delicately slides a cartridge into slot by trigger -'*click*' ...

Aims... "KOW!!!" – can spikes diagonally up ...

"heh-heh "KOW!" next can spikes... "here y'go." Handing ...

I line it... "KOW!!!!" - knocks shoulder back... cans, unphased ...

Align again... "KOW!!!!" – can flung into a twirl – arcs to ground ...

"There we are… here, I'll finish her off…"

Aims, fires, blasts can, fires, blasts last can… "Hm, one more shot…" turns barrel… points at old, sad-looking 1960's pick-up - grass growing up its sides… "I've been wanting to do this… there's old gas in it still… gas tank'd be right about… there…" –

"heh-heh, uh -"

"KOW!!!" – back of truck explodes into huge fireball – flipping truck high in air - slow spin - landing on front face – crumpling hood – bursting windshield… –

"he-*haaa yyyyyeaaah*…" squinty-eyed huge smile …

"Earl!" Greta, on deck –

"Don't worry honey" heading for shed "we'll put it out." disappears in… reappears - with extinguisher… to truck – covered in little orange flames - gushing black smoke up… –minute-long steady blast …

Greta, imploding, spins round, slams door behind her …

He tosses extinguisher aside:

"Well I'm gonna go check on my cycle – it's still where it was?"

"Hasn't been touched since last summer… – I'll go iron things over – dinner'll be on soon…"

"Thanks."

head past gun shed… to large, barn-looking shed… lift wooden latch, creek door open… step into dark, - thick, dank, mulch stench… find string, yank, bulb, illumines – moths, zipping straight to, bouncing, re-bouncing off it… here, massive green John Dear Tractor… rakes, spades, weed whackers, hanging along wall… - ah, and here, the blue tarp - shape of YZ 80… grab hold on - swoosh it off …

looks… asleep… feel tires… ~hm, kinda low…~ see motor pump, crank it to life… fill tires… pour fresh oil in… gas… wheel it outside… mount… kick… kick… kick 'BWA - BWAA!' - click in gear, cruise into field… light works… – and open it up – 'bwaAA! – bWAA! – bWAAA! – BWAAAAAAA!!' steer into familiar trail – up rocky ascent '*bwwwaaaaAAAAA!*' turn round, down… to barn …

Climb wooden stairs to second level… Memories flooding in, seeing bed by lone window, dresser, walk over, slide hand over comforter… same two books on lil' night table –Emerson's Essays and Walden… lay back, hands behind head, sinking into – memories – branching to ~oh yeah~ - *these* memories… to – in distance, outside "Hey Zach – we got dinner here!"

Tense meal... – Greta sending serious vibes – holding conversation ok – keeping it light – just, those eyebrows - ~the eyebrows give it away~ - frowning – slanted down and in to point of almost closing eyes... - eyes, that seem to be... grinding an ax at me as I... eat this... cornbread – hear my mouth chewing – Earl has to chip in a "well, quite a meal, how about another brewski on the porch?"

We ease into creaking wicker chairs on back porch in wild, brisk air, Earl, topping off the two mugs... "So you just... washed up - on shore?"

"Yeah, wild eh..."

"Sorry about your friend..."

"Yeah."

"So I hear you, passed up a scholarship?"

"Yeah."

"Why's that?"

"Ah, the college route is so 'passed down' – figure one can learn plenty firsthand – out in the real world y'know." ~firsthand(?)~

"Heard something about New York too..."

"Yeah, I'm looking to be an artist – new goal... - sounds exciting eh - see what I can make of it..."

"Well you always could draw – we still have that picture you drew a few summers ago - of that raccoon... - framed on the mantle in there."

His eyes stare out at the tree tops... another gulp from mug, smile curls on ...

"To me... if you don't live in nature like this... you... *loose touch* – get too much on the defensive... – attitude – style - gets so... reactionary – whole existence... – relating to people – so many in and out souls – people so... suspicious of one another... – won't say that's always the case – but you find plenty of... how do I say – ah it's been all said before 'cut-throat' - 'dog-eat-dog' – 'survival of the fittest' – really something to that... – but when that's it – when it's all survive survive *survive survive* – sleep goes out the window – where does it have a place in that ideology – no real room for sleep – your enemies could be up plotting – better cover yourself – up – get out the planner! – alarm goes off 6am – and it's gritting teeth through any aches and pains – because all those other eager beavers – those enemies – you know they are – it's a race – there's another cliché you've heard - 'rat race' – whoever coined that heh-heh... – and the hamster running in a wheel – man, sense of humor... – but tragic – when people really feel that way.... – not out here though – if it's for you... if it's where you belong... – and it's for me, that much I can say..."

breathes in deep, exhales... - strangely long, removes pipe from flannel shirt breast pocket... thumb, packing tobacco in pipe ...

"Well, think I'm gonna hit the proverbial hay." (~proverbial(?)~)

blue flame bending into pipe, shakes match out, tossed. "Your quarters are... as you left them sir. Have a sound one and we'll look forward to the morning."

Leave him to his ochre-cherry-smokey-puff cloud ...

Climb dark, fragrant, vibey, wooden stairs in barn... – the expected twinges of anxiety (due to exposed, rusted nails, sticking out sloping ceiling) as I slouch towards bed across the way (ah the scenes my imagination's reeled [with relation to these nails] over the years – play again – the gouging eyeballs reel – the shredding head – nail, etching on skull)... ~ah how much of our own blood we spill in our imaginations...~

Scattery dreams culminate in hugging Shannon – hoisting her up - as clothes dissolve – pleasure engulfs – jolt to consciousness – abs tight - tightening in strain - to suppress – no use "aaah you gotta be... *man!*" – thoughts race through head ~*man,* no change of clothes – you *gotta* be kidding me..."

force body up... to awkward, slouchy walk towards small bathroom... judging by light out open window... 4, 5am... – stop – eyes squint into focus - out window – a light on in Earl's – and... ~*Greta*~ – on phone – pacing back and forth nervously – looking up now – at me – electric-shock-eye-contact – her eyes widen in fear – as it strikes in ~*I'm being ratted out!*~ - hurry out of sight – jog back towards bed – grab cash wad, jam in pocket, – tie on imitation Vans – jog to stairs ~*gotta go-gotta-go-gotta-go-go-go*~ down – push bike outside – feel dew on heels – figure I'll push it out of earshot before cranking it up – but here –afar off through trees approaching – cop car – mount – kick – kick again 'WaoW-WAA' – in gear – 'BaaAAA-*BAAA!!*-BAAA!!-BAAA!!-*BAAAA!!* into trails – know the way - ~no squad car getting back here~ – up mountain '*WAAAAA!!!*' – over – into thicker woods... – black soil... a ways... - ford through a creek... other side, lean bike against a tree... here, a dear, on hill yonder, staring at me – hone in on its eyes – on one – the dark blue haze awisp in the glossy black ...

wade into creek – stinging cold... remove shorts... scrub them on a rock, waterfall, flowing over hands... vivid red cardinal flutters into scene, perches on low branch in front of me, just over head... see dear descend out of sight over hill... Cardinal flies off ...

Pull shorts on, shoes, getting on bike, tank's on E ...

Ride on, slow, contemplatively, half an hour... puttering slow up hill now, blank-faced... at precipice: 'glub-glub-glub...' ~shoulda topped her off last night...~

Prop it against a tree... walk around, breaking branches off trees... cover the cycle with them... scan scene, committing it to memory... go in search of gas... ~there's gotta be some road with some station somewhere around here...~ - ~("some"(?))~

Mind just... instinctively(?) begins praying - ~God this is happening – you – if you exist - which it's probable you do - seeing there's a design in all this – have you a hand in this... this bumbling through woods thing here then? – are chips, 'falling where they may', - or are you aligning things into place – every second afore known by your omniscience... - are you going to make chips land in best places - for rightness – for *freedom's* sake... - otherwise drudgery wins – otherwise it's just a sap bumbling through woods - who hasn't done any gross, big, bad thing – it's him just, perishing... – this... design – one of your best designs – aren't people pinnacle for you - of all your creation? – would you have me just, shrivel – game over? – inconceivable if you enjoy... 'delighting in' 'experiencing pleasure' by, in, stuff – people – a *person* – that you made – what a waste it'd be to have me... taper out the heart beats, lying on ground, shifting into a rotting corpse – and the bomb that would land in the lives of others at news of it – after Craig – who knows what you were thinking snuffing him out... – maybe it was to set me free – to this new course... – if that be the case, c'mon – throw me a bone... all that to say, I'm putting it to you – it's all on you - you'd be culpable should it all flop - it's on you to 'pull this out' – you're 'bigger' than all this... – yet you 'see it fit' I suppose, to have me crunching through woods like a... Barbarian... – Zac the Bar-barian – has a ring to it heh... - in any case – would you'd speed this up – what's with the dragging – look at me, here existing in 'prime years' here – doing this 'caveman joke on the lamb' thing... – yet how great would it be *to* pull it out – 'pull it out' – what's that supposed to mean anyway – it's a phrase programmed in... – what else to go on though? *'go on(?)'* ... maybe curling into a ball and tapering out would transfer my consciousness into more original realms – that is if I'm to be in Heaven... – *'heaven'* - is there another word for it – *'paradise'* – another?~ on and on it unfurls – mad rants – yelling out time to time – once, snapping a thick brach off, beating a rock with it... till breathing too heavy... walking on... humble little muttered pleadings... starts drizzling... "aaaaah well... I could be fifty miles in *the thick* of the woods *on all sides* for all I know..." feel fatigue setting in... ~maybe just... take a quick nap – *no!*~ raise eyes, gaze through fine black tree silhouette lines at glowing orange sky... eyes close... open... head nods – catches ...

brain registers ~movementation~... – like... the tree silhouettes are... spreading into black ghosts... - ~wha... – smoke – that's smoke!~ - shuffle to feet – jogging at it "smoke – yes-yes smoke aaaawwwyyyeeeeaahh" – scramble on hands and feet up hill – here, random bamboo patch – ~hm, thick~ – take up stick – baseball-bat-swing through... jog up another twenty feet... look down through trees: at little country tavern – made of brown wood – dark from drizzle – smoke, emanating from chimney... neon sign on roof blinks 'Brock's'... 'Brock's'... 'Brock's'... eyes hone in on... old gas pumps out front "*yesssssss...*", slippery descent down muddy hill towards ...

Walking to front door, hear music coming from inside ~Dylan?~ - swing in – guys in flannels – everyone - bathed in dim, orange glow - swivels heads over, stay staring as I walk for bar - Gun's and Roses, filling room: "Mama take this badge from me – I can use it anymore..."

Slump onto high stool, elbows on bar... "menu?" – "It's gettin' dark – too dark to see..."

"I'll start out with some water..." –

"Mama put my guns in the ground... – can't shoot them... anymore..." –

glug icewater from tall plastic translucent red cup down... and another... wolf down turkey burger, every fry – to tune of Pink Floyd's "Welcoooome my son – welcoooome... to... the *machiiiine...*" and on into album ...

Setting down tip – "do you sell gas tanks here – like a little red one – a gallon? – my cycle ran outta gas – it's out in the woods - gotta fill it up..."

"nup." Says local-volunteer-fireman-type, pug-nosed bartender... – "you lookin' for just enough to get you a few miles? - could use glass – like one a these." – points thumb back at Colt 45 bottles, lined, illumined, in cooler behind him ...

- on stereo – a matter-of-factly Morrison overhead 'Riders on the storm...'

"yeah" reaching in pocket for wad "take one a those." -

'his brain is squirming like a toad...'

"got ID?"

'into this world we're thrown...'

"Oh... actually don't have my wallet – just cash..."

'like a dog without a bone...'

"you 21?"

"18."

"sorry."

"uuh, I'll buy it, watch you pour it down the drain, how's that? – just need the bottle."

"gotta be 21, sorry... – anyway plenty of 40's got drunk here last night - just outside that door – should be a pile of 'em in the trash can – fill it up with gas, pay in here..."

Go out, press trashcan lid flap inwards – flies swirling out... it's filled with Colt 45 bottles... take one... walk through drizzle to pumps... old-school ones... figure it out, fill it to spurting overflow, cap it ~will the fumes cause bottle to explode in hand? – can air it out periodically.~

Swing in door – walking to counter - stereo: "*You know where you are? You're in the jungle baby... yer gonna diiiee...*" – hand a five... changing it, "pretty dark out there..."

"yeah, I'll manage..."

And it's up the muddy black-soil hill, down into growing-pitch-black-dark-fast woods... ~how on earth~- "heh-heh" ~'out and out' joke~ - "uuuuuuhmy, my, my..." – smell smoke – here, a fire, walk towards... a... small campfire... – see three people, huddled around it... closer... two small children... and, back to me, the Dad... they're all holding sticks over the fire... - marshmallows on the tips of the two son's - a hot dog on the Dad's... gumdrop tent set up next to them... – he seems to... sense my presence - turns head around... – 40-something guy... – he scowls at me - a wild, primitive ferocity in eyes... I give a little reassuring wave, turn around, ~disappear into darkness before their eyes~ ...

mile or two later... no sign of bike... pitch black... – rendering any further walking dangerous and nonsensical – I squat down, feel around for a comfortable spot... sandwich the bottle between two football-sized rocks to prevent tippage, and lay... staring up at stars, feeling light drizzle on face, in a ~relative peace~ – listen to a dear walk by, tapering away – not worried about heartbeats tapering off – ~if they do, it's out of my hands, what's use worrying about it...~ ~should be fine – what seeing as I've ample food and water in body now – should keep ticker pumping right along through slumber to... waking up ~at some particular juncture... – or, that particular juncture, which I *must* wake up at..."~

Sunrise – the sleep seems to have flushed out a lot of craziness - has me feeling mellow, assured, rising, peeing, breathe deep in the wild, crisp, clean, air – eyes bring in sharp, glisteny details all over on every side... stretch '*grrrrr!*' -

suck in oxygenized air, stretch… cap bottle, press on, in search of motorcycle …

things turn weary heading into second hour (or, so it feels, - no time-measuring-device ~on person~)… and thoughts… steer into… clamorous prayers again… See a tree, split down its center by lightning… climb its ~unfelled half~… look round… climb a few branches higher… eyes hone in, scanning… - "Ah!" - jump down ~why did I jump – this freegin' hiiiii*iiigh*~ -"*Oof!*" – reach over, grab bottle, up, running …

throwing branches off cycle "yyyyeeeaah–*heh-heh!*" –

"*Yo!*"

looking over – two kids – running at… – look junior high – look mean – bored-farm-kids-dressed-like-rappers types - ~base locals~ …

both stand four feet away now, catching breath – freckled thin one, hands on hip… chubby pink-faced one, arms crossed …

"That your bike?" says the freckled one.

"yeah." unscrewing gastank cap …

"guess what."

"what"

"finder's *keepers.*"

"yeah just filling it up and I'll be outta here in a jif." – tilt bottle, splashing in …

"no-no, fill it up, - but you're not taking it. – you left it on our turf…"

"he's putting beer in it dude…" says the bigger one.

bottle empty, not knowing what to do with it, lean it against tree trunk …

pull bike away from tree – freckled kid, gives a little shove – "dude, I don't think you're listening – the bike *stays*…" –

"sorry man I gotta go." – legging over… – chubby kid steps in, grabs front handlebars with both hands, pinches front wheel between legs. - "get *off* the bike man" – his pink skin, smooth as a baby's… thrust kickstart – freckles is cursing now – pulling hard on my shirt – kick again – pumping gas – again – "lay off – here let me see if it works" I reason – kicking again – freckled kid is strong – ~farm muscles~ pushing me now – shoulder hits tree - chubby kid grabs a fistful of shirt in one hand – cocks back the other for a punch – another kick – "*WA!*" – shoot head forward into his rushing fist – headbutt it – the squeal – engine's running now – freckles clutches neck, strangling, grimacing, growling – unable to breathe, see a clearing between his arms – shoot an upper-cut full force - hits square on chin – but he seems to… feed on the pain – see another opportunity to… – shoot a fist – all might – direct crotch hit –

sharp gasp, grimaced crumple to ground.... – click in gear – chubby kid's at the handlebars again – pinching front wheel between legs... - open throttle – he frowns, digs heels in – engine screams – black dirt soars away behind – hear him snarling in effort - - - I shift weight back on seat – lean down on spinning tire – feel traction catch – watch his eyes bulge - as he's falling backwards – tires. bumping over him... – accelerate up hill, down other side - calling hard on memory – gauging, – calling on senses - ~inner compass~ - figuring which way to the road ...

Find one sooner than expected – a different one – more of a highway - buzz along in grass beside it... – a shopping center appears... gas up at a Sheetz, buy a New York/New Jersey map... sit at picnic table... chewing a sausage-egg-and-cheese, study best route... ~will have to ditch the bike right... aboou-uut... here... then hitchhike - or catch a ride - at this rest stop - to get through the tunnel, into the city..."

'*bzzzzzzzzzzzzz*' - cruise along shoulder (highway to left, trees to right) – opening up at times, slowing at others – occasional weave into woods (at sight of State Trooper) ...

At pre-determined point – ~here, in reality~ - as shoulder fades away – tunnel, looming in distance – gastank about empty – steer into last remnants of woods... descend a black-soiled slope... cut engine, lean bike against tree... break off branches... cover it... ~Tyler might have a friend with a pickup or van...~ walking away: ~somewhat rough... leaving such a beautiful piece of machinery... but... well... is what it is... - system functioning as it is these days – 'has to be the case' – or risk 'getting caught.'... – 'caught' for riding a mode of transportation without a 'special plastic card on person' – 'caught' for not having a special metal plate, fastened onto the mode of transportation – 'caught' for not paying $10 (giving them a piece of paper) to enter into a tunnel - leading into another 'state' in a "free" country...~ ... - ~yes, yes, there has to be order... – seems so... rrrrr, tough though – so hoopy... whatever – *is what it is* – and that's *precisely* what it is... for one reason or other... - "acceptance" "acceptance" "acceptance" chant the masses, both arms extended out before them, "tolerance "tolerance "tolerance"....~

Sitting at counter of diner, porcelin cup of coffee on saucer, here under nose... sit, thinking... thinking things through... – words - ~angles...~

a group of students walk in... I order a refill... nurse... ~timing...~ – they drink their coffees, have their stacks of pancakes (waffles, eggs, OJ) – laughing, looking underslept... pay bill, a few hitting restroom... rise, head for door... lay down my two dollars, follow ...

right outside door – to leader-looking guy of the bunch – looking straight out of prep school – "hey are you all heading into Manhattan?"

Fake-smile-laugh-off "yeah" - starts up snap-topic conversation with one of the girls… –

"would it be ok if I rolled along – my friend lives up by Columbia – just through tunnel would be fine… – I'll chip in a five for gas or whatever…"

"Uh" darting eyes to others, who shrug shoulders, continue walking …

scrunching nose "sorry man, we just have room for four, sorry about that…" – jogs to catch up with them… I follow them to their Jetta… Squinting in, pointing "I could probably fit in the back there" engine starts, buckling of seatbelts, giggling, "sorry man…" – from back seat "just let him in." driver smiles at the girl who said it… looks at me …

"well, if you can squeeze in…"

They're Columbia students – bring me all the way up, to where they park, out front the driver's frat house on 114th… the five is refused… good-byes… walk for Tyler's …

pissing in Mexican restaurant on 116 - La Rancharo (its blinking neon sign above front door - cowboy on horse with lasso)… take seat… dim lit… juke-box playing loud… waiting for burrito, sipping at Corona, munching on nachos, dipping them in red, green sauce… watch muted TV up, left, mounted to wall… Discovery Channel… – show about Brazil –scenes of a big festival there – huge floats… – such effort, care put into making, say, - this gigantic joker head - these lobster costumes - ~how do they find time for this?~ - and thes Brazilian women – skimpily arrayed in glitter – their tan, sweaty bodies kicking up long legs, - all of them grinning wild… sudden switch to… scenes from other parts of the country – jungle terrain – people in huts - ~Brazil eh… what matters what happens there?~ as hot-plated burrito slides before… – explodes its flavors in hungry mouth …

Key in… no sign of Tyler… ~he did say he was flying over to London for a week, visit his girlfriend… is that… this week, already…~ examine his room – clean, clothes missing from drawers… toiletries absent from bathroom ~yep, guess that's the case…~ opening fridge… pulling Corona from six-pack… cutting lime for it – with Olfa razor knife – thinking of what might be going through the mind of one of those Brazilian dancers – during festival time at like 3 in the morning – blade slices through lime fast – into finger… -~Ah, *you've got to be…* for the *love of…* O that's deep… *rrrrr* that's a deep one…~ – tear paper towel from roll – wrap it round – watch red dot grow – rip another, squeeze… envision emergency room… - ~not an option – O come on *heal…*~

- dot grows - ~don't tell me stitches... don't tell me severed vein - O please stop – just stop...~ envision red blood cells scurrying to rescue – doing their job – their reconstruction - ~ you *must* heal... mend, *mend*...~ remove towel... ~nothing spurting~... wrap it in a fresh piece... kick back on futon, click on TV... half-watching news – Bronx Zoo got a new "rare albino Cheetah" - thinking about blood... – how it's such... *life* to the body - how it animates the body... – how strong the body is – when all this mysterious fluid is surging through it properly... – ~and here it is – this precious, powerful fluid – *leaking out* of me~... how about... *degrees* of blood – ~are there levels?~ – in terms of potency... – scenes appear in mind – of track star Steve Prefontaine – died right out of college - ~the *amazing* blood that must have surged through him~ – think of it spilling, in crumpled Porsche - crashed that night of his death... – think of James Dean – broken, spilling that blood of his - in his mashed lil' MGB – think of *that* blood – how precious - leaving the body – draining it of life... – ~how about *Jesus*...~

CHAPTER 12

Wake up to… loud Mexican music… playing out in courtyard – coming in through open window …

Bathroom is exactly two steps from futon couch… sit on pot… ~maybe… 11am?~ forming, ~letting form that which must form~ thoughts, blank-staring at plain white tiles… – music pouring in from lil' open window behind head – someone must have their window open - big speaker facing out of it - to produce this level volume… – the drumming is heartfelt –picture the electronic drum set – scene appears in mind - Mexican (wearing black cowboy hat) sitting at his electronic drums – sticks ablur, beating away on octagonal gray pads – head back, eyes clampt shut, the impassioned grimace – sweat beads gleaming on face…

stems into ~what is this place?… what is this vibe… – which seems so… seeping-in-through-pores – this… grogginess – this… 'upsettedness' - *madness – bitterness - foreigner angst – rage - cutting – violence – stifling oppression – pain* - in air, which just… doesn't seem to… - accept – yea, *is hostile towards* – the likes of me…. Must… find… better… location – one less… *sapping*… taxing… – one more… free, pleasant, friendly, peaceful… - conducive to thought – to inspiration…~

Pull on Vans, stumble down six flights, over to 116, into 'Taco Mix'.

Mashing in chicken taco breakfast… ~this is acceptable… yes, it is a Tuesday at like noon and I'm not 'at school' or 'at work'~ - expression zaps into mind ~"Business is America's business"~ - ~or, 'busyness' heh-heh – busybodies heh-heh – there are exceptions – ~would that I'd meet more of them! – Elliot's one – can tell – fellow artist… – hm, though, - isn't that an unspoken rule – soon as you call yourself an artist, you cease to be one – like someone calling themselves humble – second they do - humility vanishes – 'so you think you're *all that,* eh, - *Mr. Humble!'~* chewing second taco ~it's ok, - this, 'not going bonzo over 'establishing a career" – as I'm in this season – a season of... charging batteries... for next moves... which are.... – why am I rationalizing? – it's this business doctrine – hammer-inculcated into heads since.... – that drives that busy-busy-busy is good-good-good message into brain, whole psyche...~ - ~in any case (and at any rate) it all is what it is presently, and that's... pretty much that... I guess... ('guess(?)')~ ... scenes form in head, ambling forth from door - of '*reeeally* making it' in the 'art world' – and, ~one thing, having, indubitably, to lead to the next(?)~ – envision – in a planning sort of way - getting Elliot's business card from top drawer of Tyler's dresser... picture borrowing his bike - riding clear to Brooklyn – to Elliot's studio... seems this ~'may very well be'~ my ~'thing' for today...~ ~'to go do'~ ~'deed'~ ~'pupose-a-fier' for the day, what...~

Climb the mourning, weeping, stairs - tears of grief, weariness, oppression – practically flowing out from underneath the cheap-brown-paint-slopped-on doors to cascading down cracked, chipped, grime-accrued-in-corners marble stairs... – up pace – ~must... get... out... of... here...~

On dim sixth floor landing: an overturned couch... smell of smoldering wood – fresh cut – coming from – neighbor's open door... apparently... working on busted leg of couch... keying in, hear the assortment of birds of theirs, twittering from within his apartment... –hear heavy claws scraping on tiles – a brown creature appears – approaching fast – a pitbull, snarling – Puerto Rican woman in lime green tank top and white short shorts – hair pulled back tight, big hoop ear rings – "Pa*BITO!*" she yells – dog's face goes dumb, lags tongue out... turns round, takes off – scratching-claws-in-place-running on worn tiles – turning corner - looses footing – clunks jaw on marble stair, bounces right up, wriggling stubby tail – as she trots down towards me and the guy with the couch... – in passing, blows a lil' pink bubble - five rapid loud pops in a row... – "c'moon ya dumb dog..." catch breath, key in, mind playing in repeat-mode against will the dog ripping face off ...

Grab bike... – Tyler's comment a wile ago springs to mind - "anything in this apartment – *yours*..." lean it against wall again... – go in search... *~aha!~* his old ipod... wind – bike on shoulder - down stairs – here, a resident, climbing up – black plastic bags, hanging from each hand – the weight of all New York, seeming to... weigh down on his shoulders... – out front – flow onto bike – towards Columbia, plugging in earplugs... ~electronic music~ - Tyler's fav – "no time for idiotic lyrics" as he'd say... First song blares on – riding along to 'Fischerspooner's' 'Emerge' track – unlocks thoughts – Emerson's quote enters mind – or, a paraphrase - where he refers to energy being 'every-thing' – definitely a point in that... – the one on the jobsite who has the most energy – most desire – motivation – *performance* power – tends to rise to the top (granting it's fueled by knowledge, wisdom – which... does that elevate smarts – 'know-how' above energy – seeing as it directs, harnesses, calls-the-shots of energy)... crossing over 3rd Ave - here, two youth – thin black kids – one fake-throws something at me – the other (apparently) voicing some angry commentary... ~walking violences...~ - ~ - products of environment(?) - how surroundings so meld malleable youth...~ glide past MAGICAL PARTY WORLD store – two guys struggling to raise an inflatable Incredible Hulk up on thin black plastic pole... pass big cheap store – massive red sign, situated high, front, center: SLAMDUNK... ~so, this all considered, - this, here on the table, how does one go about (yeah, how ought it to be a goal eh? – to go about) getting more energy then, right...~ on through Morningside Park – Columbia campus – beaming Asian students – left on Broadway... – music – track to track – really 'coloring' things – influencing - lends – infuses - a kind of way-of-seeing... here, riding through richy UWS – music peaks into super cool segment – blazing everything up notches - to seeming much cooler than it really is – much cooler than, say, how this old lady with a walker sees, perceives it all... – and here she looks – instead of sinister – quite ridiculous, scowling at me – and I flash her a toothy grin - to communicate that ~as if she could read it!...~ weave over, ride along Central Park a while – which ~as a whole... is what it is~ – weave in again... stare straight in eye of shaggy balding bum on bench – a connect of sorts – his head snapping back at the experience ~charge(?)~

passing Lincoln Center... here – 56th Street – passing a lady – clutching her briefcase - frizzy blond hair – sunglasses – see her upside-down-U mouth – lips part - see her teeth - grit at me – yet, serious as she may be – heading to whatever business meeting she's off to – the euro-boppy tune peaks in – right on time - can't help but see her as a type of... *clown*... soar on... no hands... a few lights later – a shiny black Chevy Cavalier brakes abruptly - catch glance of driver – 35-year-old-looking guy – white - neatly-parted black hair - slight bulge of fat bubbling out from white collar, pinched by too-tight navy blue tie... as tune spikes again... ~if I were to write about this bike ride... and one were to read it – in the future - while living in a... freer time – they would have to understand – that this bike ride – in this time period in 'history' - passes through – one after next - extremely control-freaky atmospheres – words don't have enough '*umf*' in them to adequately describe - fully express - to readers just how thick, oppressive, the vibes existing here at points... – the music – a solace in it – hence all these people walking around with earplugs on – 'music bring me away – transfer me from this reality...'... ipods as crutches... what can you do...~ turn volume up ...

Time Square abuzz – here a movie set – spotlights, metallic-looking light reflectors – cameras on rolling robotic dollies – director chairs – beat-looking crew – one making a second of zombie eye-contact - ~self-actualizing are we here heh-heh~ - on through Penn Station area – its nervous, bile-in-belly, odd, foreigner feel... Chelsea – that eerie, shamey cloud, hovering, to Union Square – Farmer's Market in full swing – walk bike through... mount again... - NYU flags appearing – pick up speed down lil' slope into Washington Square, cruising across, past fountain – here, pack of college girls – all looking straight from Texas - all sporting their freshman 15 – all in jeans, flip flops, pastel tank tops, all giggling - ~American chick-i-dies~ - up ramp, other side... onto MacDougal Street – its 'hanging on, Dylan(y)' vibes - cross Bleeker – Houston, - bump over cobblestones, - dramatic head-swivel at tall, thin Polish or Russian beauty striding by – almost slam into back of cab - left on Prince – pass teeming Apple store, hang a right... – left on Spring... left on Elizabeth... pass Habana Café – chic crew out front scraping teeth over bright yellow cobs of corn... right on Houston... right on Ludlow... left on Stanton... stop in at Lotus for a tea – teabag tag reading "a cup of tea is a cup of life"... Clinton Street to... Williamsburg Bridge – crawling ascent – people zooming past in opposite direction... to leveling off – taking in view, riding along, no hands - East river, vast, below – barge passing under – white foam trailing in wake... – soar down Brooklyn side – past others, crawling their ascents – snapping power eye contacts – each spiking something inside – the strength of zap contingent on how good looking or arty looking they are – like this redhead - gesticulating alongside guy – such a longing gaze she snaps ~an eternity in it... - aaaah, *looks!* – every implication bound up in them – shooting froth from them... – ('them'(?)~

Elliot's standing (inside open garage), staring at a huge blank canvas ...

"Ey."

"Ah, - Zach right"

"yeah..." – eyes set on blank canvas... "figured I'd visit... after all this time. – had your card."

"Well, welcome."

"this," nod at canvas "looks rife with potential..."

"been staring at this for three days - four... can't seem to bring self to... picking up brush... – all seems to have... been done before..."

"thought you were more into video art anyway..."

"yeah... figured I'd, uh... give painting another stab... – but... second I stick a pigment on there, y'know – be it a dot, line, whatever... - feel like I'm... copying someone... – that it's shot-through – in a 'beating a dead horse' kind of way... – but, then, leaving it blank also sends messages – a.) that I'm wussing out – which, whatever – that's not the case... – or b.) I'm trying to make a statement by leaving it blank... – which has been done before – over-done."

"throw the thing away."

"thing cost me 70 bucks – and the time stretching it... – hours."

"Chuck it... – when in doubt – *throw it out...*"

"could start just throwing paint at it – but that's been done... – schmear it on – scrape it on with comb – done, done... – is it a sign we're at the end – nearing the end - in the end times? Anyway gotta get outta this studio – let's hit the Verb – talk about October's show."

"October's show?"

capping jars of paint "yeah – you're gonna help me out man..."

"how's that?"

"by writing up some brilliant idea - straight from your depths – we'll incorporate it into the show – albeit a smaller show – here in Williamsburg – but has potential – serious amounts of invites going out – Tyler's on it – invites sent to the right people, calls – strategic – and DJ ON will be playing at it – big draw right there..."... grabs cordless saw - *'BBZZZCHT!'* cuts a 2x4 in half - *BBZZZCHT!'* another... – two more *'BBZZZCHT!' BBZZZCHT!'* sets them on table... takes up nail gun *'BLAM-BL-BLAM-BLAM-BLAM!'* fastens them together... "the pieces are coming together, Zach..."

walking on Bedford... 6pm light in air – "so howya living? How's it going up in Spanish Harlem with Tyler man..."

"Ok... he's over in London..."

"Oh yeah... so you gonna be catering with him, or..."

"guess so."

Order up Sencha green teas... sit out front – amidst batch of smoking hipsters ...

"what a joke..."

"huh?"

"you, an artist – having to walk around with a tray of dainty meats – rather than having the freedom to tap into… creative realms within – produce this, that…"

"yeah well…"

"what's your definition of art anyway?"

"beauty ties in… – which varies, viewer to viewer, experiencer to experiencer… - whatever charges – moves y'know – that sort of slant, angle, deal of a definition… you?"

"out of box – freedom – bestowal of freedom – ideal stuff… something people get longing for… – or, could go the 'mirror held up to society' angle – that which reflects - enlightens… - agent of betterment – improvement… – can be, at least… –

I like blowing-top-of-head-clear-off… vibe – deal – however you'd put it - *factor*… - not necessarily 'shock' per say – could say an element of that in there – shakes viewer up – to bring about change… – that vibe, deal, thing… – in some cases…"

"…'in some cases' heh-heh… – 'at times' - 'to a degree' 'in part' 'to an extent' – savior tack-on's – keeps from sticking, this, that in box… - how about beauty – how are you defining that these days…"

"as it regards to?"

"Whatever, you name it."

"People spring first off the bat – I've been doing plenty of people watching recently - looks count – they really, really do… – watch a beautiful person – watch doors open…"

"what's a beautiful person?"

"my definition of a beautiful person is one who, upon seeing them, I become happy… – that simple… upon looking at them - their face, body, goes in – through eyeballs – registers in brain – chemicals snap about, happiness occurs – that's a beautiful person in my estimation… so – shallow as it sounds - I do actually stake a lot of credence in looks – what else have you – first impression y'know – if those chemicals aren't triggering pleasure chords up in the head – what else have you got going on - or to go on heh-heh… – also the Hebrew definition of beauty – heard or read it somewhere – part of the definition they have for beauty: 'healthy'…" sip of tea "makes sense. – see a truly healthy person – quite attractive… which opens doors to whatever facial, body structure you have – if you're healthy – you're beautiful…"

"what about terminally ill people?" –

"they can be healthy mentally – that shines through in the physical – it's in the eyes... – and emotionally and spiritually – it conveys outward – we pick up on it – and if someone gets all these components real healthy – we're talking a mega beautiful person..."

"Yeah, one person looks on the shell, the other is more intrigued by the ideas, concepts within the shell – sharing the ideas, concepts between each other... – that's excites – that fires pistons – beyond facial structure..."

"It's what a person – or, one could say, *art* – does to the atmosphere – is he, she, it, bettering, lifting - or detracting, poisoning the atmosphere... – elevation of atmosphere, that's what I'm talking about..."

"hm, yeah... it continues to fascinate me – that whole 'what make's art art?' thing... - can boil it down even to a *mark* – this one paints *that* mark – another paint's *this* mark – compare the two – one is dismissed as trash – the other's raved about... *what's* with that – does it come down to love – how much love goes into the piece – or coordination of hand – or depth of experience springing from artist onto canvas or into sculpture, song, whatever... what gives, y'know..."

"one 'function' of art is that it serves to absorb our anxieties – some need this more than others – big city life – as compared to farm life out in... Iowa – (more spirits floating around in big cities might tie in – the number of people – spirits – invisible forces, connected to, surrounding – guardian angels - *energies*...– it's fact – you're by yourself – the energy is one way – someone enters the room – the energy – the dynamic – vibe – rises... think of... Christ - forty days in the wilderness – that vibe... – then up pops the devil himself – talk about *tension* in air – though the devil is rather sly from what I hear – atmosphere might have been more... suave – 'let's rap' kind of a deal... – you see what I'm saying – all these people around – all their energies – metropolis - they need outlet – thus they are creating more art than people tilling the soil out in lush rolling hills, where, with all that nature – talk about life sustaining – who has need of venting or outlet... – yes there are artists out in farm country – I'm talking quantity though – by in large it's the big cities with the massive amounts of artists, slugging away... - do we see a connect in the proliferation of art (art as coping mechanism – as something that's greasing the skids of life – art as casting light on, making sense of things) in big cities – where one requires more reasons for having to cope – given all the pressures and extremes..."

"Yeah, you've expressed 'another point...' – how many more points till we grasp it bigtime y'know – comprehensive understanding... do we just keep drumming them up – are they all pieces of a puzzle – to reach completion eventually... – I'd like that... 'deep full grasp' served up on a platter..."

"write a book – there's your title... <u>Deep Full Grasp</u> by Elliot Frank... -

seems you have 'art' somewhat on the dissecting table... art doesn't work that way – too slippery... like God..."

"mm, arty sentence there..." sips from tea... "anyway, glad you visited today – everyone in this city seems too 'cool' to hold such a simple conversation we're babbling about here... - Art... capitol 'A' Art..."

"is what it is..."

"what is what it is?"

"Art... – and us here talking about it..."

"that cuts it down..."

"how's that?"

"eliminates discussion... flatlines..."

"did you have hopes that here, today, at Verb, we'd pound a stake in ground as founders of the true, all-encompassing, definition of art?.... – it is what it is – that's all it is..."

"what's 'what it is'?"

"*what it is* is what it is."

"what is *it*?"

"what it is."

growing mad "what's *what*?" he demands.

"you're acting like you don't know what's what around here heh-heh..."

..."what isn't 'it is what it is' – or what isn't 'what it is'?"

"Well., that which 'isn't' I suppose..."

"whatever..."

"anyway, what vague, leading-to-where talk this is eh..."

lightening up... "it leads somewhere... – newness – experimentation – 'unconventionality leads to new discoveries' I like to think – free flow – seeing what happens – openness... but look at what we're using in attempts to achieve this newness: words 'passed down' to us – from previous generations – generation to generation... - don't you feel like you're surfing on others ideas in a sense – every time you open mouth – unless you're really letting it fly – Lewis Carol was into that – had to do it under the label of 'poetry'... – you know he was a mathematician right..."

"yeah – he'd be one of the guys at the table if I could pick ten people - throughout all history - to have breakfast with... - yeah, words... words are a double-edged sword – define something and you bind it in a way - like... tag a

name on a thing or concept – such a 'nailing down' aspect to it... – but has to
be done, really, so people know what's going on... – sounds from mouths
causing people to form pictures in head - or feel this way or that – very interesting... - the speaker and the recipient... – and names as tags for people - a
guy named Victor – or Max - going through his whole life – having this image
of himself pop up whenever he hears or reads his name – whereas this guy
Matt – or Dick or Rob – have their vibes, pictures, to deal with through a lifetime. . . – and how names are foisted on us - without our say *whatsoever*... -
where's our say when it comes to having the name we believe we ought to have
– say a guy gets it in his head that he's a... 'Howard' or a... – say he makes up a
name... – tough to even think up one – what's left -we've used about every
possibility of sound combinations there are – we humans are very clever - and
is that another sign of the end? – I thought up a somewhat original-sounding
one - say he feels he's a 'Krealy' – well, that's a creepy name – alright "Leef...ly"
        "Leaf – like a tree?" –
        "See – sounds from my mouth have caused you to tack it to that image –
it's inextricable! ... You're referring that 'preconception bank' in your head
y'know - files... – 'pre'conception – a conception – or, 'concept' that's 'pre' –
i.e. thought up back a while ago - generations ago – locked in - handed down
to others, who just, take it, and... use it – run with it – without... really...
examining it... – just sort of... bumbling along kind of deal... - colors, too, -
blues signifying this – reds that – or are we 'wired' this way – i.e. if no one gave
us a textbook meaning – would it bubble up – the words – is it universal?
greens, yellows – pink – all so tied to these preconceptions we have in us... –
and what we bring to them, to an extent... but think about it – the *tags*... -
who tagged them thusly – who called all these shots - unbeknownst to us? -
and why are we continuing to go on their definitions – riding waves from back
hundreds of years ago... y'know..."
        "yep..."
        "but anyway, couldn't be helped – the original 'taggers' had to call it some-
thing – so everyone would be on the same page, y'know, know what's up... –
but man, how people take to loving tags and labels – get labeling people – slap
an occupation title on someone to sum them up – Oh he's an accountant – oh
she's a nurse – he's a lawyer – she's an artist – boom – they're in a ball of wax,
that's that... – and so based on what people do – here, an author writes one hit
book when he's twenty five – his fiftieth birthday he goes into a pharmacy –
buys a bottle of aspirin, walks out... - the cashier whispers to coworker "that
was *Fred Wallace* – he wrote that book "All is Rising"... - he has that *stuck* to

him to his grave – and especially after – there it is in the obituary – there it is in history books – hundred years later "he wrote All is Rising" – no shaking the label off from the grave… – makes you think twice about doing something – seeing the label that (the doing of it) will indelibly stick to your name… - goes for movie makers, politicians, whatever… where was I going…"

"…names… tags…"

"ah… and… context – it's… - everyone brings what they have in them to things wherever they go… – so, getting back to names - in our country 'mat' means one thing – we bring it, project it, - at times on our friend 'Matt' – or have it cooking on back burner – *however*, in another country perhaps 'mat' means '*king*' – *they* bring that – project that image, glory, on him… - so it comes down to sounds from mouth relating to context, pretty much… – determining feeling, response, on and on…"

"having control of the name you go by… – this cracks into 'control'… the 'control factor' as I like to call it – have given it plenty of thought… – control *definitely* having its place in 'art'… – this guy is… just a bit in control of the medium – receives… just a bit of acclaim in return – whereas *this* guy - is in complete control of the medium – to point of *playing* with it – and the acclaim gushes in – audiences show up in droves… – to see what they love: *control* heh-heh – 'mastery' as it's popularly known… –

but yeah, I see what you're saying – we're… bound – in a sense - by the past – one could say – yada-yada, this line's kinda ran its course eh…"

"heh, well it's been overlooked – underrated… – the extent to which pre-conceptions are wielding power these days… like… unaddressed… – power we should 'wrest' from the preconceptions – and usher in newness of vibes - across the board - creativity completely out of box y'know - live in a freer… *way*… state of being…"

"sounds hippie…" -

"*Ah, another* preconception – drag it on in heh-heh… – you're pro-grammed – down to your quips… – but we're all programmed to an extent… – even with, like I said, colors – we've even gone so far as to tag meanings to *colors*… – control factor ties in, what? - you know them right – you sat through the art classes… – got your browns - meaning earthy, grounded, rooted… – reds connoting action, confidence, vitality… purple: royalty… white: purity, cleanness… yellow: happiness… green: life, nature, growth… blues: dark says authority, depth – light says friendliness… gold is wisdom, wealth… black: death, stability…"

..."I'm far from programmed... - many people – poppy culture – go around, having taken their cues from TV, radio... movies – behave, talk accordingly – funny concept in that – masses taking cues from actors heh-heh – but then actors... take theirs from producers – which get theirs from... writers – could say it all traces to writers – words...– lot's in that, too – words, driving things, machines, societies... – in any case, wouldn't say I'm in the big cue-takers camp – considering I don't own a TV, radio, or go to the movies..." –

"'cue-takers' heh-heh, like that..."

"we all have our influences over the years... – which... lock into place... and we... go through life... dishing these flavors on others... pretty much... till we die..."

"'all' is dangerous man... – 'all' equals generality – 'gross' generality... – and 'we', who's that?..." –

"'many people'... happy?"

"vague."

"whatever... – but yeah – there's *influences* – and there's cue-taking – sometimes they cross-pollinate... – but cue-taking that's alone – no originality – no heart - stirred in... that's a rough call... how to describe... - kids come from Florida, Tennessee, wherever, go to art school in the city, see pictures in textbooks, watch documentaries about famous artists – see them smoking in interviews – angrily slopping paint on a canvas – registration occurs in mind – here's what a famous artist 'looks like' - few weeks later they're walking around campus, cigarette dangling from mouth – paint, spattered on shirt... - they see 'famous artists' unloading – they hop on the dumping-inner-angst-out-on-campus band wagon... - *bllaaaaahhh!* onto the canvas... 'gee, thanks for... sharing that with us...' – where's the joy – the *fun* of art – *good times* – like when you were a child and you did some small thing like... beat a level in a video game - that *ecstasy* - would surge through whole body, mind – or you found out your parents were ordering pizza or something – or Thursday night before summer vacation – recall that joy – *that's* what I'm talking about – and I'm talking about it being experienced by twenty, thirty, forty, fifty-somethings – across the board! Enough of this pissy – crap-on-viewers garbage..."

"it's not arty to ax out a type of art..."

"yeah... suppose it has its place... – you get my point – I'm talking about uplifting – elevating viewers - let other artists do what they will – who's experiencing the most joy – that's what really counts in my book... – because the vibe spreads – and it's gonna be life giving or life draining – and that goes for way more than just art.... – and as a sideline ~(sideline(?))~ – speaking of 'not being arty' - if you asked me to can a type of art - it'd be a lot of realistic-look-ing ones – paintings, drawings, on and on… - - heh, it's like – with Hitler – he had abstract art removed – called it "degenerate art" - from museums - as for me – other way around – keep the mind-expanding abstract pieces - which ignites imaginations to possibilities and beyond - opens all kinds of doors - and chuck the mass-appeasing, play-it-safe, realistic-looking - labored-for-months-over paintings of barns or bowls of fruit, a person sitting, a standing nude or what have you… be that all as it may though… - branch into this – how, so much has to do with what's going on within the artist… - your art – be it drawings, paintings, photographs, sculpture, a *website* – will be as real or fake – as authentic or inauthentic – as *you* are - on the inside… - and the out-side, I suppose - outside hints of what's on the inside – there's a connection – sends messages of what's inside – especially clothes – and stuff people own – and their pets – anyway it goes for you-name-the-work as well – locksmith, chef, architect - it's all 'inside coming out' stuff – 'manifestation' y'know, yada-yada… – talking off cuff here." ~(off cuff(?))~ - "Alfred Stieglitz pops to mind-" –

"now we're talking… – he helped kick me into photos in the first place… that and working at a movie store…" nostalgic look waxes over face… "– night shift… – got to choose from aaall the films - they had a huge collection… – I entertain the notion that I've seen the most movies - for someone my age – of anyone on earth… – got paid for sitting there, watching them, too – peanuts – but hey… anyway yeah, that lead me to uh, putting pen and laptop aside – I was an English major at NYU… heh, - I actually had a season of meditation – in my dorm… - on a cliché' - I really did… I meditated for days on a cliché'… – the one 'a picture is worth a thousand words'… I sat Indian-style in my dorm – curtains shut – meditating on that – thinking through its validity… – weighing it - all the implications of it… -reeeaally explored it – it branched into so much else… dropped out of school soon after that – or kicked out – combination of the two – the putting aside of pen and paper the picking up the camcorders… the rest is… well, here we are…"

"indeed… yeah, look at Stieglitz… opening a gallery in Midtown – inviting outside-of-box-thinking Europeans over to show their work – tapping their resources – their minds – stretching horizons, their faith – availing adventure in their lives - opening lines of communication – pushing limits – going beyond – expanding minds of his countrymen in the process… now, that was during *his* time – during his lifetime – what's happening these days – here in the beating heart of *our* time… he did it, *what* are *we* doing? - that's what I'm talking about – higher than hum-drum – and higher than that - on a quest – enrichment on many levels, across boards, setting captives free…"

"you can see why we're be collaborating for this upcoming show… – I see in you a genuineness - to point you can't – *won't* stick on mask to play the game… I've stuck on the mask and played the game - years – to where now – having made some money from the game – can ditch mask - spread wings – play by own rules - operate outside it… – I see me in you – you're me ten years ago – just better - because I see you're not going to bend into the yoke of the game like I did – and I'd like to spare you of that - I'm going to float that atti-tude – I support it – even with money - if you get any other financial support – go for it – but off bat – my guess is you won't find many *if any* others like me… – giving you free license to make art – as *you* see it – *your* definition – and, in so doing – you'll hone that definition *further* – share your discoveries with the world - I'd like to gust winds into the sails – hoop-free – hoops trip-up, con-fuse, distort, bog down, hamper – impede, disrupt flow of artist's creations… – all that minutia and paperwork – and control freaks, trying to get their hands in – all that will be out the window for this upcoming show far as you're con-cerned - leave that all to me - you just… stick thinking cap on - delve into those depths of yours and come up with something rich - nutritious - to feed many hungry and depraved 9-5 souls yearning for a drop of water - a *morsel* of originality… ok that sounded cheesy heh-heh… I digress – put pen to pad – tap inspiration to dregs and then some – whatever that be - it'll be the warm-up - the appetizer - the lead-in to my projector piece… – photos flashing up on wall to music – I got a ringer lined up… – it's at Fleishman's gallery on Driggs – they're paying me five thousand – I'll chop it in half – twenty five hundred each – you in?"

"Anything then."

"Anything. – I mean, y'know, - no going insane with costs - but we can manage providing somewhat of a budget…"

"and people are going to show to this?"

"Tyler's gonna throw the net wide… the guy knows mind-boggling amounts of people… - his network. your artistic genius and flare… my vision, experience, hands-on construction skills and, of course, video art… strong djs - we're talking a team for the art history books bro…"

…"deal."

"very well then…"

tea's finished, walking for studio… "you know those yellow legal pads?" he says "go fill a page – or a few, whatever - with your idea for a ringer warm-up piece - come see me in two weeks and we can prepare…"

"good deal."

Looking in garage… "and help me throw away this canvas."

"seriously?"

he's dragging it out… I take up other end – start lifting it at dumpster - "Eeeasy - just lean it up against it – "someone from the neighborhood will nab this by tomorrow, guaranteed. – I'll tape a 'free canvas' sign to it"

"and so force someone else to prolong the putting-of-paint-on-a-canvas tradition? It's on your head man, your call."

"you're a nut. see you in two weeks…"

Ride in dark over bridge, electronic tune playing… – adding levels… – speeding into Manhattan – orthodox Jews, hiking up in opposite direction – in black… weighty vibes to them – another – groups of them… batteries run out… quiet ride along Clinton… Stanton… Ludlow… lock bike out front of Earthmatters (healthfood store)… get a bowl of hot veggie soup… climb to second level… finish it… get cup of tea… climb up again… sit on sofa… mystical techno(ish) music playing… sipping, mind shooting off in new directions… returns to steadfastness… – launches all over… returns to an equilibrium… gets forming possibilities for upcoming weeks – a warning popping in that police will probably be checking Tyler's soon – sniffing me out – once ~two and two is put together~ – Mom knows Tyler is living in New York – knows his parents… ~will take chances there tonight – won't answer door if anyone buzzes…~ - but tomorrow… – Chelsea shelter's out… – did hear (while staying there a few months ago) of another shelter – by Grand Central… – can give that one a try …

Long, thoughtful, ride up 2nd Avenue – pit stop at Rite Aid for a legal pad and pack of # 2 pencils …

pleasant surprise of substantial stretch of hill – good speed picked up – from 92nd – 103rd… Black drug dealers in lobby stiffening as I go by with bike on shoulder, head up stairs …

Carve a point on a # 2… lay on futon, pull legal pad from bag… close eyes, look inside… open eyes… jot… repeat …

CHAPTER 13

Open eyes to Tyler, standing, holding miniature camcorder to eye – other eye shut tight – free hand holding half-eaten granola bar… smiling, chewing loud – "yes, yes, future famous person… famous person in future, rouse thyself heh-heh…"

"Thought you were in Europe."

still rolling, "just got back – fresh off red-eye man…"

"shut it off…"

wheels suitcase to his room …

"I'm gonna be cruisin' soon – I'll be staying at another place…"

"where?"

"… a place."

Emerges from room – "a… place…" …

"yeah – I kinda… escaped suburbia – parents are gonna be calling around – don't want cops showing up, knocking on your door… – at least not while I'm here…"

"hey your call man – don't let the door hit you on the behind… – you got my number – Mr. payphone…" shuts door to bathroom, hear shower start up …

grab legal pad, head for midtown …

The shelter is… higher quality – right down block from Grand Central… –

swinging in door, giving the fresh-bumbled-in-from-the-west look – they have me sign a clip board (swirl a scribble) – assign me a room number …

here, in shower – *shampoo and conditioner* – provided (or left)… scrubbing Suave 'Juicy Green Apple' shampoo into hair… move on to 'Tropical Coconut' conditioner …

Toweling off... ~feeling pretty good about this place... could stay here a while... won't be calling Shannon anytime soon heh-heh...~

And it's day after day... out for long walks around city – meet up with a friend occasionally – Scott was in city the other day - treated me to a burrito lunch – "look at you – crazy, homeless, zero-responsibility bum, heh-heh, *man*, - tough road, duping the system, eh?"... - Gavin was in city – for a job interview, bought me a coffee, sitting out front café Esperanto – him in his suit, tie, briefcase: "how the mighty have fallen, fallen, *fallen*... – you know Shannon got swept up by some Brown stud right?"

I in my stained donation-bin sweatpants and sweatshirt ('2002 Rose Bowl'), "well, is what it is... what can you do..."

"you no spine-" – his cellphone rings – fumbling it – "Hello. Yes, 2:00 is perfect. Thank you sir, I'll see you then. Ok, ok, bye now." hangs up, glares at watch – "*maaaan* – that just gives *me half an hour* – what's the quickest way to Wall Street?"

At points throughout each day, I go up to my room in the shelter, pull laptop from bag, place it on desk in front of window, open it, and type... working on a novel... called "Swedish Dreams" about a creature who exists inside the collective imaginations of ten Stockholm students – friends who've invented it – where it goes, what it does... one girl goes insane... – the creature, affected by this, another girl looses it, institutionalized... then one of the guys... – the seven unite – go on a journey - to a friend's – in Berlin – he's set up a room – 'made for imagining'... fingers type so fast... concept of time vanishes... sit at night, face close to lighted screen... deep into the morning... – as roommate - a short, quiet, reading Russian named Yuri - shines his mini-flashlight on pages of thick book in his bottom bunk ...

Madison Square Park – its fountain, spurting its middle stream up, to falling downwards, splashing on European-esque structure... – ~so many *types* about... Americans, showing up for lunch~ – has a pull to it, this spot... find myself here day after day, observing, jotting notes on legal pad, reflecting, jotting, fantasizing, jotting... I picked up a beige corduroy hat at the shelter ('Ft. Lauderdale' stitched on it) and – from it (or who knows why), I have dandruff... which trickles down as I write - constantly brushing and flicking it off... and... have a beard going suddenly... rather than the schlep up to midtown shelter – easily find half-eaten pizza slices in the trash cans here... – even occasionally requesting a burger from someone my age – or generous-looking

- standing in line for the Shakey Shack – it works about every time... and I... appear to be growing a pouch of fat over my ~once rock-hard six pack~ ...

The Saturday I'm to meet Elliot already... here by the fountain early, putting finishing touches on my outline... suddenly get it into head that ~perhaps I can scrape all the dandruff out – maybe that's how it works – just, keep at it – till scraping away that last flake – how many can there be? – not like it's gonna flake off down to the skull.~... so I begin... - rigorous (plenty of energy - having just pluckt half a fruit salad from the trash - and an untouched – though, had to wrestle it off a hissing squirrel – half of a Quizno's sub)... I'm sitting, hunched over, just... going at it – dandruff, snowing down, landing between feet... reaching the hour mark, less is falling – spurring me on ~maybe after two hours my theory will have proven itself true~ - up the vigor –

"Zach?"

slowly look up ...

recognize... former classmate – had classes together – ~French, Calc, Physics II, - rrr what's her name - she got that full ride to... Columbia...~

"It's Patricia" her eyes are wide. her nose, upper lip, a bit scrunched up ...

"Ah right, yes, how are ya?"

"eh, ok, how are you?"

"I'm alright..."

"what are yoouu... doing?

~no mention of the dandruff experiment~ – "ah, jussst... clearin' my head – what are you up to these days?"

"I'm doing an internship with KPMG this summer. – what are you doing in the city?"

"I'm uh, working on a project" point to legal pad, lil' drum-tap with eraser "working with an artist in... here in the city... gearing up to do a show soon. – experimenting with art these days... - Actually about to head over and see my colleague... – you heading back to work?"

"Yeah I'm just finishing up lunch... So..." – appears about to breach into shipwreck survival and/or aftermath subject... -

"Well good seeing you... have a fun time at work..." waving ...

"Ok, - I uh, didn't finish my lunch – bought two slices – ate one – I – I don't know if you..." -

"suuure I'll take it off your hands – thank you kindly..."

She walks away... – and the slice is still warm... biting into it, dandruff flakes flurry down onto it ~rrrrrrrr!~ crunch another bite... ~eating my dandruff... priceless... what's next... dandruff pizza... - yeah I'll take some *dan-*

druff on that slice… 'here we go: garlic, parm, oregano, *dandruff…*' slumped over… ~not much sleep last night there~ fade out …

~ … "the voice is the reflection of the soul… art reflects the peoples – peoples seeing… ZEITUS GEITUS!"~ – snap awake… pick half-eaten slice off chest, resume eating it… -

eyes focus on a gathering of young Hispanics, laughing by the fountain… ~hm~ - they've brought a folding table over - from this area, set it up, have a birthday cake on it… candles lit, they're singing to birthday girl, sitting on folding chair with big smile… one's cutting the cake - as a black guy in a lil' John Deere tractor pulls up… points at the table, telling them to return it… they pack up – the one girl in tight-fitting purple top – lower part of fat tummy exposed – bends over, picks up her JIMMY JAZZ shopping bag, as they drag table over – to this area, setting cake on again, as gardener putters away, contented look on face …

hold crust to a squirrel, who nibbles aggressively at it… ~what people fear, - 'being homeless', 'on the streets'… here, I'm… *in it…*~ … ~all in all ~~('all in all'(?))~~ it's… like a… form of… total freedom… in some senses… when looked at from… various angles… - can… sit and watch stuff, can go around pretty much wherever -outside - unless reprimanded from some authority or other – which, admittedly, can prevent you from getting hurt – say you're ambling aimlessly down the middle of a busy street… freedom… - until this or that discomfort pinches in, snaps the groove… – biggest thing… – the thing I find myself like a… constant slave to, of course, is food… – this ongoing quest – anxiety… - find stuff to cram in mouth… – kind of a dealbreaker, really – to the whole homeless thing – for a thinker…~ wrinkled, rocking, smoking, insane-looking guy, pushing himself along in a wheel chair, rolls by… ~is this this guy's lot?~ …. ~*Man, what are you trying to do with your life, Zak……* - bit broad… – how about days - break it down to days… – to *today* for instance – what are you trying to accomplish *today* – what is your *goal* for today… – other than the dandruff experiment…~ turn head, look down, on bench, to left, a Village Voice - opened to random back page… advertisement for
'NYC's TOKYO SPA' –
two Japanese girls, stare out with tilt heads… - white words:
Body
Scrub
Table
Shower

wind blows… flips pages of the Post - sitting next to Voice… – headline: 'Nation of Flim Flam Politicians.' – wind… – pages flip… Sports section… 'Seniors Shed Tears as Huskies Shred Cougars.'

Look over at table, ten feet away… a kid – looks to be a mixture of ethnicities… – he's rocking back and forth… frowning, hand motions, pausing at times to pen lyrics in little notebook… ~he's mad about something…~… cursing, frowning, motioning hands harder… ~hm, unpleasant~ – person at table next his, looking sheepishly over ~what words, actions, can do to the atmosphere…~

nod off… – into a dream… – setting: huge gathering of people – filling every square foot of Central Park - every ethnicity, gathered – each huddled together in their groups – here, the African – over here, the Asians, over here, Puerto Ricans… on and on, group by group… and they're… heading… over… to… boats… lined up… and… they're… setting… off… for their… homelands… –mixes too… – vigorous DNA testing having been done…– determining who can stay: German, English, Irish, Dutch, Scandinavians: all OK… - jolt awake… ~Hm, guess I won't be up in front of vast crowds delivering an 'I have a dream' speech with that one…~

Look over, up, at… huge clock – high on face of gold-coned-topped (aglisten in sun) building… 1:05… ~I turn 19 today… what a birthday…~

Rise, get schlepping along ~for exercise…~… crossing street, curly-haired girl, walking opposite direction, on her shirt: 'Got Gonzo?'… onto sidewalk… big poster in window to right catches attention… stand, stare a while… has a clean, smooth-skinned, pretty mulatto woman – smiling big, bright white teeth - curly hair, aspring from head… wearing spandex… on one knee… in an exercise position… big, red-lettered words above her : 'Turbo Palates.' – schlep on… stopping again… standing a while, looking through windows of 'P C Richardson's' - at the flat screen TV's… football highlights… – here, a guy, diving (slo mo) over pile of grappling, falling linemen – linebacker dives in opposite direction – mid-air collision – running back sent into slow helicopter spin - ball, popping from him – others, diving, scrambling for it… ~now, here's this… pro athlete… he's got this… body… - which can bench press all this weight, which can run such and such quick mile… – sure, he worked on it – but… some, there's no argument, are born with that extra girth and/or agility… now, look at me – not trying to play the victim – just… 'laying down facts'… - he can lift more weight… – so a helmet gets strapped on his head – ball is thrown to him – people pay to watch him run into an endzone - millions and millions of dollars… You, well, what can *you* do? Paint a picture? (hands on belly "haaar-har-*harrrrr* – tell you what – you go *paint* your picture – Oh, and have fun – haarrr-*haarrr*... now *get outta here!*... – ya *schmuck!*"~ bust into laughter, looking down, shaking head no, putting right hand up, pinch top of bridge on nose, eyebrows rise, laughing, walking on ~myyyy-my-my-my-my~ tears, rolling down ...

A lady walks towards in opposite direction... intensity of her vibe, snapping me out of it – her face, scrunched in – like she... ~ate a watermelon seed – real sour one – years ago - that she's been working, working, working on it for years.... *yow*... let it go babe...~... here, long-haired metal head strides by – ipod plugs in ears, sun glasses, all black, leather, studs, piercings... ~see you have your belief system going there hoss... how's that going for ya... – actually, pretty apparent how it's going for you... kind of a tough call ya got goin' there...~ ... ~how states of mind play so instrumental a part in the forming of our visages... –ah, *philosophies*... our philosophies – *belief-systems* - 'set of beliefs' – turning, morphing, us into what, who, we are – and what we look like, project to the world...~... ~what is what you believe turning you into?... mm, like that... - and actions, work, dealings - what's what you're *doing, doing* to you? – mmm yyyyyeeeaah~ ~and how are they perceiving me – scraggily-bearded, Ft. Lauderdale hat askew and all heh-heh...~

Look in through fancy Italian Restaurant window... Rich guy in suit with business woman sitting at white-table-clothed table, lots of silverware, two tall glasses of freshly-poured white wine... – my eyes find rest on a lil' silver bowl of... ~is that... cubes of brie?~ It is... He feels uncomfortable – puts hand to forehead, fake scratches at hairline, blocking me from view... eyes alight on cuff links... now Rolex – brain registers intricate movements of gears a few ticks before moving on, leaving them be... ~leaving them to their brie...~

Stop to think on corner... ~regain composure~

Eyes hone in on a second floor neon sign: 'Eyebrow Threading' – a TV under the sign – inside window – showing the procedure – a plastic-gloved hand adroitly plucking at, patting with napking, sowing up, a brow ...

here, a fat black lady cop pulls up in lil' police three-wheeler - with its lil' cab to sit in... gets out, serious-faced, chewing gum, pulls pad of tickets from back pocket... starts writing up one for sad-looking, long, 1980's Dodge van... –plumber guy - looking like Super Mario - appears – throws hands up, yelling, as she rips it from pad, sticks it behind windshield wiper, climbs in scooter, shuts door, putters off ...

lil' stoplight green man flashes on - masses lunge forward on both side – interweaving in center of street – a bus blasts its horn – caught in intersection, blocking honking cabs …

here, a tall model – plenty of agencies in the neighborhood – brisks by, purposeful, chic, - sunglasses on - hand beeping at cellphone, long blond hair blowing behind her – charges a surge in - ~through veins…~ turn as she goes ~nniiiiice *look*… gotta get me one a those… – sooner better than latter… just…~ turning, walking on ~the money thing…~ … ~but man, what I wouldn't do with the likes of her - (wouldn't(?)) – no-no – *would* - what I *would* do~ - shake head - ~snap out of it man… – git yer mind outta the gutter… *gutter?* – ugh, another cliché… – so programmed with them – they've burrowed in – pop up time to time… – we so go on them – one to the next… it's that… linking-meaning-via-word-pictures thing… – in this case, 'filth in a gutter'… – is that calling her filth – or what we'd do? hmm… – well, loosing self in a pornographic fantasyland with one who's not my wife I suppose is gutter stuff – cop-out stuff – pervy stuff… – in any case, gotta get me a gal *that level*… – on the list – *snap out of it!* – priorities – ducks in line before any dating game… – 'ducks in line' – word pictures – visual language – linkage – pictorial – images, in head, image to image, we exist image to image~ blind guy taps stick by - ~what about him though – say he was blind from birth – what are images to him?~

stop in tracks out front Universal Magazine store… beg 75 cents in ten minutes …

get a cup of coffee, gather a stack of magazines in arm, plunkt down on table… an hour of leafing, noting, absorbing, gauging, comparing, pondering …

just… sitting… note the kinds of magazines represented… ~got your fashion and glamour mags over here… your art mags over in these racks… Car mags… Sports mags… Fishing… Bikes… Travel mags, Photography… 'WINE' magazine, 'Money'… 'ROBOT'… over here, 'Yacht Design' (picture on front, rich thirty-something standing, yellow polo shirt, one hand on chrome steering wheel, other on power lever – it pushed fully forward, clean wavy light brown hair fluttering back in wind, pair of Oakleys on tan face, white toothy grin)… Foreign magazine section – French, German, Italian, on and on… Music mags… Interior Design ~is what it is~ mags, Health and Fitness ~is what it is~… – here, two racks devoted to weddings – smiling women in gowns on covers: 'BRIDE', 'Modern Bride', 'Perfect Wedding'… 'BRIDE GUIDE' …

elbows on table, hands holding head, which stares down at cheap wood, run fingers through hair... flakes, floating down, change dynamic – look, feel – of table ~like that~... eyes drift to right... here, a mag, left on table: 'VOGUE'... –

eyes skim over feature article headings on cover:

'Cocktail-Party Cheat Sheet
how to sound smart'

'Bad Boyfriend?
10 ways to leave your lover.'

'Plastic Surgery Baby Steps
Look gorgeous now,
Avoid major work later.'

'No Sleep?
Look rested *in a flash*

Marlboro clock says 3:14... to meet Elliot in Park at 4 ...

~hmm, forty more minutes...~

bumble over to computer store... stand perusing games ...
all the... colorful boxes... here, 'Starry Night Beginner'
remove from shelf, flip box over:
'Learn the popular names of familiar Star patterns – from the Big Dipper to the Seven Sisters...' ... here, 'Sims 4'... flip over ...
'The next generation *people simulator* ...
They're born, they die. What happens in between is up to you.
Take your Sims from cradle to grave through life's greatest moments...' -
picture of computer-animated guy with smirk and goatee – arm around waist of blond in bright red dress ...
'Create your Sims' (with its corresponding [computer animated illustration] picture)
'Push them to extremes'
'Control their world'

'Fulfill their life dreams... Or realize their failures' (picture of a grim reaper) ...

take up 'Sim City 4' flip over ...
'Create a massive Metropolitan area.'
'Construct your city's transportation system.'
'Determine your city's fate.'

~Americans must like these games... right up alley... controlling...~ -
and this one – race cars on box: '*Total Immersion* Racing'... ~distract me!
Deeper doses! – *heavier dosages now!*~
eyes scan on... 'Wingnuts 2'
and here – illustration of smiling monkey, banana in hand, on box:
'Zoo Tycoon 2'
'create your *dream zoos* – get closer than *ever!*'

Eliot likes the ideas - "Everything – it's a go..."
"So you'll help me recover my cycle?"
"Yep – my friend Kyle - lives right up the street from me - has a pickup – lends it to me whenever..."
"and if it's gone... you'll buy a new one – my choice on model..."
"yyep – just, we put it on ebay after show..."
"and music will be aok..."
"DJ ON – give him the playlist – he's got the juice – top of the line sound system..."

We cruise to Jersey next day... I point out the rest stop sign I'd memorized as a marker... pull over... crunch into the woods... but it's gone... turning to Elliot, "Just as well – a new one will send a cleaner, more powerful message at the show... – all is as it should go, be..."
"Glad you think so."
At Cycle City an hour later – select a gleaming, brand-new-looking used CR 125... Elliot handles the paperwork, credit-cards it through... ride it up a wood plank into back of truck ...

CHAPTER 14

Friday night of show... – galleries all over Williamsburg hosting openings... – "we're gonna beat 'em all" says Elliot, tilting a Stella... – "we've got *the connections*... – look at this" pointing open hand to glass front of gallery – where a line has formed, waits... "doors open at 7... it's 6:30... - that's special tinted glass, they can't see in..." – he returns to setting up his projector... - actors (friends of Elliot - locals) here, getting dressed, in cop uniforms, as DJ ON sound checks... – Elliot stands, clears throat, - to extras – ~definitely look-ing like cops~ - and Shaun Caster (fellow Williamsburger artist – straightening fake (very realistic), graying, longish beard... adjusts fake glasses)...- "Ok, Zach brought you all through rehearsal earlier – after the performance in here – let's make it a quick clean up and encourage people to come into the back room... *here* for the musical slideshow slash mime piece."- to me - "you're all set right?"

"yep," looking over at cycle, positioned central ~bristling~ on stand... – massive, standing industrial fan in front of, facing, it ...

I'm wearing full length white leather suit, long silky white cape, white leather (and shiny plastic) riding boots... – gleaming polished white helmet, with black tinted eye shield... "Alright" clapping, heading for his backroom area "everyone take their places! – we have *one minute!*" – Elliot, pumping fist, glaring in my eyes, "Alright Zach, *make it happen.*"

Feel a nervousness rustling in stomach - feel, hear, in head, heart, beating... - pointing at dj – "song's are all cued, right? – when everyone's in and ready – press play – same volume as rehearsal..." – to eight fake cops – "alright – line up against walls – four here – four over here... – look real - look authoritative."

I go in back room… pacing… hear electronic music kick on… I picture the gallery filling… -picture them picking plastic cups of wine from table… picture them examining the cycle, - some, hands to chins, pondering, - others, discussing… - music cuts off… hear one of the fake cops "Alright everyone - *behind the line* – see the line - the red tape on the ground here – everyone behind it – here we go…"

slip helmet on, buckle …

pull on white leather riding gloves …

~timing… timing…~ quieting down… people, ready… on goes music – cropped section of electric-guitar-w/-fast-drums metal song – I swoosh curtain open – cheering – assistants (on other side of divider) dump huge trash bags of glitter down as fan turns on full-blast – shooting all over semi-circled audience – *~man that music is loud!~* – mounting cycle – kick it started – 'WAA – right into full throttle *–AAA!!* (front tire set in a bike stand) – people not even brushing off glitter – spellbound by cycle's wailing – back tire shrieking – white smoke billowing from it - fan blowing cape back dramatic… - right on cue, Shaun, with his beard, acting like regular visitor-guy, crosses line – acting hypnotized – like he just… wants to touch the spectacle – "Sir!" yells a fake cop – advancing towards - and soon as I feel Shaun's finger make contact on elbow – crank front tire from stand – into wheelie – blasting fan out of way (assistants on other side of divider – yank fishing wire connected to it – drag it to wall [we'd replaced the blade with a plastic one [painted metallic [realistic] in case it flew off]) – I let go – to cycle cart-wheeling into wall – smashing 'KLOW!!' through wall (as planned – put tin sheets of drywall up – padding behind it) as I roll on ground, acting hurt, holding arm, curl into fetal position, trembling – as actor cop – with fake (looking very real) billy club full-swings down – knocks Shaun over the head – as he bursts fake blood pack in hand – sprays, splatters on white floor – and Denis (also playing a 'regular guy' actor) dives in - headlocking fake cop – other cops diving on him – two cops whaling Denis over the head with fake clubs – and (something which we'd discussed as a 'dangerous possibility' - but dismissed, hoping for the best) real audience members jump in – especially three guys - who showed up looking like they came straight from the pub – and it's an all-out melee – puncing, cursing, headlocks, smashing onto wine table – someone cut from broken glass - speed metal going loud - cuts off - girls screaming, pushing towards door – assistants from the back room come running in - and Elliot – he's hollering – "It was an *act!* Hello! Stop!" – but two guests are still duking it out - fake cops leave off trying to break it up, hunched over, catching breath – I try getting between them –

wearing helmet – punched in the chest – fall to ground, wind knocked out... – and the real cops show up - and everyone's scrambling out - as two NYPD cops walk in, billy clubs wielded... look down at fake blood smeared all over floor "What happened?"

Elliot: "It's fake blood – it was part of an act – the *first* act of the evening" - making for door – "I gotta get the people back in here for the main event." –

"Wo-wo-wo" stepping in his way – "there ain't gonna be no art show till we find out exactly what's going on here..." as a news cameraman enters the gallery rolling footage – "get *outta* here with that!" yells the cop, shooing with club ...

Never did get people in again to see Elliot's slideshow, which he was ticked about... – but the next day – our show was all over the papers – and now, here, watching on TV in shelter's common room – my face, pale, hair sticking up, giving a response to news lady holding mic (the name appearing at bottom of screen: "Zak Bar, Artist")- "yeah well it was a performance piece - people took it to be real - things got out of hand, blown out of proportion, so... yeah, I mean, it happens – no one really got hurt and I hope no one's gonna try to press charges or anything like that..." feel eyes looking at me – residents are whispering, pointing... I pull Ft. Lauderdale hat lower over eyes – "was that *you* on TV there?" rasps a smiling black guy, three chairs over, leaning towards me, front tooth missing ...

"yeah... uh"

"hee-hee*eeeeee*" smacking knee "I'll be – that was him y'all!"

"daaa*aaaam*" someone says "dat's what's up." –

"whatchu doin' in *here* fo?"

And my fingers are caressing the roll of bills in pocket – twenty hundred dollar bills ...

CHAPTER 15

Watching morning news in common room - van crashed into Bronx laundry-matte last night… "the driver fled on foot." … ~is what it is… yes, more and more 'it is what it is', day in, day out, one thing after the other… – yet… what is that: 'day in, day out(?) – another cliché' on hands? – people use it – what's it *really* mean? 'day *in*' what's that? Well, going into a day, guess that can count… – 'day *out*?' well, going out of a day… guess it holds water after all… 'after all'…– after all *what*? – are we talking after the earth is destroyed, or… – and "holds water" *aaaaarrrrgh!*~… eating bowl of instant oatmeal… sneeze – dandruff drifts down – into bowl as spoon up steaming lump, shove in mouth ~mmm eating more dandruff… *grrrrreat!*… hey, c'mon, par for course here heh heh…~

Dig round in donations box… pull out a faded red Flash Gordon shirt – faded yellow lightning bolt on it… change on the spot – returning shirt (white, blue PALM BEACH across chest - got from box yesterday) into box… step out-side – sun stings in eyes… pass a few shelter folk – scraggly old guys – ~checked-out long ago for one reason or other… – letting the days pass to till when whole existence gets swallowed up into oblivion - followed by 'quiet funeraless reality' - as all go along on their ways…~

head over to CHESTER FRIED… shelter folk, and people from the blind and retarded school up the street – sit at the cheap tables in center of space inside – this one, as I pass, plastic-spooning a lumpy steamy gooey potato salad into mouth – her lazy eye following mine as I go by – the other one whited out… pass the glass display cases with the logs of tin-foil-wrapped Boar's Head meat logs and rectangle cheeses…. big plastic jug of JIF… this guy – at table by drink coolers - lanky black guy in tank top and dark sunglasses – tall - ~coulda been a star b-ball player back in his day for all I know~ - tall can of OLD ENGLISH 800 on table in crinkly brown bag before him... – shooting breeze with companion – scrappy-looking stout black guy - flashing gold front tooth - sweatshirt with the word 'LUGZ' printed on it – lots of hand motions – using 'was' where 'were' ought to be – drawing giggles forth from deep places in tall guy, who nods his head no "Aaw no he didn't... – aaaw *man*..."... and this guy, sitting at table solo, thick, tortoise-rimmed glasses... open book before him... another book, sitting besides, inside a large Ziploc bag - title: "THE SECRET OF THE AGES" ~hmm, what does he know?~ - glance at title of chapter he's reading: "Medieval Magic"... open glass cooler door, grab an OJ... walking to cashier, take in a deep sniff of the fried chicken, which the Mexicans are cooking up on smoking griddles behind cold-cut display cases ...

head out, pass guy wearing 'Eyebrow Threading' full-body sign, handing out quarter sheets - take one ~sooner he hands them all out, sooner he's off the clock, - help a brotha out...~ ... ~aah promotion... we're all promoters for something to one degree or other... *what* you promote is the kicker... – I'm on path to promote art - and what else is art besides praising things -places, concepts, colors, shapes, people, sounds, on and on... – promoting praise...~ pass a Hispanic lady talking loud on flippy cell phone "That's right – you guys went and saw Madame Butterfly togethah... – and we saw – that's right uh-huh..." – fades into overhearing this guy on cell: "I was kinda – it skeeved me out at first..." – fades away... -

Woman sets down dufflebag full of bananas and green apples – hands me a banana – with flier: 'Free Spinal Checks'... guy wearing sunglasses, stack of papers in arm, tries handing an 'Epoch Times'... here, two Asians - arguing heatedly in their language – over two boxes of lightbulbs, both held in the one's shaking hand – the brand printed on boxes: 'SKYLARK'.

Wander over, into, Whole Foods in search of free samples... an employee squints a glare as I fish third helping of pear slices out from plastic orb shielding them... head over and find a table next to the deli covered with small paper plates – each with a dice-sized chunk of energy bar on it... As nibbling on second featured flavor, hear lady next to me – at deli – "*no-no* – not so many carrots..." – tight perm ~wound~ – small Mexican guy gets picking them out... – "that's right – a few more... – there *there*, that's good – now if you put some more of the other stuff in – *no-no* that's another carrot there – that's right... – a little more..." she senses my staring at her, melds on a tight, intense smile, glaring at the pasta salad... - and it zaps into mind – a scene of me walking around in Whole Foods – with a small stereo in the inside pocket of jacket –

one that puts out a good sound...– at strategic times – such as one just wit-
nessed – or barges in line – or even intense reading of ingredients – or by just a
particularly intense look - pressing play - and on comes the tune *"Freak out...*
(that distinctive lil' guitar) aaaaaAAAFeak out!" – video taping it all perhaps
~possible seed for a film to appear in an upcoming show? – edit – choose best
bits – be strategic in inviting as many of that (type A) crowd to big gallery
opening, - gauge facial expressions, reactions – film that as well?~ ... ~then
again... who has the time?~ And I buy a big 79 cent bottle of water (though
they say these things don't break down in landfills) and walk out into a
depressed, eerie 2pm Chelsea... to meet Elliot in Brooklyn at 3 ...

"Our next show is at Philadelphia's 'first Friday' – you've been?"
putting Verb coffee to lips "heard of..." (all the galleries open up in Old
City section, first Friday of each month – streets teem with students and arty
crowd) ...
We're sitting out front – next to a mastiff dog, leash tied to chair, ears up,
peering in café for master ...
"put that pencil to legal pad – you got a week – make it rich – *just don't go*
ruining my act again heh-heh"
"you're gonna have to open the wallet wide for this next one..."
"You've something in mind already?"
nodding yes... "I'm living in a homeless shelter these days."
"Thought you were up in Spanish Harlem?"
"that was just a one bed room – he let me stay a while on futon..."
"Denis is looking for roommate – you have some cash in your pocket
now..."
"Seriously? I'd fork over a deposit tonight..."
He beeps at cellphone... and

here I'm a week into staying with Denis – who, discovered first night, is an
admitted insomniac... – when I go for bathroom breaks he looks up from the
couch in dark living room - some obscure foreign film, from local video store,
on the TV ("went through all the others – working through foreign films
now...") ...

Saturday morning before first Friday... ~must... go in search of... inspiration...~
search online for hiking in the area ...

Ride a bus out to Bear Mountain ...

Start hiking up... – here, a group of orthodox Jews ~hm~ congregated – ~some sort of... retreat? daytrip?~ - the kids, in black, stare sets of wild eyes at me, passing by... – curly forelocks dangling down from black skullcaps... press forward... up rocky winding path... through afternoon... - insisting some profound... ~revelation~ awaits up top ...

... ~what is it... beyond what it is?~ - ~define *it*... – but it's contextual... – slippery like that... – ('that(?)')~

incline begins leveling off – gray clouds rush overhead - lightning flashes - ~oooookay~ - speed-walking down... down... down... forty minutes... no rain... just... wild, semi-darkness... – here, the Jews again – reacting strongly to storm clouds – and me – one has a boomerang in hand – long wooden one - tips painted red... – cocks it back – powerful throw... - far – rises - the bend – return – reactions from friends – screaming – running - himself running, hands waving in air... – last second stopping, facing – catching ...

And here, waking on Tyler's futon – having stayed over after arty party at his place... eyes scan room, getting bearings – bottles and cups all over ...

rise, walk out ...

walking on 116th street... early June, early morning – merchants getting an early start on a Mexican or Puerto Rican weekend festival – setting up their tables – here a guy arranges cowboy hats (with Rican flags sown on them) just so on a table... – a woman, positioning a large, plastic, transparent, neon pink, lime green, purple, etc – alien-head-shaped containers for daiquiris, margaritas – plastic straw tubes sticking out of them... here, a guy seated with a mass of balloons and inflatable super heroes at his side, ready for the day's sales... – eyes linger on an inflatable Scooby Doo sledgehammer in passing.... subway to Chinatown – all the black gum dots passing under feet, heading for the buses... pass vendors – glistening fake watches... pass jewelry stores - 'POPU-LAR JEWELRY'... - "LUCKY JADE JEWELRY"... pass a parked cop car – motto on scratched door:

Courtesy

Professional

Respect

gnawed buffalo wing bones scattered about its back wheel, half sunk in a black, rainbowy puddle. . .

Board China bus, dollar cup of coffee from 'White Swan' bakery in hand –
dollar Poland Spring in other... take seat back right... gaze out window as we
pull off – listening to Metallica on ipod as barrel through tunnel – emerge -

stretch of factories, sending up their puffs of smoke... billboard:

GOD BLESS AMERICA

HOME OF THE BRAVE

crossing bridge... – look down on gas station overhang, black... – lighted
red word on face of it: 'POWER'... - overhang next it – lighted red word:
'DIESEL' ...

here, an airport... – a plane, forcing its way into the air – soars over bus ...

read through today's New York Times... till Philly skyscrapers appear – a
light turquoise – in distance, as we cruise over enormous bridge ...

sitting in subway heading for 2nd Street – here, bearded black guy, reading,
wearing t-shirt: picture of a green alien – big almond eyes, one hand upraised,
words arching over it: 'TAKE ME TO YOUR DEALER'

And here we are – Elliot, Denis, Shaun and I, eating big cheesesteaks at 'Liberty Bell Pizza' on Race Street, hammering out details for the show ...

And here we are at 'Gallery Stark' on 3rd Street, 7pm.

2nd and 3rd, Cherry, Market and Arch: swarming with people – weaving in
and out of galleries, plastic cups in hand, - live bands set up, playing out on
sidewalks... – artists with their work laid out on blankets for sale... guys calling out – selling their "collections of short-stories – based right here in Philadelphia!"

At our space Elliot pumps and pours cups from keg (got from local 'Yards'
brewery)... standing room only – DJ ANSER (famed Philly dj) pumping out
avant garde sounds - Euro dance, trance, electronic, techno, house, his own
creations... – paintings on wall are huge abstract pieces by Shaun – which he
allowed Denis to draw on – thick black and white geometric shapes ...

7:30, Elliot gives the nod... Shaun gets up on a table – music cuts off... –
calls for everyone's attention – requests a semi-circle form around one piece
(which he, hours ago, covered with Vaseline and gasoline) – "here we have a
painting of mine!" – puts lighter to it, flicks, flicks again – 'foOF!' – up in
flames – a girl screams – runs for door – "carry on everyone" – music blares
on... – and I've 40 minutes before I'm on... - many here – tuning into a few
conversations - have read about our Williamsburg show ...

press through crowd – a bunch of New Yorkers mixed in – and out door...
~go bumble through the galleries a bit – blow off steam...~ – left on Market,

left on 2nd – into big space – cartoonish paintings on wall – packed with people on ground level – plenty upstairs on loft as well… stepping in – here, a painting of a … ~fantasy planet of sorts~ – robotic things lurking about on it… – next painting over: a scowling cartoonish girl - bright purple hair - perky breasts about bursting through purple tank top… ~well, plenty of skill required to make something like this – tip hat to that, but uh… who's gonna hang it over couch… – or anywhere for that matter… – who knows – maybe it'll sell – some comic book store owner or…~

Half a block to 'Artist House' – a quick look in window… detailed realistic paintings, lil' realistic sculptures… walk on - ~snap a picture, save yourself some time… – consider the village scene painting there – 'ooookay – I catch the vibe – 'a village', 'relaxing'… uuuh – oookay… that's like… *it* then – that's all the bone you're gonna throw me – that's all I got to work with here?… hmm, ok, a village… yeah… well… is what it is… – been there, done that – (bye-bye mystery)… – ok-ok, golf clap – I'll grant you that - you have a very steady hand – you've copied the real thing masterfully – if fact, cookies for you – someone get this man a cookie…~

Pass a bunch of galleries… dip in one – here, a cluster of cut lil' segments of garden hoses, glued to a piece of wood… ~ all those hours that went in to making this… – was it all fueled by… hope of someone writing out a big check for it?…~ walking out ~and how about the auctions – like at Christies and Sotheby's…– 65 million for a Jasper Johns painting of a flag… someone could throw the 'meanwhile children are starving in Africa' at that action…~ - ~and how many galleries have I walked into – polished – owner stiffening – restraining message of 'you are a poor student, you can do nothing for me – *there's the door!'* – I can pick up on it soon as walking in - ~the money tip~ – can sniff it in air …

slip in another - huge photos of mountains on walls – people in awe at them "can you believe the *scope*…" one says, wide-eyed.

look it over… ~well… is what it is… big mountain… lake…~ -

and here, the old artist - two people congratulate him - suddenly walk off, and I'm standing close, face to face…. guard down, he offers a hand "Roy Shelling."

"Ah" shaking hand "right…"

dynamic turns thick at my lack of praise or chatter – I'm just… standing here… – his eyes beginning to dart… – he can't contain – even at this age – his *displeasure* – being caught with ~one whom he can't get anything from~ – not even a smoothing-things-over silence-breaking… it's apparent – large gulp from cup - he doesn't have the time for this - to speak to me – ten years ago, maybe, - now though, no time to make a new relationship – at this stage in life - he watches his time – gives it to a select few – watches his words – watches who he gives them to – only important people – and look at this moment of time he's currently in – how he perhaps had such grandiose envisionings of how his opening, would happen – and now (could it be!) he's standing with this teen-ager wearing a corduroy blazer, orange t-shirt, thrift store dress pants, sneakers? You'd think you'd reach a stage wear you can mask it – but not Roy Shelling – as he attempts relief via another quick sip from clear plastic cup – which is already empty though - raising of eyebrows – "heh-heh" - eyes darting – lock on one more important – smile snaps on – "HEEEYyy *You!*" – breaks away, engages …

Out, over, into F.A.N. – wind up rickety Old Philly Historic House stairs – to where a string band is playing upstairs …

down onto Arch Street… pass the 'Betsy Ross House' ~is that where she sowed the flag?~ - right on 3rd… here, 'Iron Works Gym', ~getting in on the 1st Friday spirit~ – doors open – promotional girls pouring Peroni beer into cups – handing to rowdy students, clubby girls, packed, packing, in… turn in… walk through bright-lit gym – all the glossy-white-painted equipment – dolled up girls, tough guys, arty guys ~quite a mix~… swing into bathroom, sit on toilet… visualize through performance - in… look at watch – twenty min-utes… as drunk guys barge in and out door – pissing, farting, cursing, laugh-ing… rise, flush… wash hands… make way through gym again – more have showed – look up on balcony – girls, dancing, amidst (this one, on) nautilus equipment – mc on loft chatters into mic – commentary on the cheerleaders – in bikinis - performing a dance on the main floor – boisterous cheers from crowd… – now, a boxer – covered in tattoos – punches at hand pads of trainer – "this guy is an ab-so-lute animal, people – that's right he's fighting tomorrow night – I've seen him in the ring – he's a bell ringer – ladies and gentlemen, the man, is a beast – look at that power…"

right on third – weave in a few more galleries – and over to 'Stark' – as Elliot pulls case of wine from back trunk of his old, silver Saab - "you're on in like ten minutes man…"

Back stage, Brian Chirnowski (big construction worker from Green Point – friend of Elliot's) ties on a pair of cleats …

dutifully pull on my gorilla costume… fasten mask on head… – look in backstage mirror… – ~very realistic…~ – hear Elliot introducing the show –

"and after Zach's piece – be sure to *stay* and see my projection show - just in the other room here." –

Brian puts football helmet on (wing on its sides – matching his Eagles football uniform) opens door, walks into main space… stands… all eyes on him… laughing, cameras flashing …

Electronic music blasts on – I barge out door - run in – jump on his back – he lashes round – growling, trying to throw me off… – till, stops, stands, winded – music stops… "can I have a volunteer from the audience?"… laughter… pause… Denis (in disguise) shuffles in… – music blasts on - I jump off – dance around both of them – Brian, grabbing Denis up in bear hug – to… lifting him over head – "yyeeeaaaAAH!!" – I beat on chest "OO-OO-AA-AA!!" – and Shaun and Eric (also in gorilla costumes) enter scene – rejoicing, beating chests – as Brian throws Denis to ground – Shaun and Eric diving on him, pinning him down, flat on his back, legs kicking – as Brian struts over to his sports duffle bag… pulls out a can of whipped cream – "hold 'im down fella's!" shakes it up… straddles Denis' chest (Deidre – Shaun's girlfriend [acting as Denis' girlfriend] – starts intervening - tries to pulling Brian off "that's enough – let him alone! – someone help – this has gone too far!" - Steve Isner (Elliot's friend from Philly - playing fake cop) steps in, shoves her away… - Brian sprays the whipped cream - forming a big pile, overflowing out Denis' mouth - his legs flailing - in a kind of… death struggle – as I'm doing a crazy gorilla dance, circling them… to perfectly-synched, hig-speed electronic music – gauging expressions of horror through eyeholes… – Denis stops kicking – legs go limp – loud voice from sound system (Elliot speaking into mic backstage) "Now it's *yeerrrr tuurrrnn!!!*"

the other two apes jump up – to standing on either side of me… – we do a (pre-choreographed) dance for ten seconds – then leap at crowd – grabbing whomever –

I notice lots of tattoos on the arm of the guy I have a hold of – and it's ~*the boxer from the gym*~ – feel his right hook slam into the side of head – stars burst into streaming fireworks – as I… stumble backwards – half-see him through eye holes – in fighting stance – frowning – closing in – the wind up – another explosion of colored flashes… -

I'm in the hospital – the doctor, looking me over – frowning into my eyes – "hi there… – we're, uh, looking for some kind of identification…"

"Oh… I… don't have my… wallet…"

"well what kind of insurance do you have?"

"Insurance?"

"Yes, what medical plan are you on – or what's your name – we can look it up in the computer…" –

blackness – swirling colors – "Zzaaaach… Zzaaach-ch-ch…" – sounds in slow motion – looking up… – it's… Brian – helmet off – and Elliot – looking down – panic in his eyes – "*Zach!*" - senses sharpen – rightening of speed… Brian: "Zach – you alright buddy – c'mon, get up man…" –

"I'm good – I'm good – on with the show…"

Elliot stands:

"He's alright everyone – he's responsive – everything's aok – '*on with the show*' he says – right over this way everyone – slideshow's about to begin… – that's right – riiiiight in there…"

roll over on side… groggy-headed rise to feet… unzip, pull off costume… pour a cup of wine… walk in other room – jammed full – a young crowd – as music kicks in, slides flash on – the piece is called "Then. Now. To Come" - "Then" appears on screen – flow into a series of photos (he shot through the years) – of European Architecture – the exquisite detail, quality, craft, *TLC* that went into it – here, the Doma in Florence – here, buildings around the Louvre – Hamburg's Rathaus (city hall), - Prague – view from Charles bridge… – Rome shots… – Berlin… Budapest… Zurich – line of well-built, colorful houses (glossy paint on wooden shutters, flowerpots) curling up cobblestone street… – London - smart architecture – Cambridge… Oxford… – the vibes they all throw off… "Now!" – 70's architecture – square buildings – New York, Philly, row homes, suburbia – plastic siding on 'cookie-cutter' houses – sped-up video clips – the building of a 'McMansion' – 2x4 frame – drywall – siding – SUV pulls into driveway… – shots of big, looming, brown, high, rectangular, projects – all the balconies exactly the same (barred railings…) music, tying in – coloring - so well – Elliot, sweat aglisten on face – whipping hands between two Macbook Pros and many-knobbed equalizers… "Then!" – beautifully crafted – extraordinarily detailed Venetian glass chandeliers – here, brass-wrought ones – silver – bronze – the craft! the intricacy! the love! Flash to Tiffany lamps – the stained glass, kaleidoscoping colors - vid shot, circles round it… – pictures of hand carved wooden chairs from England, France, Germany… the designs! claw-footed ones – lion heads carved in – foliage – delicate patterns… hand woven chairs: solid… – "Now!" – pictures - shot at Home Depot – chandeliers - looking fresh churned-out off assembly line – ~just pluckt from conveyor belt…~ - painted black cheap steel frames – ugly shape –

alabaster... – shots of Home Depot metal-framed chairs – manufactured patterns on beige fabric padding... – cheap-looking futons... on and on – pics flashing so quick – crowd, transfixed – "Toooo *Coooommmee!*" – the cue for Denis - flips switch in other room – setting off sprinkler system – Elliot, shooting plastic tarp over computers in time – lights and music cut off - people scrambling, screaming in the spray – bumping about – tripping over, spilling wine on, each other – hollering – running out... cop car arrives – and I just... break off... bizarre walk... blocks after block... here, into... ~rougher area~ ... group of black guys playing dice game on front steps of run down row house... frown at me... ~'City of Brotherly Love' eh...~ look around... lowrider car rolls by – loud bass rattling it – lyrics –"bullets flyin' – *rat-tat-tat - straight rueffless!*" gauge vibe... ~more like 'city of open hostility'~

hours later, here, 30th Street Station ...

middle-of-night train to Trenton station, where new day dawns, study times on TV screen - for next rain to New York... - see 'New Orleans'... scenes form in mind – ~what if I were to just... go there ~ – play it out... – how wild would *that* be... – on like a Monday morning – just... going there... what to do upon arrival there... walk around the sunny streets... with the palm trees – and what that would do with regards to time... – who it'd baffle, - who it'd infuriate... – and why can't I do it... just, go, explore – how about just catching a train now to... Memphis – change trains there, proceed on to... Austin? – ~guess I could... – just, wouldn't be real... smart... – would kinda... 'jack things up' – why though... maybe it all has to do with relationships – 'being there' for people... and when you're not there - confusion and pain 'not-rightness', a 'void' - and people... 'give up' on you – (what a tribey element to people) - and you... turn into a 'drifter' and the years drift by as you... morph into a 'nobody' – and 'carry pain' around with you - which can't help but laser beam out through your eyes – into those of anyone you interact with – and they sense the eeriness – the unrest – a feeling of discomfort tingles in – and so they want to 'get away' from your presence – go find solace in tribe...~

buy trail mix from Arab mumbling into clip-on ear phone... $2.50 worth (a small brown paper bag)... awaiting train on platform... – you-name-the-culture: represented... song playing on outdoor speakers overhead "Heylaaa, heylaaa - my *boyfriend's back* – yyyeeeeah...".... I imagine a quicker way – ~perhaps the way of the future(?)~ – to get to NY from Phila... – ~would be via these... see-through tubes, which extend between cities (include Boston as well - DC too) - picture a business man or woman, climbing in - lay horizontal inside a thin cylinder in the tube... – this... *capsule* - powered by a jet engine –

shoots the business man or woman to NYC – they arrive in a matter of minutes...~

on train... guy across isle, watching a kung fu movie on portable dvd player,
eating Twizlers... look out window... passing a 'train parking lot' – hundreds
of train cars, sitting... ~think of all the stuff that gets hauled to a fro across the
country... – seems so like, 'grown up'... –when you whittle it down to core
though – it's really... pretty simplistic – stuff getting shipped from here to
there to keep people alive – or add to their pleasure... – depending on your
income – you have this or that level of pleasure-enhancing stuff available to
you... here, two of the cars, sitting next to each other – identical twins – clean,
big, bright white – across them: red, all caps: 'WISCONSIN CENTRAL'.

pull laptop from bag... ~another thing for the future, of course – enable
wireless in all trains – in whole cities – across the entire land... - I heard Philly
was gonna be the first city to go totally wireless – but 'Tempe Arizona' (of all
places) beat them to the punch, made it happen... that's what I'm talking
about - enable wi/fi all over NYC, Boston, name the city – rapid increase in the
spread of knowledge... – think how faster things would go – how much
quicker you'd have answers to this, that – how much good reading you'd get
in... all the music, films... – how you'd get to places faster (directions at fingertips) – and global communication - so much more of it – video conferenc-
ing with video cams - cultures fusing... – think of some war breaking out –
friends effectually snuffing it out – sending a few e-mails – what's going on
here? what's the deal? – Ah, ok, that's the beef, eh... Hm, interesting, well, what
do you think, let's work it through... How's it going over there?" - communication between youth – eliminating possibilities of older egotists throwing
them into armies - to go spill each others blood... – think Expansion of knowledge! putting laptops in people's hands – moving progress forward faster...
Our generation: huge leaps!~

CHAPTER 16

The show is all over the papers in Philly, New York, beyond …

Reporters and artists show up unannounced at Elliot's studio. –

"I can no longer paint with my garage door open… – then the fumes get to me…" sitting at Style café on North 11ᵗʰ, latenight – "but it's been driving me out more – shooting more footage - speaking of which I'm gonna need your assistance – you with your… *presence*… – I have a few locations over the next couple days… – I can edit it all up in time for a Chelsea show we're signed on for - at the end of the month – Tyler has a *lot* of people on board – we're giving him a pretty big cut, in fact, - if that's cool with you."

"fine… you handle the money matters…"

Shannon and I myspace occasionally… comments on what she reads about me in the papers… – and here, she's… visiting a friend in Brooklyn this weekend, suggesting we meet up …

Type a reply – give the venue of the concert Elliot and I are heading to tomorrow night …

In morning, her reply: "cya ton" …

Standing, kind of… in a daze, staring at band, setting up on stage… – Elliot, lurking off to the side, along wall… Shannon shows – looking very pretty - radiating joy – exaggerated, clingy hug, stretches a long time… – her friend – "this is Sara" is gorgeous… -

"Yeah this place cards" I say – forgot to mention… – my friend got me in – you got in somehow?"

"We have fake i.deeeees."

We're catching up – the cocktail she's sipping at, giving her a giddy vibe – as she launches into how she "hates" her new internship – how "HR" won't let her "take off two days - even though I'd have the work done…" – on stage, acclaimed band "Schternburner" continues setting up – with their tight black jeans, tight t-shirts, long hair… start sound checking - I feel a gripping in stomach… looking over at Elliot, he smirks, gives the nod, pulls cam from pocket, points it at band – lil' red light turns on – points it to me… – cutting Shannon off – "I'll explain later – I gotta do something real fast." – step forward – put hands to mouth to project voice, call up to lead singer: "You're bound to your guitar man!" –

"what are you *doing*?" Shannon hisses, grabbing arm.

Pointing at base guitarist "you're *bound* to you're guitar – these have all been passed down to you – you're all taking cues from the past – you too drummer! You're all just doing, repeating what you've seen!"

"heh-heh, thanks dude." says lead singer "thanks for sharing."

Elliot panning back and forth between me and band - I call "it's been this way years and years – decades – you're falling in line with it… - guitar plus microphone plus drums equals rock band! You're in a box! Where's the thinking outside it? where's originality? – where's newness, innovation, evolution?" faces are frowning, cursing at me… "*let's get out of here.*" Shannon snaps, yanking me away by sleeve… "have another dude." the lead singer says into the mic, tuning his guitar – as I see the red dot on cam blip off …

– the bouncer – shwooshing in – powerful over-reaction – grabbing sleeve – pulls me through bar area - shoves me out door - into a run to stay on feet …

"Are you *crazy?*" demands Shannon – Sarah, covering her mouth in nervous laughter …

Elliot: "way to go bro – catchyalata" – jogs into night… "That's Elliot – my… artistic *colleague* – we're collaborating on a new piece – he was filming off to the side in there… – it'll be in an upcoming show we're doing. – I'll invite you to the reception…"

night unravels into Sarah's friend's party (the fashion crowd – Sarah, a model and stylist – met Shannon in London – studying abroad - roommates in a dorm) – to Shannon and I having words in the hallway "you're *flirting* with Sarah – right in front of my eyes!" – a door opens, neighbor's head sticks out "hey could you keep it down, - we're trying to sleep – the music – people in hallways…"

"Sure, I'm going now…"… to Shannon's… sad… beautiful face… "I'm gonna be filming with Elliot tomorrow – but on Sunday let's meet up – we can have one of these… 'serious talks' you've been so keen to have…"

"call me"

"aalright, ciaaooo…"

Elliot and I… walking through Pratt's campus… sensitive students, being arty, sitting in clusters, talking… - some walking solo, broody ~broodily~ …

Elliot's friend Brett signs us in - at desk with security guard - to one of the buildings, brings us to his painting class – "alright, here we are… – here's where we go our separate ways – do your bit and go – and *don't* get me expelled…"

We wait in hallway… looking in through window on door… see professor call students together for a demo… he talks… lecturing… then – soon as he swipes a brush stroke on canvas – red light illumines on handy cam, and in we go …

"You know you're bound to that paintbrush." I say to the professor – student's heads snapping swivels… – fear entering into old, gray-bearded professor - "who are you? – get that camera out of here - or I'm going to call security."

"no matter who we are. – just here to say – that brush, those tubes of paints – the stretched canvas, gessoed – you're bound to it – and it's all passed down – you've seen it called art – and so you've picked up those same tools that others have used – in search of, perhaps, a piece of glory – and where did they get the idea to use brushes and canvas - followers following followers – can this be called art anymore – this – going on a system passed down - which *others* thought up?"

"Who let you in here?" standing "I'm trying to teach a class here… I'll have to ask you to *leave*." – "I'm calling security." – he takes up phone, dials …

to petrified (save Brett's smiling eyes) freshman students: "just letting you all know you're paying hefty sums to take cues from the past – doesn't look like he wants you hearing this, does it - but hey… here to say it's time to think outside the brush-and-paint box."

The guard who signed us in grabs hold of arm – Elliot rolling –

"juuust exercising my freedom of speech here in this free country…" –

"well that's good to hear" says guard "but you're gonna have to exercise that *outside*" –pulling to door …

"heyyy now" pulling arm free - and he snaps into over reaction – diving into bear hug – knocking over an easel - clangs across tile floor – dramatic push out door… – Elliot flicks off camera and we sprint from the campus, flee on subway …

to MOMA, where, Elliot (discreet, off to side) films as I examine a huge Cy Twombly scribbly drawing/painting (one of his Four Seasons canvases)… – I lean in veeery close – "'scyuze me sir – please step back from the art" says tired-looking guard, walkie talkie in hand… give him a confused look, resume examination… slide # 2 pencil from behind ear, pointer and thumb pinching back tip, move it slow towards piece– "*scyuze me* sir – *sir - no touching* the art-work." – stop the pencil's advance, look over at him –

"Oh, I'm just going to make it better. – one line – right here – it would make it a *stronger* piece… just gonna jot it in." –

"sir *step away* from the art" – he whispers something into the walkie talkie… – "sir you're going to have to *put the pencil away*." – I quicken pace of pencil towards piece –

"I'm just going to make it better that's all – one thin line – right here…" - he karate chops my arm – sending pencil bouncing on floor – "now I told you to put the pencil away" – I swipe it up - quickly move it towards canvas again (Elliot circling – getting angles) – and guard hooks arm – to behind back – other guards jogging in – this lady – eyes wide in fear – this guy – grabbing shirt collar, hooking other arm - bumping first guard aside – pain shoots through body as he wrenches a… full nelson – pushing me out of the room – hear side flap of handy cam snap shut - Elliot wrestles me away - "it's – ok – it's ok – he's here with me – he's a little unstable – I'm here now – I wandered away – sorry about that - we're leaving now – it's ok – it's ok… we're going…" we're brought to the front door – seen out, - Elliot, walking along, serious-faced in concentration, viewing footage …

CHAPTER 17

Rise next morning... feeling like... ~a depressed fly, caught in a web of insignificance – the spider, fast closing in~... walk from bed – as is – no shoes outside ~is this... 'on a whim' or... insanity... or...~ - big coffee from Verb... over... down stairs – stopped at turnstile 'INSUFFICIENT FARE' blinks... pull wad of cash from pocket... feed machine... card pops out... to platform... speakers over heard: "If you see a suspicious package or activity on the platform – *do not* keep it to yourself – tell a police officer or MTA employee... *Protect yourself...* Remain alert and have a safe day." ... L to Union Square... "where to next?" bumbling round... step in random subway, pulled up ~wherever it takes me... 'takes(?)')... looong, eerie ride over Brooklyn bridges... nodding off... – ~where's my... place?~ repeating, over and over, uncontrollably... to... swimming colors... -

"This is the *last* stop on this train"- head snaps up, automated voice - "everyone *must* leave the train – thank you for riding MTA *New York City Transit...*" – doesn't really register though – plump, black lady - gold necklaces, bracelets and rings - wearing fluorescent orange vest, navy blue pants, sweeping trash into scooper – "you *gots to go* hun."

Bumble onto platform... sign: "Coney Island" ~par for course~

Down stairs... head for ~main draw~ – the ferris wheel across the way... stop, pick up a payphone receiver, roll in two coins... "yeah Hi Shannon, about our talk today..."

"What about it?"

"Uh, I'm in Coney Island today."

"Okaay..." emotion entering in: "are we going to meet?"

"Up to you – if you're up for cruising out here – pretty interesting place, really – kind of a fantasy land of sorts… – an attempt at – which counts for something…"

"Are you ok?"

"Yeah I'm fine – come on out here – we could have a heart to heart – I'll be right in the center of it all – just go to the central-most - epicentral-vibe-point - and you'll see me there – say, - the Cyclone roller coaster – at two o'clock sharp."

"Sarah and I were going to go shopping –"

"go then – whatever you feel like doing. – everything is totally fine with me - perfectly acceptable at this point… – I'll be there at two – show if you show – be it all as it may, one way or other – aaanyway, have fun shopping dear…"

"Zach what's wrong?"

"nothing's wrong - gonna get going though… – if I don't see you - I'll… send you an e-mail or something – ok ciiaaooo." Slam down receiver… proceed to… bumble around - wrapt in thought - solid hour or two – out-of-head stuff – seemingly *out of body* at times – concepts reeling themselves over and over – fuller force each time through – most about direction – *directions* – ~possible routes to go in life~ – the number of possibilities… – here amidst booths filled with stuffed animals – guns mounted – ~hit a target, win a stuffed animal…~ – guy with microphone clipped to ear: "Yaaankee *Doodle Dandy* time – let's step right up and give it a *whirrrll!*" in head is storming: ~how could one think of going a road past generations have trod – thinking their thoughts – emulating their activities – *being what's already been?*~ - catching a glance of my reflection in the plastic of an arcade machine – hair all over… people staring at me as I go by… – suddenly zaps in that I'm supposed to pay Denis rent today ~gotta pay rent… gotta… pay… rent… to live in a sheltered space… gotta – have to… pay paper bills – which I got from doing activity to allow for me to stay in out of the rain… – to 'keep me warm' in winter… – to 'keep me alive'… gotta… pay money… to stay… alive… to… live… in… current… system… by paying… feed… the… engine… – the mode of things… perpetuate… the system… – it… pats me on head… "good pawn…"~ shake head "*rrrr!*" - ~solutions over griping – choose solutions over griping – solutions over griping… – solution-orientation pro-active (pro*activity*).~

look to left - at booth - black basketballs, lined up – lime green alien heads printed on them – basket ball hoops set eight feet back – Puerto Rican gal chattering into head-set microphone, doing a little dance to loud music playing… make a certain amount of baskets, win one of the stuffed playboy bunny heads, hung up about the blinking walls... – or a stuffed Dalmatian... – the climax of the song peaks as I walk by – she swirls into a dance move – long ponytail on head leveling horizontal... –

and this guy again... "Yyyyankee doodle dandy time folks – step right up - step up, step in, *geeet* ready to winnn..."

can't find a clock anywhere ...

hone in on a guy's watch – as it blurs around, yanking at arcade game joystick... *1:50 already!*

Lean against entrance to Cyclone... hear it run through its cycle... again... again... - a nearby video game repeats – "Yyyeeeaah! Contra *Strikerrrrr!* - with its drumbeat - about every thirty seconds... watch the Cyclone about ten more times through... ~well after two... hm...~ walking, sunk, away, ~aaaaaahhh well~ - feel hungry... – head for Nathan's ...

Sit, sad, pushing hotdogs into mouth ~solace~... one... two... three chili-cheese dogs... wrap fourth for the road... walk through carnival area – past 'Virtual Reality Rocket' (shape of a minivan – people in line to board... it... shakes around for 5 minutes – some kind of screen inside, simulating this or that)... walk up slow incline... onto boardwalk... ~try my luck~ at... getting a cup of beer... the small Mexican guy hooks me up... sit on bench... watching the ocean, drinking it down... look at the people on the beach... here, two fat Hispanic girls - bodies hanging out of too-small shirts, having a giggly, falling-down catch with a beach ball on the cold sand... and all these other ethnicities ~like the United Nations around here~... unwrap fourth chili cheese dog... – still steaming... four big bites... rising, heading, chewing, into carnival scenes again... sunny... feeling buzz... – eye contact with carrousel horse as it glides by... – buy a yellow corn on cob on stick – gnaw at it, walking along... no line at the Cyclone entrance, pay the $6... here, pouring down last gulp of beer – fold cup, stuff in pocket – get in car near the front... – sit alone... here, a girl – looks 14 – perfect skin, clean gold hair, sky blue shirt and eyes - ~so innocent~ - looks at me – sees the teeth, chewing at corn... – the fresh chili stains on shirt... – frightens her... - hesitation – steps back, will wait for next run ...

~old wooden coaster... gonna be a joke~ here, clicking upwards... arch... into... *descent* - stomach feels like it shoots up - knocks against back of teeth... butt, raised clear off the seat – pen behind my ear flies out... – third drop - mind goes code orange – picture a stream trailing from mouth – showering into all the screaming mouths behind me – them tasting – it registering in their heads... to go from experiencing elation to revulsion - *like that* – do to communication of tastebuds to brain... ~Oh, oh no, here it comes~ - ~man, I, -I

thought these accidents just happened to others - - - am I gonna be *'that guy'*?~
- cheeks bulge – but I lock it in - ~sheer power of will~ - force it all back down
again… and we clank into the boarding area… legs wobble as I exit - "hey"–
smiling guy with his girlfriend, passing - "think you might wanna hold on to
this." – my pen …

walking around, queasy… feel liquid rush up - cheeks bubble out – eyes
lock on a trash can – the lid is a big clown head - its mouth opened wide… leer
over to it – fall to knees - loud - projectile - solid minute… senses slowly…
coming to me… ~I'm insane~… ~it's ok though… seeing as everything is the
way it is – is going to be the way it's going to be - can't be any other way –
acceptance of this – of what is –of what's to come…'~ ears pick up – registration in brain - automated laughing – "heeeeee-hee-hee-hee-hee… hhh-
heeeeeeeee-hee-hee-hee-heeeee" look over, up… - a furry, mechanical ape ~of
course~ wielding a banana, gun-like, in hand ~naturally~ – laughing…
~laughing at me…~… wipe mouth… eyes scan to right …

Shannon… serious-faced… arms crossed… – little-girl frown on …

"I've been following you…" she says.

"Oh?"

She helps me to feet… we go, my arm round her shoulder… up onto the
boardwalk… sit, look at ocean… – "I'll be right back – can I get you a
drink?" –

"Uh, Sprite?"

go to the same Mexican guy …

"Sam Adams and a Sprite…"

see the Sprite on counter and start guzzling it down – "another Sprite
please…"

hand it to her over at the bench… –

"Are you drinking a beer?"

"Uh, yeah – Mexican guy – could care less – we have an… *understanding*
thing going… – you know in Europe it's 18 – that's more like it – I go by a new
set of rules now – guess you know that by now." ~besides, I'm insane.~

"So, relationship talk…"

"Ah yeah…"

"What is it? How does it stand?"

"Stand?"

"How -"

"I know – I know – I get the question – I like how you communicate… –
you're very frank – unlike other girls – that was a big attract initially - when we

first met – I picked right up on it… – I give girls time – it's like a game – to see how fast they bore me… – usually happens when they blow a fuse over some minor thing – I see their limit in that - and interest in them just kinda… goes… – but I stuck with you because you're unique in how you get right to the point and you're very much about the truth – into what's going on – *really* going on - through and through…"

"ooookay, glad you feel that way – back to the point -"

"*see* – heh-heh…" gulp from beer "aaahhhh… yyyeah *Coney Island*…"

tongue working at dislodging a piece of corn, stuck in teeth… -

"I now see – what one could say – the 'raw essence' of things – this all a preface of sorts – to our talk… - I mean" sweeping hand to refer to the carnival scene behind us – "look at all this – it's all… clear to me… everything is just clearer and clearer to me… – bares itself before me – ever since the shipwreck… – something happened with my vision… – and thinking – whole psyche… – it all ties together… - I *see* things for what they are…"

"a regular Superman on our hands here…"

"one could say…" – dislodge the piece of corn, "cheekily." think of the yellow piece, not digesting, making its way through… -

"I'm serious – I look at - and gage the energies of people – I *read* people – see inside them – see motives – right off bat – things just unravel naked before me – and organizations – their driving forces – everything, clear as a bell… – I look in your eyes and I see concern for the future – what to do with regards to school – which degrees, which career… – very American…"

"that Sam Adams is kicking in."

run hand through my hair – pang of embarrassment - flurry of dandruff falling… take up, finish the beer …

"you're wasting away in Margarittaville…" she says …

"I'm on the cusp of something *big* – correction, I'm *in* the bigness already – dwelling here in it – day to day - these are *prime* years… – just… – in a stage of sorting it all out, plotting, – gauging…"

a boredom sweeps over her… – amazing how you say one sentence and you open someone up – say another and things close down… – good communicators learn to surf this – control conversation – renew and renew and renew the vibe - sustain the amiability… ~I've dropped a 'cut off' bomb – no real redeeming things – seeing that 'forcing the envelope' would hint desperation – exacerbate awkwardness…~

"So you're not going to talk about our relationship. – I came all the way out here -"

"Ever think that we're to be figuring something out here – like – matching up names to meanings – cultures to functions -"

"So now you're not even going to listen to me?"

"Ok, ok…- again, you're different from other girls… – ugh, that word, 'different' – you get what I'm saying – unique – 'distinct' (no) – 'special' (no no no)… – this is another dilemma I have – the language we're like… caught in – limited by – I tip my hat to the Russians – a friend told me – 'Yuri' – a roommate at one of the shelters I was living in – he said their language has like *eight* words to English's one word… I'm big into – all for -more variety… - the extent of our vocabulary – the extent of our language – those borderlines – are the borderlines of our world – how, what we experience - our 'realms' – yeah, of our *experience* – there, *hit* it…"

"You're out of control."

"You used to like hearing me blab about 'philosophy'"

"You've gone too far."

"Anyway – I changed my name, did you know that – a while ago."

"to what?" –

"I like the sound of "Zach" – dropping the "ch" – make it a "k"

"Zak?"

Yeah, sounds the exact same – why 'ch' when it could be a 'k' …

"I guess… how about your last name?"

"just drop the second 'r'…"

"Are you going to go to the government - have it all cleared?"

"Too many hoops."

…"Change you're social security number while you're at it…"

"don't get me started… – like I was saying about structure - ever think there's a structure to things - that we're slowly to be finding out – slow revelation of how all the cultures were meant to work together - like a fine-tuned machine – each serving its function – like, Italians being the cooks - fashion designers, Germans the engineers, Chinese the factory workers – and pumping out all the plastic stuff, Mexicans the construction laborers, that sort of thing? – seems it's already… unraveling that way – but it goes out the window when you have cultures which are strong in more than one field – don't want to hamstring anyone…"

bored: "yeah that would be sticking things in boxes…"

…"I'm on safe ground in that I phrased all that in the form of a question… you can get away with anything, framing it in form of a question… – though, interesting, - I have a somewhat… ambivalent relationship with the question –

on one hand they get you out of tagging things – out of preachiness – yet, on other, can - if ill-used (and how often they are these days [though, people are catching on]) they can be drainers – they *want* –they demand… – so it's a 'hitting up' of sorts – which, sometimes people are up for – other times it's like 'dude, let me be' – depends pretty much on context – and *that's* a *huge kicker* in my book – context - you get that right, you're in, you are *set*…"

"that Sam Adams is really holding forth…"

"Ah, maybe loosening the tongue a hair – but the ideas I'm blabbing out – they were drummed up back whenever - when I sat, or walked about, sober as a judge… –

in any case, all this" - motion with hand to scene around us - "it's all… what it *is*…"

"Captain obvious… what's… *life* to you?"

"it… is what it is…"

"*which iiiss*"

"what it is."

"what, do you level everything with that now?"

"well,-" -

"It's like you think you're all special with your 'new vision power' – but really you've just like, melded into an android – ever since that shipwreck – you've become like… a pod person – what's that movie – the *body snatchers* – you and your arrogance – and no feelings…"

"I've become an artist… - actually I have very intense feelings – for ideals higher than these – styles that go *beyond* this – *way beyond*… - you see hints time to time – flashes of ideal y'know… – what I'm into – what I'm studying how to implement – and I think Elliot is too - though we've yet to vocalize it – is this concept of – this *duty*, now – of *elongating* the flashes – that Saturday morning vibe – ushering that clear into Monday morning –Tuesday - that's what I'm talking about - Wednesday, 9am – usher it all into a *permanence*… see what I'm saying? Feeling this? – more than stretching the vibe out - *creating* it – creation of joy – know how - and ongoingness y'know…"

"Yeah, well, good luck with that.".

"An extremely intelligent girl uttering the word 'luck'?…"

"you flatter me."

"it slides out…"

"It's Sammy. the goggles are firmly in place."

"vomited too much out - into clown trash can, you'll recall…"

"You're a nut… – what about this ocean?" – hand, sweeps, taking it all in – "surely this must… *move* you…"

"it is what it is…"

"What about relationships – between people – what does that mean to you?"

"… they… are what they are…"

"What about our relationship?" see tears well up in her eyes "what do you think – *feel* about our relationship, Zach?"

~one of those 'crunch times' in life I suppose… but… what… more… can I… say… than, well "it…" looking in her eyes "is what it is, Shannon."

Tear streams line down cheek – caught in lifted hand …

"Well I think I'm going to go now Zach…"

"Nipping-it-in-bud time?" – ~hm, bit flip.~

"Might as well…"

"Well, ok then…"

She rises, hurt smile, walks away …

~what was *that?*~ watch her… disappear in crowd …

Sit a long time… fall asleep - head propped on bench back, mouth open… wake up, sun-burnt face, no concept of time …

Bumble into amusement area again… as clouds roll in overhead, light rain falling.

passing go karts – a line. filing in – step into it – right to handing over bill – getting ticket – handing that to white guy in sunglasses, cigarette dangling from mouth – who rips it – walk past line of youngsters – revving engines in cars - painted colors of countries (flags on spoilers of each) – take seat in the red and white Japanese car… ~go-kart riding alone in the rain… *niccce*…~

Waiting for signal – more people filing in… a commotion in left periphery… looking over… a girl, lying on the ground, her friend, bending down, lifting head up, distressed – people just passing by – this one, canines, ripping top of a corndog off – piece of fried crust falling to sidewalk by lying girl's feet - her friend, fanning her now, wakes her up… she slides back – to sitting up, back against fence… fat Hispanic security guard/first-aid lady in dark green polo shirt appears, shooing people away, talking into walkie talkie, kneeling, attending to, in Spanish… hear the line of engines ahead of me racing off… foot mashes pedal to floor …

rain has the track slick… lay into the first turn full throttle – back end fishtailing – spun roud – French car – head-on… - straighten things out… pedal floored 'BRAAAAA!' lap. go on to pass everyone… – head, resting on hand, bored… feel the engine cut out, at times… – at strategic times… – see the guy with sunglasses and cigarette has a… remote control device - ~cutting engines at will…~… ~I see how it is…~

CHAPTER 18

sitting on swaying Q train, just three of us in train car, clanking over bridge, sun, setting, amidst skyscrapers in distance… stand up, walk over, put face to scratched up window… sky is a glowing honey sherbet color behind purple and rose buildings… off, somewhere in imagination land… – snap back into subway reality, soaring into black tunnel… slump back on bench… look up at posters – lined above: "America runs on Dunkin'"

and I have stacks and stacks and money – and I'm fed up with Denis' odd (growing odder) nocturnal behavior (hand-making masks for Halloween – in place of foreign movie watching… – looks up at me with crazed eyes as I walk by to bathroom at 3, 4am) – yesterday I awoke randomly – looked over at doorway – where Denis stood – his silhouette, there – hair froed out - holding a hot glue gun… "uuh, Denis?"
"yeah"
"you alright man?"
"….fine…"
"uuh, ok… could you, uh, close the door – thanks man - have a good night…"
coughed a hacking-death-rattle of a cough, and closed the door… – I stayed awake an hour …
~time for a new place… a better place…~
switch to L… emerge onto Bedford Avenue… pick up a latte at Verb… sit, looking out big window… ~quite the *scene* here~ – kids reading thick books, pondering, sound of cappuccino machine… – feel that… compel – muse - to snatch up pen - pin down essence of vibe on napkin… 'Movable Feast' floats to

mind – that first chapter… ~how top that?~ … ~this type of scene, here, that I'm, in, here, presently, - been so written about over the years – by so many…~ – ~another subject that's been written about, hashed through, harped on, book to book, to book: the whole leery daily-routine-of-life thing, notion: the whole 'eat, sleep, be entertained, repeat' concept - the 'where's the significance in it' – 'what's the use' thing… – how many writers have lamented on that one – how many packages can it come in? - yet where's the solution – after all these years – all these books – see them piled on used book store shelves, carts - no novel can really drive a stake into a cure-all… - People continue to bend brain over it – why we're here, what's going on – what's it all for… – unless you've checked brain at the door, are just floating along in the fog with the blissy masses… – all that said – could write about it these days – could work – can crackle – because times change… – new material, new possibilities…~

~energy, energy, energy…~ – remove new, long, # 2 pencil from pocket…– fresh-sharpened tip – tap it on yellowed marble circular table… – loud song playing – "I'll come running to tiiiee your shoooe – I'll come running to tiiee your *shooooe*"… over and over… Sunny out, table opens up… go sit in front… song shifts into (spilling out open door) "Who do you *neeeed*, who do you *looove*… when you come *undoone*…" guy leaning against mini-mall here – wearing yarmulke… forelocks… smoking – ~aren't they like… supposed to be holy? - why wear the yarmulke?~ reminds of a guy - in Madison Square Park a while back – hot day… eating lunch on bench – business guys to right, lunching as well – the one – in business attire – yet, wearing a tightly-wound, bright red turban - *dropping f-bombs* – the others, laughing it up… – doesn't the turban have something to do with holiness or… - why wear it at all? aaaanyway…~ -

here, a lady – curly, frazzled hair, head, jutted into shoulder, clamping phone to ear, frowning, baggy eyes glare at laptop screen on table, fingers chittering at keyboard… mannish voice firing orders… it strikes… ~everyone just… going around… trying to get what they want… is that how it is – is that pretty much it…. hm, thinking there's more to it…~

Sit… considering… options… right elbow propped on a metal-frame-covered-in-fabric divider, enclosing, separating us from sidewalk… people-watch the hipsters going by… a girl in red dress (big white flower designs on it) and ladybug sunglasses – stands, paging through book at bookstore next door - sudden wind gust – little tornado kicks up - of bits of leaves and dust – sudden clattery noise - heard above – wind blows her dress up – she shoves it, clamps it down - a square of styrofoam, falls from overheard, striped awning – floats down to… landing between us – and a kind of… shame seems to set in to her… she puts her head down, walks to the next rolling bookstand - faces me - quickly picks up another book… see her looking through her big glasses – gauging my response to the dress flying up like that… – but I'm in another world – which she perceives, relaxes – and the strong winds have passed - and an ice cream truck's jingle is heard… louder… passes… big dog – great-dane-mastiff-mix, here – owner, holding leash in pocket, looking grundgy under-slept… ~arty local~… ties leash to a small tree… dog, whimpering… till he emerges, large coffee in hand, spring water bottle under arm – talking on cell-phone – laughtery grumbles about last night's party… lights a cigarette, pulls water bottle from under arm, unscrews cap, pours it down into dog's lapping mouth… pours rest out along, over dog's body, back and forth – "ha-*haaaaaaa*" - into phone - "daaamn straight heh-heh-heh-heh-hehHA! – daaamn straight – heh-heh-heh—" – bottle empty, tosses it on nearby pile of droopy trashbags – as dog shifts into shake-off session – the spray – whole pel-lets - mingled with spring water - splashing up and down the side of my shirt, face – into hair …

"it's alright…" … slip into observation mode, people watching… the many sizes, shapes, of… bodies… passing… – the amount of… plump behinds, tired eyes… ~how the body conforms into what you constantly have it doing…~ so many… sitting at desks these days, gulping coffee, stuffing sandwiches in faces, staring at screens – then manic mania time - treadmills at the gym – trying to burn fat off belly, hips… – as they steadily expand bulge outwards and out-wards, ~metabolism, throwing up hands~ over the years …

someone's left a glossy art magazine on next table over… enter into an arti-cle on 'the best art books ever'… rip it out, fold, stick in back pocket, head for bathroom… lock door - ~…why lock bathroom door?~ - even atheists do this – why? – someone comes in and sees a partially naked body – is this from les-sons over years – instructions, norms – or is it built in – conscience… nurture or nature? (and what's 'nature'?) - are atheists following a moral code in clos-ing the bathroom door – a 'common sense of decency' – have they put the folder labeled 'going to the bathroom in a public place and leaving the door open for others to see me on the pot' into a cabinet labeled 'indecent'?…~

stand pissing into toilet, staring at quote, markered on wall:

"from each according to his abilities,
   to each according to his needs." – Marx …

~yep, looks good on paper (or wall)... doesn't account enough for the 'sticking of the brilliant and the slobs all in the same boat' factor... – can tie up – 'stymie' - some serious geniuses...~

zipping up... a pain, felt in stomach... ~that tuna from last night... well, might as well get it out of the system...~ turning round, sitting... eyes alight on another quote - in red:

"No talent – maybe,

But ideas..."

scrawled in black under it:

"Everybody has ideas.

That's the easy part."

unloading diarrhea... – *feel* the pain in stomach – ~unpleasantness~... ~suffering... – and how much more in store? – how many more instances - for how many more years... what's my lot in regards to pain... and what for? – why? really...~

but then... recall a retarded girl – used to live on our street... "a*why*'" she'd say... to just about everything... and it was kind of annoying... "why" can be needy, irritating, draining... yet there are times where it's necessary – *vital* - to ask it... and the pain leaves, flushing, unlocking, walking out ...

into mini-mall – into 'Internet Garage'... feed machine two dollars... - Bowie's 'The Man Who Sold the World' playing loud over head... type another paragraph for my 'Swedish Dreams' novel... press print, take, fold, slip in back pocket... bunch of new emails... click on youtube link - sent from Evan (up in Boston)... – a Vietnam Vet – pulled over by a cop... – all caught on tape by a camera attached to cop car... the Vet is drunk... resists arrest... – reaches in car for something – cop runs toward camera – guy fires once, hides behind car door... appears, aims, fires, disappears... cop shoots back... Vet appears, fires, hides, appears again, fires, fires, hides... cop, blasting rounds... – Vet appears, fires, hits... charges towards, cursing, fires again... gets in vehicle, brake lights go off as duel exhaust pipes puff smoke – car, shrinking into distance ...

go get a refill at Verb... sit inside, staring out window as Alan Parson's "Eye in the Sky" plays overhead... suddenly a kind of... feeling - *unction* sets in... – ~epiphany(?)~... an almost overwhelming feeling - *conviction* - that I *must* go for a walk ...

walking along... questioning, things, reeling in head... - ~is *this* what it is? – this high speed of thought vibe... venture forth in this 'avenue of thought' – this one... - is *this* line of thinking legit? – is *this* one right – more of a feeling, that one – requires words to elucidate, 'make-understandable' it... – *must* it be understandable? – how about this line? - does *it* hold any credence whatsoever – is it something I ought to be spreading – or am I totally off base? Could it be I'm… out of my mind? Is this where I'm going – is this where I'm at – is there a… threshold? – could I be beyond?~ - Suddenly feel compelled to… look up… two swallows – stare down on me, from their nest, attached to an old wooden beam… – we stare a long time… they look concerned for me… then they… seem to… grow in intensity… to like a… glowing state… and… *communicate* to me – like I… hear their voices - inside my head - "it's true, Zak… it *is* what it is… and that's all it is… – it's true… – *keep* going with it… you *must*… we're depending on you…" -

"Zach" –

"Elliot, heey…"

"you buggin' out or somethin'?"

"huh, oh – the birds - yeah that's, - I was just, staring… what's up?"

"heading over to Verb… you up for a coffee or…"

"Just had one… I was heading into the city…"

… - whisking ringing Treo from pocket, looks at screen "gotta get this – talk later ok – and c'mon"- snapping fingers - "snap out of it already." walking off "hello?"

~big cool art guy…~ … walking along… mind reels into the "heavy hitters" of the art world - who dwelt within this city over the years… the thoughts direct feet towards subway – to, here on platform, awaiting L… - ~too much coffee~ – mind ~reeling on rapid-repeat~ – the words 'patent pending' – repeat over and over… - now 'panzer tank' – picture it bashing through a wall – again and again… - to 'Gainsevorte Street' (a street from childhood – can't quite place where, just, it was… there - in neighborhood - dreamily -back then…)… next… 'Alexander *Girken*' – steady repeat… - on to a new name (never heard before): 'Sterges Terkle…' - ~Sterges Terkle – or 'Tirkel' – wait, yeah '*Terkel*'… – 'Terkles'(?)~ Union Square… up… outside …

to here, standing in front of famed "Cedar Tavern" on University Place… used to be *the* artist's hangout (De Kooning, Rothko, Kline, Motherwell, Pollock…)…. yet… ~what *is* this?… – look at it… - even back then… *look* at it… - where's the fun? it… *so* is what it is… - a dim bar, people drinking… a *physical* place… 'bye-bye mystically wonderfulness vibes' the pedestal I put that scene on – a few years ago up in Mass, daydreaming in Art Histoty class…. – *here it is* and it is what it is, cut and dry…~

Order a beer, get carded, exit, bumble round neighborhood in thought… – walking by brownstones… - ~new street – first time ever walked down it…~ -

~down(?)~ ~walked(?)~ – that's *past* tense – I'm walk*ing* it… 'first time I'm *walking* down it' - (down(?))… (~it~(?))…~ – hear a window sound – metal screeching on metal… look in that direction… a window, just opened – see the girl – don't quite catch face – brown hair swirling as she turns to go – see her body though – in black bra and panties – young – somewhat plumpish – not fat – just, healthy – curvaceous… ~functional…~ disappears behind lacey curtains - which flutter a bit by the motion of her going, nonchalantly, first-thing-in-morningly, away inside, ~to go do this or that… – what?~… and that's that – as I walk on –mind shooting off in new directions… try battling into focus again, striding through Washington Square arch… A list of famous artists reel in head… ~in this line of… what you do… tagging – sticking with you, again…~ the list of names rise… - like credits at the end of a movie… - now authors… ~could go on and on – movie directors, famous actors, musicians… politicians… – how each of them scrambled to… 'leave their mark' in this way or that – how they poured all that energy into that book – and then… that was it – out went the lights… - think of all these artists – 'famous' people – name the accomplishment that made their names live on… they, just, did stuff, pretty much… – this one did that, that one did this… they all seem after 'that praise'… for what they did… - fill-in-the-blank (their biggest 'hum-dinger' accomplishment)… does that strike vain or tedious or… what's the word… – 'trivial' – at this point? – Kerouac sat typing all night – night after night – to make a book, which people would read… – to put his *thing* out there before his lights went out… – Fitzgerald – wrote while battling off depression - to 'put his stuff out there' before his earth experience packed up and was no more… – all those who drew up the big Jap Animation hit movie Akira – all those hours, nights – chucking their ball of wax before it's over and done with… – then that thing – that thing they poured life into – latches onto their name – Daniel Webster – 'Oh yeah - he's *that guy who made the dictionary*'… – Jesse Owens – 'yeah *that fast runner guy*'… Salinger – yeah he '*wrote that Catcher in the Rye book*'… – man what a way to machine-gun down ambitions – the thought of what you put your mind and hand to – turning into that thing that people will stick on you as a label – as you live – and even after you're dead… – you're inextricably attached to what you do – it so becomes you – 'well, what does he *do*?' – 'what did he *do*?' (answer this or that) – gears aturn in head – registration – head tilts back – 'aaah, ok' – the guy's been categorized, filed – boxed… – and actors – boy they really get it… – James Dean – forever attached to 'East of Eden' (i.e. someone else's thought bubble idea dream vision accomplishment) – he got latched into it - it latched (is latched) to him – him (his name

now) to it… - and 'Rebel Without a Cause'… – puppet strings – writers, director, yanking at the strings – sure the actors infuse their style, flare, attitude -
but it's all in the confines of someone else's structure – someone else did the
arranging – the actor – 'memorizes the script…' - people wonder why he came
off so pent-up-with-angst! – think of you having to be remembered by your
connection to some *movie*! - and musicians – type into iTunes the name of a
dead rock musician – up pop five of their "top songs" – ugh, it's like, *'that's
them'* in a sense – 'that's there thing' – could it be! their… 'ball of wax'… - yet
some have more than one ball of wax –

the ambitious ones… – and what is it (these balls of wax – accomplish-
ments) other than building stuff up inside them – till out they throw it on others… more stuff building up over time – another hurling – on and on it goes…
– is a key figuring out how to – making surroundings conducive to – stuff –
unctions –building up inside – anything to this?~

…~heh… I could probably use (do for a) good punk show – proven anti-
dote when you're waxing too analytic on things – dissecting everything – chilly
scientist hat on… – ripe time to hit up a bonzo punk show – drummer going
bonkers - everything being just… *turned on its ear*… - explodes mind's con-
structs - blow all the lil' control-freaky boxes to bits…"

shake head, deep breath …

~I have a lot of thinking to do… very serious thinking… thinking that
requires… *solitude*…~

CHAPTER 19

I convince Elliot to get me a room at the Chelsea Hotel ...

I give him the money... He arranges at the desk... hands me the keys ...

"This looks like sitting on laurels to me..."

"We have shows lined up..."

"An apartment would be more logical - as I've already lectured..."

"paperwork, necessitation of identification... hoops... – as I've... made clear..."

"see you at the gallery tomorrow."

walk into the lobby – the couches, the fireplace, the art on walls – here, big painting of an off-white horse's head, facing viewer... and up to my room, top floor, plopping on bed ...

and it's show after show... bigger and bigger attendance... magazine interviews ...

and I can afford to stay at the hotel – and the staff treat me special, having seen me in the papers, on TV... –

and it's Elliot, popping up unannounced – "let's go – Mazda" - (his beat-up 90's van filled with video equipment) – "is out front..." and it's into it and highspeed to location – today – the financial district – suits all over the place, rushing hither-dither, ebb and flow ...

help him set up a white sheet to serve as a screen – right in midst of the morning rush – near big famous sculpture of a bull – video camera on tripod, catching it all... Sheet up, he grabs projector from Mazda... sets up generator... plugs projector in - connects laptop... calls up a video – "shot this in

Chinatown last night – got the go to get into the kitchen – and out back by the dumpsters."

Video projects big up on to screen… – mice, stuck to sticky traps …

People slowing to view… – the mice, in different stages – the initial fear-filled thrashing, struggling ones… the rapid-breathing, spasmodic ones – in middle stages - bouts of ~wriggling~ - and the later stages – helpless quivering, twitches – see resignation, setting it to the eyes… as life… goes from them… ~something… leaves the building… then… spark goes – just… belly breathing…~ – catches in one shot – close up - that *moment* of death… the change… last breath and… us all… standing, with others, who've stopped, watching… - "there goes that" says Elliot …

"no-no" I say – "there *that goes*…"

"whatever" –

"no-no, not whatever" –

"enough!" –

"*grave.*"

Graduated-from-top-colleges-go-getters-who-jog-in-spiff-paddy-running-shoes-and-spandex-in-Central-Park-on-weekends types snarl remarks in passing – sneer …

Here, a cluster of mice up on screen now – all stuck, one alive, quivering… helpless, scared …

Two cops approach… "You got a permit for this?"

and it all goes… so fast… Boston shows (old friends turning up, here, Shannon again)… Charity dinners… – here, one, raising money to fund building fresh water wells in Zimbabwe – in pitch-black of ball room, Elliot's video projects bright, crisp on huge screen – kicks off (loud – perfect match – electronic music playing along) with vids of families in Cambodia (Elliot flew over there to shoot it) who spend their days picking for redeemables in vast, mountainous trash dumps – bulldozers (blurry in heat waves) plowing heaps in the background – dirty birds flying all over… – the kids, sad-faced, barefoot – ankle-deep in green water… – flash to East Hampton – on beach – a family – Dad in rugby shirt, sunglasses, red Polo hat, reading thick book, Mom in sunglasses, sundress, sunhat, lifting black-red bottle with white label from yellow picnic basket, pouring the wine into two wine glasses – ~she always longed to be something bigger – go make it out in L.A. – up on the big screen with her 19 year old looks – but she just didn't go for it – now she drinks it off her mind on the beach next the rich 'husband' with kiddies!~ - blond little boy and girl pat at big sandcastle - happy Golden Retriever frolicking about – dark gray Range Rover – parked here, on beach, front wheels turned just so... kids now grabbing snacks from igloo cooler – 'Gogurts' – 'Polly-O' string cheeses – lil' OJ cartons with straws... now, putting on their fluorescent life vests, helmets... – trot giggling to their lil' waverunners – thumb full-throttle – into bouncing over surf out towards setting sun on horizon... long close up on their smiling laughing faces – spritzes of water splashing on them... – flash to close up on Cambodian child – music cuts off – those dark eyes, jittery, a fly, landing on nose ...

popularity grows and grows – and we're going to richy parties – and here, just signing some big contract at 2pm in a Midtown skyscraper – scrawl signature on line – happy handshake from suited Luxemberger... Elevator down ...
   through frigid glamorous lobby... spin through solid revolving door... hit by heat – feels ~120 degrees easy~... - as dark-skinned Arabic guy with beard across sidewalk – standing slouched next his smoking 'Yummy Halal' cart – enormous pile of red-sauce-slathered chicken, sizzling on its black griddle – where he stands – with all that smoke – temps probably upwards of 150 degrees or so – he's been there all day – I stop, stand, watch him execute an adroit chop through a piece of meat on the griddle – he scrapes spatula – it, held vertical – just its sharp blade tip making contact – towards himself, to stopping at edge – whereupon, he turns, his whole body, towards me - a sound is... coming out of his mouth, growing in pitch – like, two voices, together: "EEE*EEEE*" mixed with: "OOO*OOOO*" - simultaneously... I'm just... staring at him – he's, finished turning – is, looking... straight... into... through... my... eyes – making that noise – mouth opened in a kind of... square – ~guess this guy's... met his cracking point - this second - of all people to witness it... here... I... – ~poor guy... probably thought it would never happen to him...~ people are stopping, staring... the guy who just received a Styrofoam container from him, holding a five in hand for him - visibly uncomfortable, self-conscious at the staring – the... connection to, association with, this... and time's... going slow – it all seeming... staged – still happening – ~uuh~ - cellphone explodes into vibrations in pocket, stride off, answering "yeah."
   "we got the show in Geneva man..."
   "good deal" – phone into pocket... feeling heat... stick ipod earplugs in, press play, electronic song... influencing perception... everything looking zainy... crossing 6th Ave – right as tune climaxes– a white Lincoln (driver) hits a Mexican on a bike – up he flies through air – like a rag doll – leg bent odd –

plastic bags, still attached to handlebars, discharge plastic soda bottles - see he's... wearing white painter's pants – scene flashes in mind of his painter buddies - awaiting their sodas... having to get back to work eventually, wondering the whereabouts of Pablo, later finding out the news... he continues his arch through air - his clean black hair (in pony tail) - catching the sun, shimmering – mangled bike, flying along, following – its front rim, bent into a 'V' - and he hits the ground tumbling – to limp stop... – sodas bursting, fizzing, tapering off... but I, turn head forward again, crossing the street - observe people's reaction – one guy's jaw, dropping like a ventriloquist dummy – cigarette falling slow to ground... – cellphone buzzes alive again in pocket - "yeah?"

"we got the Brussels show."

CHAPTER 20

sitting here... been months and months... in hotel, in comfy chair facing window – open – wintry gusts blowing in – spiking up white lace curtains ...

~I've been sitting here for... what... two days?... – sure the bathroom breaks but... it's...~ slouched in chair here... – no drugs involved... just... deep sighs... blank staring... letting what happens, happen, within... - ~it's... – it, well, is what it is... hatcheting things down to size – to cores - stripping frills... – laying *it* bare, naked, quivering... – it, though, just, being so... *what it is,* nothing more... – how can it... and how can it, then, matter that much... seeing that, well, that's just... what it is...~ ... ~am I... hardening into a cynic? Is this... how that goes...~ – ~why is it (this, that) so... *more* to others... – and such... boring littleness – or series-of-hoops(y) to me...~ it occurs I... don't... know... the... date... - ~what does that matter anyway - if it's Tuesday, Wednesday, one way or other... – think it's Wednesday, actually... – what month?... uh, snow falling... December? January? ... – and this whole 'what does it matter' – how cliché *it's* become – so hashed-out, through – and what to answer from all the hashing?... – who has something to answer – send them to me – let's talk, reason together...~ -

a knock at the door ...

again ...

slow rise ...

creaky walk to ...

opening door ...

Tyler. Smiling, large Jamba Juice smoothie in hand ...

"Zach. Found out you were here."

"from who?"

"Elliot."

Turn, walk in, plop down in chair, resume gaze out window... hear Tyler enter, walk towards, slow... –

"Man, somebody's gotta get a sound system set up in here – stick in a Police CD – cue up song "So Lonely" – stick it on auto repeat, *crank* the volume up, and let it *rip*, heh-heh..."

"...He's in L.A. this week. He call you?"

"yeah, asked me to check up on you... *man*, it's been a while... rockin' a beard I see..."

"yeah, well... you got by the desk?"

"Elliot told me to drop his name, which I did – they got him on his cell, that was that... Elliot's big man... – and looks like you're making it big too, Zach... looks you're on the road to making it *real* big..."

"days just... seem... balls of yarn... Tyler... get it rolling in the morning... unravels... as it does... to till... night... fall... where it's... the lie... down... – ball ravels itself up as you slumber... – awaken with a new ball – and here we go again, unraveling time... life as a series of raveling and unraveling balls of yarn... and how much more of this... y'know... once you've... seen it... this way..."

Tyler, sits, sucking smoothie through straw, thinking..."

"... I used to listen to rock" I continue - "metal... - it would soar me up into such *heights* – it would so *charge up* – excite - *inspire*... and certain videos - was *so* into that concept of watching, say, Bruce Lee – then go listen to best electric guitar licks ever – I'd crop them from songs – on computer - - - harnessing that energy - transference of it - that energy - *into* my paintings - channeling it into other forms of art... – how music and films would launch me into... *elation*... - now... it's all just... so... *what it is*... to me... anymore... – One band after the next – listening to them – can see – gauge – that they... can only go... so... far... and that's... it... far as they can... go... I see the cores of everything – through cores even..."

"ooo, yerr *speeciaall*"

"seriously... with this clarity – this clarity I have – have had – a long while now – since the shipwreck - nothing gets close to upping things to those – to near those levels anymore – talking about *next* levels – *higher* levels... - see these books" – point to novels scattered about on floor – "they have... I'll have to hand it to them - they've been reaching – 'elevating me', if you will – to highest heights these days..." turning, looking him in eyes... "what was your most powerful reading experience Tyler?"

His eyes dart to ceiling, squint… "let's *seeeee*… aah… remember how I had to go to summer school that year… – that summer – between junior and senior year – I skipped classes one day - it was during a stage where I experimented with throwing everything off – any 'demand' on me – whenever I was totally expected to do something – or *had* to be somewhere, doing something at a set time – I'd just, jet off - to somewhere totally random… and just… gauge - the air, the ripples… – anyway yeah, so I skipped school and I was reading 'Dante's Inferno' that summer – and there was a heatwave on – it was like 110 degrees – and I went to the train tracks – by the Ber Wynn stop there…" I nod – scene of the affluent area appears in mind – "on that grass hill island - the streets on either side there – Range Rovers and Beemers rolling by – to in under – and emerging from - that stone bridge – where trains would cruise by periodically – man the *vibes* of that day – Shaun Dilks had a huge party set for that night – everyone was gonna be there – you were probably there – if you weren't traveling over in Europe or whatever… – so yeah I had that expectation thing happening – Andrea was gonna be there – Lisa – Rachelle - Eileen – all the hot chicks – all our buds – whole crew – so I had like a… comfort, haze, bubble that I was in, up on that island – and I just… read so many pages – so into it – so immersed – sweating – sitting in grass – reading of that… passing in through entrance – sign overhead 'Abandon Aaall Hope' – in that hell – *so* in that hell – as the heat was having its effect – and… walking over to 7 Eleven – across the parking lot – getting a quart of ice cream – Ben and Jerry's – Cherry Garcia – for lunch – and a, like, Pepsi Big Gulp – loads of ice… returning to hill – vehicles rolling buy – rich control freaks looking up at me – sheer derision in their eyes… as I ate that ice cream, reading – hours – in that wicked heat – about hell – very, *very* vivid – and heading to the party that night – completely off the charts - spanning clear into Saturday – returning to that hill – 7 Eleven breakfast sandwich in hand – vibey, wild, cloudy day - finishing the book – whole book in two days – no small book, as you know…"

nod, "nice one… - what's with 'nice' – 'great one' bro – very cool – what's with 'cool' - really 'awesome.'"

"what's with limiting yourself – say what you say… - you feel like saying 'cool' – say cool – let it flow natural man… – bag restrictions…"

"I'm uber-analyzing myself, language… pretty much everything these days…"

"gotta balance that man – strike that right balance - watch it doesn't get to be paralysis by analysis y'know."

"heh… anyway thinking of steering into writing – seeing it delivers – or "packs" – the biggest punch – most crackle y'know."

"What about that – "a picture speaks a thousand words" cliché – read to someone for an hour about hunger in Ethiopia and they're falling asleep – show them a photo of some skinny kid – glaring rib cage – big eyes pleading – viewers are welling up…"

"Selective writing - subject-matter-wise – i.e. writing about the ideal – where people would love to go, experience -"

"where's that?"

"Thinking it through, thinking it through… give me time… time… – and doesn't necessarily have to be a geographical place (obviously) – soaring readers up into worlds of new ideas – blowing doors off stuff that's been written – stuff sprung from cue-taking – monkey-see-monkey-do stuff y'know… – 'please publishers – check signers' stuff… – love this idea of advancing people into new realms – think of the composer Shostakovich in the 1700's – his music, unveiled in fancy orchestral halls – so out of the box – so *stunning* – it created *uproars* – he got *handcuffed* after one show - he went for it - *blasted* a new style into heads of monkey-see-monkey-do stodge-muffin control freaks – triggered in them something that just… *snapped* in their brains – to a point where they like, upped and started *throwing wooden chairs* – their blinders were *exploded* – and they were never the same since - unleashed into new realms – beyond realms – into new levels, heights of thinking, being, living… *that's* what I'm talking about…"

"Zach, you're hitting stride at *nineteen* in the art world – do what you like – do what you enjoy – do art, write, this, that, the next – you're gonna be big, man, - huge…"

"So…"

"So that's terrific…"

"How?"

"…well consider the alternative – aim for making it big and making it big, or, not aim for making it big, and *not* making it big…"

"define 'big.'"

"successful – don't play dummy – or pseudo-intellectual with me – we grew up together hoss – I got you pegged…"

"doesn't it require that you be 'bigger' than I before you can 'peg' me?"

"in any case you're on the road to super-stardom - should you choose to go that route, of course."

"what's in it for me?"

"you name it"

"how's that?"

"well you'd have money – and that would... open up... you-name-the door..."

"money eh..."

"money... - you got a better thing one could have – *practically speaking* – skip getting holy or heady on me... – practically speaking – it's money-money-money – gets you food, shelter, clothing. – and degrees of these, I've found, affect in terms of degrees of joy – to a pretty significant extent..."

"it's all what it is..."

"but it's worth something – pleasure is – have to hand it that..."

"roller coaster..."

"you're caught up in thoughts... – time to get out more – get a girlfriend or something – what good are you holed up in this room?"

"what good am I being a cynical nut out there – looking down on everyone who doesn't see like I see..."

"it's connecting with others, lifting them to new levels, or continuation of this... clammed-up... sorrowfest..."

"it's all dealing with death..."

... "what is?"

"what's the use of pursuing to further develop art – seeing it's... dealing with death..."

"how is it 'dealing with death'?"

"artists deal... with materials, which they know will eventually deteriorate into nothingness... – be it a painter – that canvas has a future of dust, ulti-mately... – or be it a director – they're dealing with actors, who, 80 years hence are gonna be rotting corpses... – you name it and it's gonna pass – why toil – to be first at dealing with something – things – that are going to – in future – inevitably – die and disappear... why I should expend such enormous amounts of energy to compete with - be better than - others, down through the ages – doing something that's... bound to fade..."

"how about beauty, dare you to dismiss beauty?... - would you be creating beauty in the process - in that expenditure of energy..."

..." what else would be the goal?"

"there, if you're spreading beauty – that count's for something, wouldn't you agree? -"

"for *what* Tyler – *specific* - enough of the *vague*..."

"count's for uplifting people – making people feel good – laugh... – or advance to higher levels – experience more profound... *feelings* – awe – joy – freedom... – lifting of soul – lightness – eliciting praise in them – unshackling – sending to other levels – realms – adventures - psyches – spiritual awareness – clairvoyance – infusion of strength – impartation of life – into people – animation – invigoration – power – heightening – hearts - bursting with zeal – mirth, ecstasy – what else - overflow abundance – spreading - changing air for better and better – glory to glory - enhancing feelings – pleasurable experiences – newness of life – life – love – growth – perfection – the ideal - expansion of the ideal – ideals - perfection - all senses - fully-on – spreading this power – via your art – spreading richness, magnificence, potential, glory – glory to glory - to glory!"

..."*why*, though..."

... a pause... inclination hints in... - into my... being... that... something... crucial – some 'message' for me – straight from the highest Source - registers in Tyler – for me ...

"why not?"

and it's like... a sledgehammer over head... - missile through chest ...

He rises... leaves... wind blows up lace curtains, clouds rolling in, snow falling ...

~it's going and doing this, that, in this life... or... not going and doing this, that in this life... why not go do this, that? why not go for it - full-on while at it... – dealing with stuff that's going to fade, disappear – be that as it may... i.e. you can go do stuff with stuff that's gonna fade, disappear hundreds of years in future – or *not* go and do stuff with stuff that's gonna fade, disappear in future... - it's yay or nay... – go for it or don't go for it... why not 'go', 'do', rather than... 'not go', 'not do' – let's do this *do* thing – and *bigtime* eh... eh - eh – eh!!!"

Rise, step to window, close eyes, look up... feel flakes falling on, melting, or tumbling off face... suck in a deep breath... smile forming on face ...

~oh we're gonna do this alright - especially here with 'youth factor' in tact – while I *can* write – really *produce* – when old - who has the energy – *now's* the time – the time to push – *push it out* – be it books - art - films - what have you...~

go into bathroom, strip bare, stare straight into bearded, insane visage in full-length mirror... a long time... go to door, open it to hallway... ~no, you're gonna get clothes on~ close door - ~you're not that crazy...~ take up big puffy coat, bought other day, pull it on... pull dirty jeans on, big boots, bought other day… elevator down… over a few blocks… to Duane Reade… searching isles… select a pair of hair clippers… scan shampoo isle… select a bottle… to counter… "do you have a 'Club Savings' card?"

"uh, no."

"Would you like one?"

…"yes."

head over… up to room… ditch coat… can't… quite… ~rrrrr~ get this plastic package open …

turn, open drawer, pick out mini-scissors, bought other day… gnaw at it, cut through… plug in… 'BZZZZZZZZZZZ' – lay in to hair 'ZZZZR-RRRRRRRRRR!!"

look down at sink… full of dirty blond hair… take up scissors… snip at, hair between brows - eliminating uni-brow… eyes hone in on exposed dandruff flakes on bald head… "aaawwwyyyeeeeaah – out in the open now are we? *exposed* baby – *laid bare* – I'm aall over you…" pull bottle of 'Head and Shoulders' from plastic bag… "wooord to your mother…"

crank shower full blast… step in, squeeze large dollop on head… work it in with fingers… let it seep in - ~seep in deep~ - *steep* a while… feel the… tingle… feel it tingling… - picture it invading, saturating, overthrowing, conquering, ~making all things new~ …

towel off, pull on jeans… out into room… search for… find, Yellow pages – open it, on bed… flip to… "Spa". Run finger down… to… a… Madison Avenue location… take up phone, dial …

"yeah I'd like to make an appointment…"

"what time?"

"what time is it now?"

"two o'clock"

"Ok, three o'clock…" …

look round… can only find… one sock… my one other change of clothes: too dirty, smelly to wear… pull on holey '1992 USA Dream Team' t-shirt… pull on puffy coat… open top drawer of dresser… filled with hundred dollar bills… grab a handful, stuff it in right coat pocket… grab another, stuff it in left pocket… pull on pair of boots, get key, head out door …

Swing in Jamba Juice on corner.

"I'll have a… 'Coldbuster'… – with *accai* berries… – yeah… that one '*Accai* Supercharger' – ok, yeah, combine the two…"

"Free boost?"

"yeah, uuh – 'Energy'… – and add the… 'Vita' boost – and 'Fiber' – 'Protein' too – and 'Matcha Green Tea' – throw it all in there – I'll pay whatever it is…" -

"what size?"

"Large."

The spa is 77th and Madison… – dim-lit lobby, swirling yellow marble floors and columns – enormous gold chandelier… red-capped bell hop guys… Elevator to the 9th floor… swing in through MICHAEL CALVIN door… – eyes of hot chick with super clean straight brown hair, smooth olive skin, widen at first sight of me – gain composure …

"yeah I'm that three o'clock appointment."

"have a seat over there Mrrrrr… Barr – we'll be right with you."

Framed pictures of celebrity clientele on wall… sit leafing through GLAMOUR… VOGUE… DETAILS… ~hmm, wonder if make up and Photoshop had anything to do with how good these people look…~

"Zach, we're ready for you." says the receptionist, standing, full view, clipboard in hand… ~Oh are you?… hm, lil' big in the hips~ …

follow her down a hallway ~what a walk!~ and into a room – colorful abstract paintings on wall… where a squat old lady sits, wearing a white doctor's jacket - smooth, glowing skin - dyed black hair – pulled back in ponytail …

"Zach this is Doctor Wolf, - if you'll just have a seat there…"

she leaves, closing door as I recline back into dental-like chair …

"you asked for a makeover?"

"yeah – celebrity style – what you do to them…"

"We'll start with the beard – is that coming off?"

"Yes, go for it."

After putting a hot wet towel on face, experience the smoothest, closest shave ~to date~… "we'll move on to the blackheads."

"black heads?"

"yes you have a bunch of them on and around the nose area… - here" - holds a mirror over me – points plastic-gloved hand at the small red dots on nose."

"I thought they were… pores" –

"no, they're blackheads."

"I thought blackheads were zits – or wait, that's 'whiteheads'."

She's nodding her head yes …

"So what do you… have in mind with the blackheads?"

"Eliminating them."

"Eliminating them? How?"

"We use a machine… – it shoots steam on them – opening them up – then it switches to a *suction* device, which removes the grease and grime abiding in the blackhead sacks – completely cleansing them out." –

~to think – goo, *abiding* in lil'… *homes* on nose – getting a free ride!~ -

"then I apply a face cream that *deep* cleans… – wash that off… – and apply a special cream which heals, seals, restores skin – which I'll give you a bottle of – which you'll apply over the next two weeks for a complete rejuvenation and smoothness…"

"Ok…"

the steam machine is a… portable box - looking like a small vacuum –

a hose extends from it - has an attachment – shape of those plastic pieces athletes suck oxygen from on sidelines – but just fits over the nose… She turns it on – machine purrs - out shoots the steam… she places it – seals it - on my nose – feels like a direct flame – pain surges through body – teeth grit - ~yet what is pain – it is what it is – it's *temporal* – so what – so overrated - *rrrrrr!*~ - picture, clear in mind, the pores – the blackheads – opening up - having to yield – *forced* into yielding ~ha ha!~ by the heat – having to give way - ~the lil' *buggers!*~ - opening up – like doors - sticking hands up – *submission* – mmm opening wide yyyeah ~*having* to~ -

with adroit hand – she flicks a switch on machine – and, continuing to blast searing steam – the suction *kicks in* – actually *feel* the grime being sucked forth out – picture it, vivid, in mind – the goo - in strings – extending – screaming – shrieking as they go… ~ha *haa!* – *do it to it* Wolfie! *yyyyyeeaah!*~ - she flicks another switch – machine buzzes louder – suction power made stronger - ~sucking free any holder-oner's – any residue~ – steam feeling acutely hotter – ~now that there's no slime blocking~ - now that it's hitting sensitive clean inner walls of pockets straight on - ~*yowwrrrrrr!*~

she whips sucker away – her hand scooping into jar of thick white moisturizing cream – smears it vigorous over nose area - so cold! - Noxzema smell to it – feel it seep into the clean, open, caverns – filling in all gaps – taking over – regulating - having its way ~*yyyyeah*…. that is *the stuff*~

washed off – another applied – Vitamin E cream smell to it – feel ~healing in its wings…~

washed off… face, buffed dry… mirror, held up ~wow… blackheads go bye-bye~ "excellent" …

Over into massage room... – where intense Asian guy wordlessly wrenches multiple stress-knots out... jelly walk to hot tub... sit in bubbles with a bunch of celeb-looking types, reading their newspapers, or sitting with eyes closed, head back on tiles ...

on over to sauna... inside a good ten minutes... the showers... the forking over of ~hefty sum~ ... the walking out on to busy 77th Street – face... feeling... so clean – lighter even – heightened sensitivity to – this... sharp, cold breeze on it – and, here, a thirty-or-forty-something - frizzle-frazzle frosted ~(fried(?))~ hair – very intense frown-scowl – overly make-uped – looking to have the weight of a hundred years of guilt weighing down on her head – glares into (blasts through) my eyes – communicating a message to... 'get out of the way *now*.' ~*niiiiice* look heh-heh... niiice one. yyyeeeeah.~

Walk seventeen cold blocks ~note: get scarf – big, substantial puffy one... plug up draft-hole...~ to swinging in solid heavy doors of Bergdorf Goodman ...

To a fully-suited guy with clean-cut hair, smart glasses, "do you have... shopping carts here – I'm gonna get a lot of stuff."

"I'm afraid not, sorry about that." English accent ...

~hm, would like this to line up with vision... – (line up(?))~ "uuh, is your... manager here?"

"Em, yes, may I ask what it's regarding?"

"Have a question for him."

"Right, - with regards to?"

"utilizing a cart in here – no way I could carry all that I intend to buy."

"Right, em, might I suggest bringing your own cart?"

... "yeah... I... suppose I could do that..."

Big smile. "Great. – would you still like to talk to the manager, or..."

"think I'm alright now..."

walk out... catch 6 train to Astor Place... walk into K-Mart... –

to bored, round, Hispanic girl in red K-mart apron: "where are those rolling cart things..." –

"you mean shopping carts?"

"no – the ones you see – like, old ladies transport groceries with them – they're often red – two large wheels on each side..." –

"if we have them they're on the second floor near bikes and sporting goods..."

Escalator up, ask around, find… pay the $21… 6 train to 59th… into Berg-dorf's – wheeling cart – in its flat (untransformed state)… – see full-suited guy from before ~looking so refined – sophisticated – affluent – arrived – yet, working a retail job – his paycheck, only allowed to be, that which it has to be, after taxes…~ - at sight of cart, curls on a sympathetic smile …

"Yep, just picked it up – beauty eh? – you just…" (unfolding, transforming it) "go… like… *this*… – viola… eh?"

pained smile, "yes, well, right, then, yees heh…"

"well, gonna get shopping here. – is the underwear section up here or…" –

"yes – right that way there."

roll red cart along – past sturdy wooden circular tables covered with deli-cately arranged ties… past displays of manikin torsos in polo rugby shirts – sleeves attached to vintage tennis rackets… balls set out just so… past black and white photos of the Hamptons and on walls… more Oak, Mahagony tables of – here, a large vase of fresh cut flowers – spilling (contained) forth… to table with underwear, boxers, spread out on it… – the white of them ~so brilliant~ – seeming… from another world… eyes scan… find size 32… start dropping them in cart… ~,10, 11, 12… – let's make it 13… - 14, there we go…~ - ~(let's(?)) (we(?))~

The white t-shirts… so clean… ~screaming radiance~ … count twenty… into cart… wheel over to socks table… ~yyyyyeeeeeeeaaaahh booyyyeeeeeeeee~

Another fully-suited employee frowns at the cart… appears to be having some sort of… inner crisis over it - whether or not to… question me… looks like he's working to direct attention away… to… here, smoothing out a cash-mere sweater on top of a pile – refolding it… he walks off into another showroom …

Loose count of how many pairs of puffy, high quality, cotton white socks went in… here, a few pairs of black… gray… navy… ~mmm argyles~… cart is nearly full… over to the rugby shirts… pull one on… perfect fit… – "pardon me sir," calls the suited man from other room, peering in, pointing to my left… "the dressing room is right over there"

"Ah, yes, thanks…" note size… put a cashmere sweater in… and a wool one… 4… - 5 dress shirts – sky blue ones ~color meaning: friendliness~ white ones ~purity~ striped ones ~authoritative~… four pairs of dress pants, vary-ing colors… wheeling to cashier, eyes alight on scarves – laid out so plush on solid round table… select the thickest – a white one ~chunk-meistro-licious~ - set it on top of the pile… check out… – everything placed in two handsome, sturdy paper bags with strong handles, which slide right in, fit perfect, in new cart… which I push through heavy doors – cold blasts, bites, neck… pull scarf from bag… wrap it round… and again… and again… tuck… push… go …

CHAPTER 21

Standing on deck of yacht... – big one... – new... – gleaming, in sun... in white, cotton robe ...

It's been ten years since that Bergdorf shopping spree... Elliot and I went on to do shows in L.A., San Fran, Chicago, Tokyo... Europe again and again and again... countless New York and Philly shows... I wrote four novels – one a best seller – writing fifth... look to left... here, Julia Denton – *Bar*, now – Germany's highest-paid model, lying in bikini on white recliner sun chair – positioning sun reflector on chest – intensifying light on tanned, perfect jawline... look over at the table we just had lunch on... - half-eaten slabs of pink salmon, aglisten in oil... opened ziploc bag... of brie cubes... half a bottle of red wine, glasses, half full... half a bowl of mixed raspberries and blueberries... open container of Greek yogurt... On the walnut dresser down in the sleeping quarters sits my wallet... and yes, in it you'll find my drive's license... and bank cards... Passport is in my briefcase on the floor by the bed – iPhone next it, charging... – social security card is in my desk at our apartment on Greene Street... It's true... I achieved 'fame' without the degrees, without the identification cards... - made a lot of money without all the cards... looking over at Julia again... ~didn't get her without the cards though...~ – ~wouldn't have seen Asia and Europe without the cards...~ in a way I was more free, bumbling around as a crazy, homeless bum... but that woulda... got old... – could have gone that route... – before tagging me as a 'sell out' – another schlub who's gone and googlemorpherborgered into the Googlemorpherborg... note... that I can learn, feel, *experience,* more, going this route... it woulda been a span of years, shaking angry fist in gutter – wrecking body on sloppy joe and cigarette diet – or a span of years... experiencing clarity to clarity – like I chose, went, am in... – it's kind of like that quote I read in that flight - over to Stockholm – or was it Hamburg? – one of these cities – which read: "while it's good to have an end to journey towards, it's the journey that matters in the end." - cheesy as it may sound it plays in, here, to this, what, will it be... a minute? 5 minutes? of reflection... Enrich journey, eh, heh-heh – 'do-it-to-it-one-shot' cliché is what I guess I, after all that, am... getting at, here, slipping brie chunk in mouth, chewing, washing down with wine...~... ~('getting at(?)')~ - ~ - and how wonderful would a clicheless experience be... ongoingness y'know... – tagless, boxless, labelless, cueless... - would it be wonderful? would it be insanity? – you'd probably be interpreted by the cue-taking masses to be a nutcase - dangerous... – ostracization... key is... not getting mad about it (about you-name-it) – meld mad and you're shot through... – and those who don't have a strong foundation... have they any other route to go... any option other than growing madder and madder about how things are so off - and destroying themselves harder and harder and faster and faster...~ ~('key') – is that all we have to express that(?) - a lil' picture(?))~

Looking up at clear, Bermuda skies ~it's true... as things currently are, here in this current system – with how it operates, runs... I simply... would *not* be here without the cards... - plastic cards with numbers on them... here with the way things go these days – which we allow to just... continue rolling along, unravel as it does.... and here, at twenty nine – yes, today's my birthday – I've who knows how many years remaining to devote every ounce of energy, every fiber of my being, to change this ungenerous, stodgy, entrenched-in-fear, choppy, mechanical, freedom-strangling system for good...~

~(good(?)~

and I look at the clean, clear water... and it's perfectly calm, still as glass... sparkling ...

978-0-595-43189-2
0-595-43189-5

Printed in the United States
81095LV00003B/289-306

9 780595 431892